CW00553498

To the Advantage of Both

A Pride and Prejudice Variation

Lory Lilian

Copyright © 2023 Lory Lilian

All rights reserved

The characters and events portrayed in this book are fictitious. Any similarity to real persons, living or dead, is coincidental and not intended by the author.

No part of this book may be reproduced, or stored in a retrieval system, or transmitted in any form or by any means, electronic, mechanical, photocopying, recording, or otherwise, without express written permission of the publisher.

Cover design by: Lory Lilian

Contents

Title Page

Copyright

Author's Note

Chapter 1   2

Chapter 2   12

Chapter 3   23

Chapter 4   34

Chapter 5   51

Chapter 6   60

Chapter 7   69

Chapter 8   78

Chapter 9   86

Chapter 10   94

Chapter 11   101

Chapter 12   110

Chapter 13   119

Chapter 14   127

Chapter 15   134

Chapter 16   141

Chapter 17   150

Chapter 18   158

Chapter 19   168

Chapter 20   178

Chapter 21   185

Chapter 22   194

Chapter 23   203

Chapter 24   212

Chapter 25   222

Chapter 26   231

Chapter 27   239

Chapter 28   246

Chapter 29   252

Epilogue   262

The End   265

Author's Note

Chapter 28 contains a romantic and rather steamy description of the marriage consummation, but this part can be skipped by readers who prefer, without altering the quality of the story.

LORY LILIAN

To the Advantage of Both

Chapter 1

"It is a truth universally acknowledged that a proper young lady, and especially a gentleman's daughter, is in need of a husband to provide her with a happy home," Mrs Bennet declared during breakfast. "Just as much as any young man in possession of a good income must be in want of a wife."

"Indeed, my dear madam," Mr Collins readily approved from across the table, chewing noisily on his bread and nodding towards his cousins. "Lady Catherine would agree with your statement, I am sure."

"I am certain nothing would make Mrs Bennet happier than having Lady Catherine's approval," Mr Bennet declared.

"Only a mother can understand what is in a mother's heart," Mrs Bennet continued. "My only concern is to see my daughters happy."

"And I am sure that will happen, my dear Mrs Bennet," Mr Collins said. "I wish only the best for my cousins. I was telling Sir William last night how I congratulate myself on coming to meet you all."

"Oh, yes, Sir William. His daughter Charlotte is a lovely young woman, and intelligent too, but she is not so lucky as to possess much beauty."

"Mama!" Jane interjected with apparent distress. "Charlotte is our friend, and she is a wonderful person."

"Of course she is! Who would say differently?"

"You seem to have spent a pleasant time with Sir William

and Mr Phillips," Elizabeth said to Mr Collins. A moment later, she regretted her imprudence, as the clergyman turned to her with a broad smile.

"Indeed, my dear cousin. I am glad you noticed. I would never have dared to assume you would pay attention to what pleases me!"

"I did it most unwillingly, I assure you," Elizabeth answered. "You appear to be well suited to their company."

"Mr Wickham is the most pleasant man I have ever met. And the most handsome," Lydia declared suddenly, causing Mr Collins to pause his chewing and frown, his mouth open to reveal the disgusting contents within.

"Yes, and he is so charming!" Kitty added. "Lizzy, you captured him for the entire evening! I hope you will not do the same at the Netherfield ball."

"I did not capture anyone," Elizabeth defended herself, her cheeks flushed. She had enjoyed Mr Wickham's company more than any other man's before, but she felt embarrassed under Mr Collins's censuring glare.

"Indeed, my dear cousin, Lady Catherine always says that a young lady should never forget decorum in her behaviour and not show too much familiarity towards a man she is not related to."

"But how much familiarity may a young woman show to a man she is not related to, if she intends to be related to him in the future?" Mr Bennet enquired quizzically.

Elizabeth covered her mouth with her napkin to prevent a most unladylike chuckle, while Mr Collins was clearly disconcerted by a question to which he seemed to have no answer.

"Oh, Mr Bennet, you and your teasing," his wife interjected.

"Well, well, it was another most entertaining breakfast. Now, if you will excuse me, I shall retire to my library."

"I may join you, sir," Mr Collins readily offered.

"You are very kind. If you do, I must warn you that I have a book to finish, and I shall not be loquacious company."

"I see… Then perhaps I could stay with Mrs Bennet and my fair cousins," the clergyman declared, much to the girls' despair.

For another hour after breakfast, the Bennet daughters were forced to bear Mr Collins's pompous statements. Then, after another glass of wine and with the tiredness of the previous evening's party, he decided to take a nap, and the ladies readily encouraged him.

Once Mr Collins was gone, Elizabeth sighed in relief. His increasing attention to her annoyed and worried her as much as her mother's obvious approval. Even her father's constant tendency to make sport of everything and everyone was becoming tiresome.

She feared she would have to face a ridiculous marriage proposal soon, and she was determined to try to avoid such a confrontation that could have only one ending but be the beginning of a continuous scandal in their house.

Elizabeth prayed that Mr Bingley would propose to Jane soon, for her sister's sake but also her own. The engagement of her eldest daughter hopefully would make it easier for her mother to accept a rejection of Mr Collins.

After a little while, Elizabeth lost patience in listening to chatter about dresses and lace. She knew no better way to acquire some peace than a long walk on such a misty autumn day, so she took her coat, bonnet, and gloves and left the house, despite her mother's warning about catching a cold just before the ball.

It was chilly and smelt of winter. Elizabeth's shoes slipped from time to time on the frosty ground, but she kept up her hasty pace, leaving Longbourn behind. Dark clouds were covering the sky and blocking out the sunlight. She decided not to venture too far away, so instead of keeping her usual path to Oakham Mount, she took an alternate route through the groves, among the lifeless and bare trees. She enjoyed every season of the year, but that specific month, between the colourful autumn and the white, freezing winter, was quite gloomy.

The solitary walk allowed her to think about one of her new acquaintances — Mr Wickham — and the story he had revealed to her regarding Mr Darcy. Despite her profound dislike of a certain gentleman, she had never denied that he possessed some good qualities too. Therefore, she had been both surprised and appalled to discover his cruelty and lack of loyalty towards his childhood friend, and specifically how he had disregarded his father's dying wish. It seemed even more astonishing that he shared such a strong friendship with an amiable, honest, and goodhearted man like Mr Bingley — the man who had stolen Jane's heart and had become the recipient of her family's hopes for safety and a comfortable future.

So deep was she in her musings that, for a while, she did not notice the man walking towards her, holding his horse's reins.

Despite the howl of the wind covering most other sounds, a sudden noise made her look up and see him. He stepped closer and closed the short distance between them.

The stallion was black, tall, and impressive, looking very much like Mr Darcy's own horse. The man leading the beast was no less intimidating. His posture was stiff and his countenance severe.

They stared at each other for a few moments, then he bowed shortly, in a rigid, military fashion. He was likely in his late fifties, still handsome enough, his appearance betraying confidence and self-sufficiency.

"Forgive me, miss, do you know the way to Netherfield?" His voice sounded polite but as severe as his figure. His tone was demanding rather than questioning.

"Yes, sir. In that direction." She gestured with her hand.

"I see. Very well. Thank you." He bowed again and stepped away.

Elizabeth hesitated a moment, wondering why he was walking instead of riding.

"Sir, are you hurt?"

He turned and frowned, his eyebrow rising in challenge.

"Hurt? Why would you assume I was hurt?"

Elizabeth glanced towards the stallion, and he quickly understood.

"My horse slipped, and I am afraid he may have hurt his leg. I do not wish to risk worsening it, so I shall not ride him until we have attended to the injury properly."

"I see. Well, these grounds are rather dangerous for riding, if one is not familiar with them. And Netherfield is only two miles away, but you are quite far from the main road, and there are many alternate paths. I had better accompany you out of the wood, to be sure you take your horse in as safe a direction as possible."

Elizabeth smiled with her usual affability, and he appeared astounded.

"Are you going in the same direction, miss?"

"Not at all. Quite the opposite. My father's estate is a mile and a half away. Over there." She pointed.

"And are you alone?" He sounded puzzled, and she smiled.

"Yes. I have taken long walks alone through these lanes since I was a child. Come. Please follow me."

He did do so, still reluctantly, she thought. "You should not walk alone — it might be dangerous for a young lady. There could be robbers, kidnappers, or many other sorts of prowlers."

"Not around here, sir. But you are right, of course. I am always careful, although I have never had to face any danger of that kind."

"Yes, but in such matters, one cannot be too careful. Once is enough for a tragedy to occur. And you surely should not offer to accompany a strange man alone in the woods," he said with increasing seriousness. "I am thankful for your help, though. Please do not consider me ungrateful. I am only thinking of your well-being."

"Thank you. And that is precisely why I offered my company, sir. I did not fear that I may be in danger from you."

"And why not?" he enquired further.

"Firstly, because you are on your way to Netherfield. No

acquaintance of Mr Bingley's could be a danger to anyone. Your appearance is impeccable, and although you also look severe and unfriendly, there is something in your expression that speaks of integrity and honour."

He clearly did not expect such an answer and needed a few moments to fully comprehend it. Elizabeth was leading the way, attentive to her steps, so she missed the amused grin that softened his expression.

"You are familiar with Mr Bingley, I assume?" the man asked.

"Yes, very familiar. I am proud to call Mr Bingley a friend of our family, and while our acquaintance is not one of long-standing, he has proved himself a most worthy gentleman. Everyone in the neighbourhood approves of him."

"Well, that is good to know. Bingley has always been a pleasant fellow, ever since he was a young boy. And a loyal one, I might say. I know he also has some family and friends here. Are you acquainted with them too?"

"Yes," she answered, after a brief hesitation which the gentleman did not miss, judging by the pointed look he gave her.

"And you? Are you alone, sir? You are surely a stranger to this place," Elizabeth continued.

"I sent my carriage and servants ahead — they must have arrived already. I wished to enjoy the view on horseback, but it seems I am not as sharp as I hoped to still be at this age, and I have lost my way. It is the first time in my life I have needed a woman to guide me."

Elizabeth laughed heartily.

"I am sorry to disappoint you, but women know that men often need guidance, although they are rarely aware of it."

It was his turn to laugh. "You express your opinion quite decidedly for someone so young, Miss…" He seemed to suddenly mind his behaviour and stopped, making Elizabeth turn.

"I beg your forgiveness, miss. I have lost not only my path but also my manners. Allow me to introduce myself. I am Admiral Thomas Andrew Pembroke."

He bowed, while Elizabeth stared at him in disbelief, silenced by astonishment. She finally recovered and curtseyed.

"Forgive me, sir. I am Miss Elizabeth Bennet. It is an honour to meet you."

"Please do not be so formal, Miss Bennet. It is a pleasure to meet you — a very fortunate one. Your father owns an estate, you mentioned?" he enquired, as they resumed their walk.

"Yes. Longbourn. It is three miles from Netherfield," she answered, her voice altered by emotion. Never had she met an admiral, nor considered she ever would. She wondered how he could be connected to Mr Bingley, whose father had made his fortune in trade.

"Do you have a large family, Miss Bennet?"

"It might be called so. My parents and four sisters."

"Five daughters? Your mother must be quite distressed with you all."

She laughed. "Indeed. She mentions it several times a day!"

"And with four sisters, you walk alone?"

"Well, we do not all share the same interests. My eldest sister, Jane, often keeps me company, but not always."

"I see. So, you are friends with the family at Netherfield," the admiral continued.

Elizabeth hesitated again. "Mr Bingley is on friendly terms with everyone in the neighbourhood. His sisters are rather different from him," she said, choosing her words carefully.

"And Darcy? I imagine he is not as desirous of company as Bingley? Or am I wrong?"

Elizabeth concealed a smile. "You are not wrong. Have you known Mr Darcy long?"

"Since he was born."

"Oh…" she replied.

"Oh? You do not seem as impressed with him as you are with Bingley." The gentleman laughed.

Elizabeth cleared her throat. "I have spent a little time in Mr Darcy's company. Enough to recognise he possesses some excellent qualities. He is well-educated, well-read, has in-depth knowledge of the world, and appears to be very fond of his sister, his family, and close friends. But his character is not easy to sketch, as he is always distant and severe."

"On the other hand, those who are too open and too willing to reveal their character might be deceiving, would you not agree, Miss Bennet?"

She paused and considered it a moment. "Do you refer to Mr Bingley?"

"Bingley? Not at all! That fellow is honest and fair. What you see is what you get. I am speaking in general."

"In general, you might be right. That is why I am restrained in speaking too much of Mr Darcy or Mr Bingley's sisters' true nature until I feel confident in my judgment."

"Bingley's sisters are the same as him — what you see is what you get," the admiral declared, and Elizabeth held back a peal of laughter. "As for Darcy, yes, I can see why someone outside his close circle would find it hard to recognise his true nature. I may easily say he is one of the best fellows I have ever met in my life."

Elizabeth was surprised by such praise. Could the admiral be Darcy's relative and therefore partial to him? What was the connection to Mr Bingley?

With Mr Wickham's sad story in her mind, and due to her growing familiarity with the admiral, she said, "But speaking of deception, is it not possible that one shows himself in a different light to his close circle of family and friends than he does to those outside it? Could his manners and behaviour be different?"

The admiral glanced at her in puzzlement. "Are you referring to Darcy?" he enquired.

"I am speaking in general," she said, repeating his earlier words.

"Well, well, you certainly are as spirited and bright as you are charming and helpful, Miss Bennet. I hope we shall have the chance to meet and speak again soon."

She blushed at such an honest compliment. "Thank you, sir. I shall accept your praise, although I am uncertain why I deserve it. So, there is Netherfield, and there is Longbourn," she indicated when they finally reached the main road, and the view finally opened up.

He glanced around and sighed. "Quite a lovely prospect, I would say!"

"Indeed. You only have to follow this road, and it will take you to the manor's entrance."

"Will you not come with me and let me send you back to your home by carriage? I feel uncomfortable letting you walk such a long distance alone."

"You are very considerate, but that will not be necessary. I have walked from Longbourn to Netherfield more than once. I am only half the distance now. I hope you arrive safely and your horse is well."

"Thank you, Miss Bennet. Your assistance is much appreciated. It was a delight to meet you."

"I am happy I could help, sir." She curtseyed again; he bowed and offered a smile of gratitude that intimidated her even more.

Then she turned and departed at a hasty pace, while he gazed after her a little longer before he turned his horse and walked towards his destination.

The entire way back to the house, Elizabeth wondered and speculated about the strange encounter. The presence of such an illustrious character in their vicinity was as thrilling as it was disturbing. Mr Bingley certainly did not belong in the same circles as an admiral. Were they mere acquaintances? Or was it only a quick visit with no other meaning? Perhaps the admiral would be gone the next day. The meeting impressed her in a way she could not explain. The man himself had seemed impressive, even before she had learnt his identity.

So absorbed was she with musing about her new acquaintance that she forgot the annoyance of the old one, until she entered the house and heard Mr Collins's voice.

She decided not to mention the encounter to anyone in her family, at least until she had heard the reports from Meryton or from Netherfield. If the admiral was in the slightest way connected with their lives, she would surely find out soon.

Chapter 2

When the admiral's carriage arrived at Netherfield, it sent the entire household into chaos. They did expect the important visit, as it had been announced by an express. Everything was already prepared, but the anticipation still overwhelmed them all, besides Darcy, whose eagerness was moderate as usual.

But the carriage arrived empty, except for the servants, and the gentleman was delayed further. Worry enveloped them, with speculations and concerns growing with every passing moment.

Eventually, Darcy and Bingley asked for their horses and decided to go in search of him. There was no time for such an endeavour though, as the man himself was soon seen approaching on foot, with his horse following behind.

The first thing Admiral Pembroke. did was to take care of his horse. He made straight for the stables and, together with a couple of servants and assisted by Darcy and Bingley, made sure the horse's wound was looked at and was reassured that rest and good food would heal it soon.

Only afterwards did he greet Bingley and Darcy properly and enter the house. The Hursts and Miss Bingley received him ceremoniously. He replied in the same manner, then asked to be directed to his room and returned only later, for dinner.

The admiral's presence made Miss Caroline Bingley and her sister, Mrs Louisa Hurst, even more conscious of their importance and made them consider once again how superior they were to the people of Hertfordshire.

"Upon my word, just imagine what a disaster it would have been if Admiral Pembroke had arrived while Jane and Elizabeth Bennet were still here," Miss Bingley declared.

"Why is that, Caroline? Why would it have been a disaster? Both Miss Bennets are exceedingly pleasant company," Bingley interjected.

"Brother, please be reasonable! Try to see beyond your first glance! As charming as Jane might be, her family is terrible, and you cannot expose the admiral to such a grotesque spectacle," Mrs Hurst said.

"Quite," Miss Bingley added, "and—"

"As little as I approve of the Bennets, surely the admiral has met much worse in his military life," Darcy interrupted her. "And I agree with Bingley that the eldest daughters are pleasant company under any circumstances."

Miss Bingley rolled her eyes. "It surprises and pains me to see that you have become as blind as my brother to the Bennets' flaws, Mr Darcy."

"It gives me no pleasure to mention that not everyone who thinks differently from you is blind, Miss Bingley. But I am afraid I must do so."

Darcy's severe reply offended and silenced Miss Bingley for a long while, and she spoke no further until she had finished a full cup of tea. For the rest of the afternoon, the ladies amused themselves, while the three gentlemen shared drinks in the library.

The admiral joined them only before dinner, and his presence seemed to impress and intimidate his hosts as well as the servants.

The table was exquisitely arranged, with dishes worthy of any fashionable party in London.

"Thank you for receiving me," the admiral said from the place of honour to the right of Miss Bingley. "I hope my visit did not interrupt your plans. I loathe intruding on people."

"Not at all! Quite the contrary!" Bingley answered

enthusiastically. "We were thrilled to find that you would pass through Hertfordshire, and we prayed that you would stay with us for a few days. I hope you approve of Netherfield. Darcy advised me to choose it."

"I have had no time to see much of it yet, but if Darcy thought it was suitable for you, I am sure he knows best," he said with mock seriousness. "However, I heartily approve of your neighbours already. I had the pleasure of meeting a young lady — exceedingly charming and witty — who kindly helped me find my way through the woods and even accompanied me for a while. Without her, I would likely still be wandering the lanes, searching for your house."

Darcy sipped some wine, struggling not to ask more about the unnamed lady. But Bingley did so, clearly very much intrigued.

"A young lady?"

"Yes. She spoke very highly of you, Bingley. She said you were a friend of her family, and she trusted me for merely being acquainted with you. That is quite a compliment." Bingley still looked puzzled.

Darcy put his glass on the table and said in a voice that he hoped sounded composed, "It must have been Miss Elizabeth Bennet. I know she enjoys solitary walks and is quite familiar with the area."

"Precisely," the admiral confirmed. "Miss Elizabeth Bennet. A charming young lady, and very handsome, I might add."

"Yes, indeed," Bingley approved. "Miss Elizabeth is very bright. And very amiable. She is Miss Jane Bennet's sister. How fortunate that you have met her!"

"Oh, please, Admiral! Surely you would not wish to see a lady of your family walking alone in the woods, through the mud, all by herself. That is hardly proof of intelligence or good breeding, or even decent manners," Miss Bingley said with a frown.

"Most likely, I would not approve of such a habit, and I told

Miss Bennet as much. I am opposed to any activity that might put young ladies in any danger. But for me, her daily walk was good luck, and I cannot hold it against her," the admiral said.

"Miss Elizabeth's manners are unusual at times, but she certainly does not lack in any other qualities," Darcy spoke again.

"Well, we must agree to disagree on this matter. I hope you enjoy the meal, Admiral. We have prepared five dishes for tonight." Miss Bingley ended the annoying debate.

"Thank you. Your care is much appreciated, Miss Bingley. I am sure everything is delicious," the guest answered. "I already appreciate Bingley's wine and brandy."

While the first course was served, the admiral seemed lost in his thoughts, glancing around the table several times. Darcy remained composed, but Bingley looked slightly distressed after the argument over Miss Bennet. Yet, it was not brought up again during dinner.

The rest of the evening passed following all the proper customs of society, with a neutral conversation, card game, musing, drinks, and a brief separation of the sexes.

"Admiral Pembroke, would you do us the great pleasure of staying another week with us? We are hosting a ball, and we would be delighted and honoured by your presence," Bingley said.

"A ball? This is quite unexpected. But I shall consider it, I assure you. Is there any special reason for the ball?"

Bingley's face coloured, while his sisters exchanged an exasperated glance.

"No, it is a simple private ball," Bingley answered. "I rented the estate two months ago, and I am trying to become better acquainted with all the neighbours. It was suggested to me that the people in the town would enjoy it. There is also a militia regiment stationed here for the winter, and where there are officers, there must be entertainment, must there not?"

The admiral laughed. "That is a very accurate statement. Where there are officers, there must be balls! Except if the officers are on a ship in the middle of the sea. But the militia have a reputation for enjoying themselves."

"Well, that explains some of my puzzlement," Darcy mumbled, barely heard by the others.

"Charles insisted on hosting this ball, but neither Louisa nor I supported it. And I know Mr Darcy is displeased to be part of such a tiresome event," Miss Bingley interjected.

"Balls are such a waste of time for a married man," Mr Hurst declared from behind his glass of brandy.

"I am not displeased," Darcy intervened. "It was Bingley's decision, and he is entitled to it. Just as everyone may choose to attend it or not."

"A very wise statement," the admiral declared. "Well, Bingley, I thank you for the invitation. I might accept it. I shall ponder it tomorrow and let you know."

"Admiral, just please do not entertain high hopes regarding the company. After all, most of the participants will be mere country people, with simple manners, to say the least," Miss Bingley added sharply.

"I must say, I am rather partial to country people and country balls," the admiral replied with a trace of annoyance in his voice that only Darcy noticed.

It was rather unwise of Miss Bingley, the daughter of a man who had made his fortune in trade, to continue to criticise other people in such a pompous, disdainful manner. In truth, she was so below an admiral herself that she would have never had the chance to eat at the same table as one, if not for the peculiar circumstances. The gentleman's cold and unsatisfactory reply disconcerted her, and from that moment, she refrained from speaking much.

Eventually, the admiral excused himself and retired for the night. Only then did the others follow his example, and the evening came to an end.

Darcy remained in the library, enjoying another glass of brandy. For many days now, his thoughts had been filled with the image of Elizabeth Bennet. And in the solitude of his chamber, in his own bed, just before sleep took pity on him, things usually worsened.

He was tormented by the feelings aroused in him by this young daughter of a country gentleman. He did admit he had been wrong to call her tolerable and accepted that she had the most charming bright eyes he had ever seen. They sparkled with wit. Her beauty was not flawless, but it was natural and lively. Her manners were questionable at times but always open and unaltered by pretensions.

In all, she was different from any woman he had met before, and she stirred his mind and his soul in a way no other woman ever had. He was fully aware of the danger he found himself in, and his only protection from such unexpected weakness was the inferiority of her connections and the appalling lack of decorum displayed by her mother and younger sisters.

And recently, another barrier had been built by her apparent friendliness towards Wickham. That scoundrel had crossed his path again, in a most annoying way, and he seemed to have already gained everyone's favour in Meryton, as he had always done. To his disappointment, Elizabeth was among those who had quickly fallen for Wickham's charms; Darcy had heard reports about the growing friendship between the two, despite being barely acquainted. But then again, that was Wickham. Very few women resisted his charms, and the second daughter of a country gentleman, probably lacking in any experience with men, could not be an exception.

He briefly considered it was his duty to warn Mr Bennet about the danger Wickham might pose to his daughters. But he had to be cautious. Any argument with Wickham would mean the threat of revealing his past, and consequently, Georgiana's indiscretion. He could not afford to put his sister's reputation in such peril. Not even for Elizabeth. The idea remained, as he could not possibly allow Wickham to deceive more innocent people. But what was the best way of exposing him? He still needed to decide.

"Darcy, did you not hear me? Are you ill?"

He startled at the sound of an insistent voice and rose to his feet to face Admiral Pembroke, who was staring at him.

"What happened, my boy?"

"Nothing... Forgive me, sir, I was mulling over some business matters. I thought you were already asleep. Is there something I can do for you?"

"No, all is well. I wanted to speak to you, and Percy told me you had not arrived in your chamber yet. He led me here. I hope I am not disturbing you."

"Not at all. Would you like another drink?"

"Yes. A brandy, please. We did not have time to talk much today."

"Indeed. Bingley and his sisters were too enraptured by your presence."

"Much too enraptured. For a man who has rarely eaten more than one course at any meal his entire life, dinner nearly killed me."

"Well, they meant well."

"I know, and I am grateful for their attentiveness."

"I am glad to see you, sir. It is a great pleasure that you decided to visit us."

"When Richard told me you were in Hertfordshire, and knowing I would be so near the county, I could not help but come to see you. I have not seen you in almost two years now. How is sweet Georgiana? You look well, I must say."

"I am as well as can be expected, and so is Georgiana. We have spoken of you often."

"I know. I receive regular reports about you from my sister and brother-in-law. But I know they see you rather rarely too. You are not often in town."

"True. Georgiana is not yet out, and neither of us is too fond of parties and balls. For me, the Season is rather tiresome."

"I remember. I am surprised that nothing has changed in that regard. I had thought you would be less restrained as time passed after your father's death."

"Little will change in that regard. It is simply a matter of preference."

"Well, you have Bingley to balance your lack of social skills." The admiral laughed, and Darcy smiled in approval.

"Were you talking about me?" the master of the house asked from the doorway, looking rather puzzled. The other two laughed again.

"It seems we have a late-night party," the admiral said.

"Is everything well? Are you troubled by something, Admiral?"

"Everything is well. Do not worry. I went looking for Darcy, and I found him here, so we thought we would talk and drink for a while."

"May I join you? I do not want to intrude. I wished to talk to Darcy too, and since he was not in his chamber, I imagined he must be here. But it can wait until tomorrow."

"Of course you may join us," the admiral answered. "Besides, it is your house."

"Thank you. Did you find the brandy? Can I fetch you something else to drink? Or to eat?" Bingley offered.

"Calm down and sit with us," the admiral invited him. "We have everything we need at this late hour."

"Is there anything urgent you wished to talk to me about?" Darcy asked his friend.

"No, it is just…I have been invited to dine at Longbourn the day after tomorrow, but since the admiral is here, I shall decline. I should call on Mr Bennet tomorrow and inform him about the change of plans. And then I shall pass on the invitation to the ball to Colonel Forster. I had hoped you would come with me, but you had better remain with the admiral."

"I would rather stay at Netherfield. I have no desire to meet the officers — at least not some of them. As for the Bennets, I am sure your visit will be a brief one. You do not need my assistance," Darcy said.

Admiral Pembroke stared at them, sipping from his glass.

"I shall not accept you changing any plans because of me.

I have taken the opportunity to see you since I happened to be travelling through Hertfordshire, but I would be upset if I interfered in your other engagements."

"Do not worry, sir. I am sure I can dine at Longbourn another evening, after the ball," Bingley offered.

"Longbourn is Miss Bennet's estate, is it not? I remember her mentioning it."

"Yes."

"And only you were invited? Not the others in your party? I would say that is rather impolite."

"Oh no, sir! The invitation was for all of us. But my sisters do not support my friendship with the Bennets, so they declined the invitation."

The admiral raised an eyebrow. "Would it be fair to assume they do not support your friendship with Miss Bennet?"

Bingley's face coloured. "They are also friends with Miss Bennet, but they believe we should not visit so much. Everybody who knows Miss Bennet can see she has nothing wanting. She is not responsible for her family's situation in life and lack of connections."

"Again, I would dare to assume Miss Bennet lacks in dowry too. That might be a proper reason for your sisters' disapproval."

"I am not interested in Miss Bennet's dowry. She is a remarkable lady, with the sweetest nature, and the most beautiful I have seen."

"She is beautiful, and she does lack in dowry. But there is much more than that to be considered," Darcy interjected. "And in a small town like Meryton, any gesture or action could raise certain expectations."

Bingley rolled his eyes and said, "Darcy is not very fond of their company either, so he has also decided not to join me. And I decided not to insist, even more so since I know they also have a cousin visiting. A certain Mr Collins to whom Longbourn is entailed and who seems to be a pompous fool. Spending an evening with him would be insupportable to Darcy."

The admiral glanced at the two with a frown. "The

pompous cousin sounds unappealing. But may I ask what is so condemnable about the Bennets as to refuse a dinner invitation?" he asked Darcy.

"Mrs Bennet and her youngest daughters are not company one would want to encourage. They are ill-mannered, ill-educated, and the matron would do anything to secure husbands for her daughters," Darcy stated severely.

The admiral's frown increased, then he sipped some more brandy before speaking.

"Really? Does not any mother — including the royals' — search for husbands for her daughters? How else could a small country gentleman's wife, the mother of five daughters with no dowry and few connections, secure their future? Can one blame her for that? Did your grandparents not do the same for your mother? Is not your aunt Lady Catherine doing the same?"

The unexpected reply and the rebuke in it surprised Darcy.

"This is different," he said. "Mrs Bennet is too obvious, too loud, too...improper. One must see her in order to understand."

"Now I easily understand why Miss Bennet was so generous in praising Bingley and so restrained when she spoke of the others from Netherfield. I can see the feeling is mutual. Well, Bingley, I congratulate you on your excellent taste in women. I, for one, fully approve of your friendship with her. I agree that she seems to be remarkable."

Bingley's eyes and mouth opened in astonishment. He blinked a few times, then finally comprehended the man's words.

"Oh, you mean Miss Elizabeth? No, no, I meant her elder sister, Miss Jane Bennet! Miss Elizabeth is remarkable too. And I do consider her a friend. She is very clever. And very direct. In a good way! Miss Bennet is very gentle and kind-hearted and sweet. They are very close to each other, very loyal, but very different in nature."

It was the admiral's turn to be dumbfounded. "So, there are two remarkable Miss Bennets in the family?"

"Yes," Bingley replied hastily.

"Miss Bennet is beautiful and gentle in manners. She smiles too much. I would say all the time. Miss Elizabeth is witty, well-read, sometimes too opinionated, and tends to misjudge people. But she is remarkably different from most ladies of her age," Darcy declared.

"You forgot to mention Miss Elizabeth is very pretty too. And yet, you still refused their dinner invitation," the admiral mocked him.

"Darcy and Miss Elizabeth have never been friends. Actually, he offended her the first time they met, at an assembly. He refused to dance with her, as he thought she was not handsome enough to interest him," Bingley said.

"That is nonsense!" Darcy cried. "The circumstances were of a peculiar kind."

"Well, well… This evening has proved to be more entertaining than I anticipated. Bingley, I am thinking of joining you when you call at Longbourn tomorrow. I would like to thank Miss Elizabeth for helping me today, and it would be a good opportunity to meet the family."

Both Darcy and Bingley looked at him in disbelief, while the admiral's face wore nothing but a large grin of contentment.

Chapter 3

The following morning, Darcy woke up with a pounding headache. Caught up in the entertaining conversation — which was often at the edge of propriety — with the admiral, he had indulged himself with one too many brandies. He had decided to keep his distance from Longbourn, and from Elizabeth, in a poor attempt to overcome his growing inclination towards her.

However, since the admiral was unmoved in his plan to call at Longbourn, he could not let him go with just Bingley for company, even though he was distressed at the mere thought of sitting in a small room with Mrs Bennet and her younger daughters. When they had visited Netherfield, he had been able to withdraw into a corner, but since he would be the guest this time, he would not have such a luxury.

Although the admiral had seemed amused the previous evening during the discussion about the Bennets, it was unlikely that he would bear their company for more than half an hour. He looked at Bingley, who was clearly joyful about the upcoming call. Undoubtedly, he was completely enchanted by Miss Jane Bennet, but Darcy had seen his young friend in love too many times to take him seriously. As quickly as he fell for a pretty lady's charms, his inclinations never lasted more than a few weeks. Miss Bennet could be no different. After the ball, Bingley intended to return to town for a fortnight, to attend to some business, and very likely that would be the end of his infatuation with Miss Jane Bennet.

Soon after breakfast, despite Miss Bingley and Mrs Hurst's disapproval, the three men were ready for the visit.

The admiral took a stroll to the stables to check on his horse and was pleased to see an almost complete recovery. However, he chose another animal from Bingley's stable for the ride, and all three left for Longbourn.

"It is a little early. Would you like to take a longer ride so you can see the estate?" Bingley asked the admiral.

"Of course. A ride would be beneficial regardless, after how much we abused your food and drink last night."

"True," Darcy admitted. "I do not remember drinking so much in a long while."

"Speaking of drinking — what else does your brother-in-law do for a living, Bingley?" the admiral enquired.

"For a living? Nothing. He is a gentleman," Bingley explained, slightly puzzled.

"Of course he is," the admiral replied with mockery. "I might have misjudged him since we have only just met, but he seems indolent and lacking interest in any part of life."

"Well…" Bingley mumbled.

"You know, I have always wondered how that sort of man accomplishes his duties in the marital bed — or out of it. The image in my mind is quite pathetic."

Darcy and Bingley stared at the admiral in complete shock. Having his sister somehow involved in the conversation, Bingley forgot to breathe.

"Forgive me, I did not mean to make you uncomfortable." The Admiral laughed. "I am speaking in general, and my puzzlement remains."

"We should find a more appropriate subject of conversation," Darcy suggested.

"Yes, we should. But it would not be equally amusing. However, I do not intend to make sport at your sister's expense, Bingley. I hope she is reasonably happy in her marriage."

"Louisa had an impressive dowry of twenty thousand pounds. She had the liberty to choose her husband, and she chose Hurst."

"I see. He is from a titled family who are rather low on money, I assume. His father must be at least a baronet," the admiral speculated.

"Do you know the Hursts?" Bingley asked.

"No, my boy, but I know the story. I have always been surprised that women and men with the means to select their spouse often prefer the security of a comfortable social position over affection and admiration. If one cannot choose, it is understandable. But when a choice is possible, it is sad to see young people deciding their future based on the chances of being admitted to Almack's someday."

"Those who have the means to choose often must take into consideration their duty too. They must think of their family and social requirements. Wealth never comes without responsibilities. When one is choosing a wife — or husband — they must consider whether that person would meet the expectations of their position in society and whether they would be able to fulfil their own responsibilities towards everyone who is affected by that marriage," Darcy said vehemently.

"Yes, yes. I hear you. That is why so many marriages are sad to see. Why so many men visit their marital beds only when duty requires it and keep mistresses whom they spoil. And why so many women are miserable and never know the pleasure and the joy of a man's company. Or they do — with rakes and rascals, or even with stable boys."

"Admiral!" Darcy scolded him, but the gentleman laughed again and urged his horse into a gallop, leaving his younger companions behind, still in astonishment.

As they approached Longbourn, Bingley looked anxious, and Darcy felt apprehensive. A combination of the admiral and Mrs Bennet might become lethal. Fortunately, there was nobody from outside the family to witness the calamity. Elizabeth, however, would surely be amused, and most likely her father too.

Darcy could imagine her eyes sparkling with laughing comprehension, and her lips twisted in a quizzical smile.

The thought of being near her made his heart race. He felt like a lovestruck schoolboy, and what worried him the most was the realisation that he was indeed lovestruck. He had been infatuated a few times in his youth, but all the sensations he was experiencing with Elizabeth were completely new to him. Therefore, he had to leave Hertfordshire as soon as possible.

He did have the liberty to choose, as the admiral had said. However, that liberty was restricted by his duties and responsibilities. There were so many people depending on him, so many expectations, so much relying on Mrs Darcy's position that he had to select the right woman, for everyone's sake. And Elizabeth could not be the one, despite her wit and charm. Her family was the main obstacle, but not the only one. She was bright, but she lacked the experience necessary to run a large household, to take care of her tenants' families, to fill the place left empty by his mother's death. The entire ton would likely reject her, Lady Catherine would create an enormous scandal that London would hardly forget, his relatives — including Georgiana — would rebuke him, and she would suffer and feel miserable. She could quickly come to hate him, and his only gain would be that he had satisfied his weakness, his desire, his lust. That he would finally have the chance to taste her pink lips, to enjoy her company, her laughs, her gazes, her sparkling conversation, to share his bed with her. He would only satisfy his selfish wishes, hurting everyone else. Including Elizabeth herself. No, that was not entirely true. He would have certainly satisfied Mrs Bennet's desire too. What a comforting thought indeed!

"Darcy! Darcy, what on earth are you thinking of? You could at least pretend you care about our presence," he heard the admiral mocking him.

Darcy cleared his throat. "Forgive me, I was a little distracted. I see we have reached Longbourn already."

"We have, but you have been absent half the way here.

I hope there is nothing important you are worrying about," Bingley said.

"Nothing special. Just my usual musings," he answered as they all dismounted. A servant came to fetch the horses, and the front door opened, inviting them in.

∞∞∞

"I think a ball would be proper entertainment for a clergyman," Mr Collins declared solemnly.

"Well, as long as Lady Catherine approves of it," Mr Bennet replied, winking at Elizabeth.

"I am sure she would, my dear sir. And I hope my fair cousins will do me the great honour of saving a set each for me."

Lydia glared at Kitty, then at their mother, who paid no attention to her and replied, "They will certainly do so, sir."

"Good, good! And if my cousin Elizabeth would be so kind, I would ask for her hand for the first set of the evening."

Elizabeth tried to keep her eyes on her needlework, wondering how long she could pretend to be ignorant of the request or how painful it would be to sprain her ankle a day prior to the ball.

"Lizzy will be happy to dance the first with you, I assure you," Mrs Bennet declared. "What a pleasure for me to see my eldest daughters opening the ball side by side! I am sure Jane will stand up with Mr Bingley. What a joyful moment that will be."

A servant entered, interrupting their discussion, and, to everyone's astonishment, announced, "Mr Bingley to call on Mr Bennet. And Mr Darcy and Admiral Pembroke."

Silence fell over the room; the girls exchanged astounded glances, while Mrs Bennet seemed to forget to breathe. Mr Bennet stood up with a frown, confusion clearly writ across his face.

Elizabeth felt slightly distressed. She would never have imagined seeing the admiral in her house the day after their brief encounter — or even to see him at all, ever again.

The three gentlemen entered, Mr Bingley with a broad smile on his face, looking at Jane, whose cheeks coloured with pleasure. Behind him, the impressive figure of the admiral dominated the chamber. The last to enter was Mr Darcy, barely stepping beyond the threshold, as tall as the admiral and almost equally imposing.

It was the first time Mr Darcy had visited Longbourn, but the family disregarded him almost entirely in the presence of the remarkable stranger.

"Welcome, gentlemen. Please come in. It is an honour to receive you," Mr Bennet said.

"I am happy to see you all," Mr Bingley said joyfully. "We do not wish to intrude. We only came to greet you briefly. Allow me to introduce Admiral Thomas Pembroke of His Majesty's Navy. He has done us the great honour of visiting Netherfield on his way back to London."

The ladies mumbled a greeting and curtseyed, Mr Bennet bowed, Mr Collins put a large grin on his face and bent very low, with equal solemnity and ridiculousness.

"It is an honour, Admiral," a chorus of voices responded, while everyone tried to find a place to sit. Mrs Bennet quickly rang for refreshments, despite Mr Bingley's assurance that they had just finished their breakfast.

"Thank you for your kind reception," the admiral said with an unexpected amiability that contradicted his frowning countenance. "When Bingley told me he intended to call, I asked to join him. I wished to take this opportunity to make your acquaintance and to express my gratitude to your daughter Miss Elizabeth for saving me from a rather trying situation yesterday."

His words astounded the party as much as his appearance, and a moment of deep silence followed. All eyes turned to Elizabeth with wonder and reproach, and she glanced at the admiral, who gave a small shrug and an apologetic smile, obviously understanding he had committed an indiscretion and that Elizabeth had never mentioned the encounter to her family.

"Saved you? Lizzy? When did this happen? Have you been hurt, sir?" Mrs Bennet asked agitatedly.

"Mama, I met the admiral yesterday while I was walking. He missed the turn to Netherfield, and I pointed it out to him. That was all," Elizabeth explained, then turned to the admiral. "There is nothing to be grateful for, sir. It was an honour and a pleasure to meet you yesterday and to see you again today. I hope you find Netherfield to your liking so far?"

"Very much so — from what I have seen," the admiral answered. "Bingley made a good decision in renting it."

"It was Darcy who advised me. I mostly owe this decision to him," Bingley admitted.

"In that case, we must thank Mr Darcy. It would have been such a shame not to have you at Netherfield, sir," Mrs Bennet said, glancing at the haughty gentleman with a small trace of amiability.

Mr Darcy remained silent, but Elizabeth felt his gaze on her from time to time.

"Mr Bingley, your sisters are well, I hope?" Jane enquired shyly, and Mr Bingley looked happy to be able to address her directly.

"Yes, very well, thank you."

"I hope we shall have the pleasure of seeing them tomorrow, at dinner," Jane continued, and Mr Bingley turned pale, tangled in an attempt at excuses.

"I am not sure...they were not sure yet, but...there might be a change of plans and..."

"Oh dear, I hope you will not abandon us too, Mr Bingley," Mrs Bennet interjected in a desperate tone.

"No...I mean...I shall not abandon you, madam. It is just that the admiral arrived and..." Mr Bingley was looking from one to another, clearly so alarmed that he could not find his words.

"Oh, how silly of me!" Mrs Bennet cried in revelation. "How could I be so rude? Of course, the admiral is invited too! We would be greatly honoured and exceedingly pleased if the admiral would agree to join you!"

Mr Bingley turned even paler; he looked at Mr Darcy, as if begging for help, but the admiral immediately said, "That is very generous of you, madam! I gladly accept your invitation. How could an old officer deny himself the company of six lovely ladies and the prospect of a good meal?"

The entire Bennet family, as well as Mr Collins, remained silent, with apparent bewilderment. Mrs Bennet, who received the compliment with even more pleasure than her daughters, smiled sheepishly, her face changing colour several times. Mr Bingley looked relieved, and Jane's eyes regained their serenity.

"How lovely! This is wonderful, indeed! What an extraordinary surprise," Mrs Bennet repeated several times. Elizabeth knew that having an admiral at her dinner table was something her mother had never imagined, not even in her most daring and grandiose dreams, and she could hardly breathe from her eagerness to share the news with the people of Meryton.

"I never knew Mr Bingley had a relative who was an admiral," Lydia suddenly interjected. "And the officers from the militia that are camped in town will be surprised to hear it!"

"Oh, the admiral is not my relative. I have only had the honour of knowing him for a few years," Bingley replied, and several pairs of enquiring eyes turned wordlessly to the admiral, who returned a friendly expression while he explained the connection.

"I apologise, more details are required since I have invited myself into the midst of your family. I am the second son of Lord Archibald Pembroke, the Earl of Carlisle. My sister Amelia is married to Lord Matlock, Darcy's uncle."

"Oh…" Mrs Bennet gasped, followed by another moment of long and solemn silence.

The maid entered with refreshments, and the astonished gazes were finally dropped. Drinks were offered to the gentlemen and tea to the ladies, a welcome moment for the family to reflect on the latest details. Suddenly, not only was the admiral's presence an unexpected honour, but also Mr Darcy's consequence had grown significantly.

The first to speak was Mr Collins, who stepped forwards and bowed deeply again before Elizabeth or her father had the chance to stop him.

"This is indeed the most extraordinary moment of my life! More wonderful than any dream! I understand that both you and Mr Darcy are closely acquainted with Lady Catherine de Bourgh, and I am in the happy position to inform you that her ladyship was in perfect health a week ago when I left Rosings Park!"

Mr Darcy and the admiral gazed at him in puzzlement, while Mr Collins seemed to experience a moment of complete rapture.

"Thank you for informing us, sir," Mr Darcy replied sternly. "I did not know you were so well acquainted with my aunt."

"I have been lucky enough to benefit from her ladyship's noble patronage. I am the parson at Hunsford, and my house is on the edge of Rosings Park. I have the privilege of seeing Lady Catherine daily! In fact, I confess I am here with her approval."

"This is quite a coincidence," the admiral said. "I have not seen Lady Catherine de Bourgh in about five years, I think. How is she? Still stubborn and annoying and always demanding to have her way in everything?"

Almost everyone choked on their drinks, appalled at such a question. Elizabeth bit her lower lip to repress her laughter, glancing at her father, who was fighting a chuckle, and then at Mr Darcy, whom she expected to be scandalised by such a remark about his illustrious aunt. Instead, he was pressing his lips together to crush a smile — a gesture that shockingly revealed a pair of dimples in his cheeks. The amused expression changed his features so utterly that Elizabeth felt strange chills across her skin.

The admiral looked entirely composed, while Mr Collins was red-faced, fighting for air.

"My dear sir, I assure you that this is far from the truth!

Lady Catherine de Bourgh is the kindest, most generous, and most attentive person in the world! She is considerate and cares for everything and everyone. Even me! She insisted that I should come to renew my acquaintance with the family and even recommended I find a wife. I am forever grateful to her."

"I am sure you are, Mr Collins, and I am certain she is very much as I remember her. Come, do not distress yourself. How is Rosings Park? As beautiful as it used to be, I imagine." The admiral's attempt at calming Mr Collins met with some success, as he readily started talking about Rosings' windows, stairs, and park, forgetting some of the offence given to the most important person in his life.

∞∞∞

The gentlemen's visit lasted a full hour, and when it ended, everyone in the party had some reason for satisfaction. Darcy suddenly decided that he would join Bingley and the admiral for dinner, pondering that Mrs Bennet and her younger daughters had not behaved as insupportably as he had expected.

While they were waiting for the horses, with Mr Bennet accompanying them to the door, they heard Mrs Bennet's loud voice demanding Elizabeth tell them more details about the previous day's meeting with the admiral.

"I hope I did not upset Miss Elizabeth by revealing our encounter," the admiral said to Mr Bennet.

"Not at all, I am sure. To be honest, I am grateful to Lizzy for not sharing the story yesterday. If she had, I would have heard little else but speculations about an admiral's presence at Netherfield. As it was, we had the pleasure of hearing the details from you, and we saved countless hours of distress."

"I am glad I could help," the admiral jested. "You must know that I told Miss Elizabeth I disapprove of her habit of walking alone in the woods. It could be dangerous for a young lady."

"I have told her the same many times," Mr Bennet said. "But fortunately, the roads are quite safe in our neighbourhood. Besides, one can hardly convince Lizzy to do something against her will. The line between steadiness and stubbornness is very thin, and my Lizzy crosses it at times."

"Well, she must consider her safety! This is a very serious matter," the admiral insisted. "I have known several situations where young ladies have been harmed or abused, and I have always warned my acquaintances to be particularly cautious about exposing themselves to any danger."

"Miss Elizabeth is a wise lady. I doubt she would do anything to put herself in peril," Darcy said, surprising even himself.

"She will be happy to hear of your trust in her judgment, Mr Darcy," Mr Bennet said with a hint of mockery. "Surprised, but happy."

"Well...yes," Darcy mumbled while collecting his stallion from the groom.

"Admiral, it was an honour to make your acquaintance and a pleasure to receive you at Longbourn. I look forward to seeing you again tomorrow evening," their host said.

"Likewise, Mr Bennet."

As they bade their farewells, a new party of three gentlemen arrived, interrupting the cordial exchange. The new arrivals were clearly surprised too, waiting in awkward silence as the others departed.

If Darcy had a good impression of the visit, it immediately vanished, replaced by anger and disappointment when Wickham and two other officers greeted Mr Bennet with familiarity and enquired whether Mrs Bennet and her daughters were at home.

Chapter 4

As soon as the three guests departed, the speculations and comments burst out at Longbourn. Mr Collins attempted to express his opinion, but nobody was interested in it, and the ladies were too joyful to worry about his sensibilities. Consequently, they mostly disregarded him while debating the admiral's astonishing presence.

However, shortly after, the three officers arrived, and the ladies' enjoyment increased.

So absorbed was Elizabeth by the previous visit, that she had forgotten Mr Wickham and his companions were expected too. She wondered what would have happened if Mr Bingley and his party had remained a little longer or if Mr Wickham and his fellow soldiers had arrived earlier. Did the admiral know Mr Wickham? If so, how much did he know about the injustices he had suffered at the hands of Mr Darcy? And what would Mr Darcy have done, faced with the prospect of being in the same room as the man whom he had so grossly wronged?

"My dear gentlemen, do come in," Mrs Bennet uttered. "What a lovely day this is! If you had arrived only a few minutes earlier, you would have had the chance to meet Admiral Pembroke! Yes, yes, I know it is astonishing, but it is true! An admiral was here, at Longbourn, and he will join us for dinner tomorrow night! A happy day indeed."

The three seemed disconcerted, looking for a place to sit. Mr Wickham appeared slightly distressed and undecided whether to sit near Elizabeth or not. Eventually, Lydia asked him to sit between her and Kitty, and he obeyed.

Lieutenants Denny and Pratt expressed their curiosity about the admiral's presence in Hertfordshire.

"He is visiting Mr Bingley and Mr Darcy. He is a relative of Mr Darcy's. He got lost in the woods yesterday, and Lizzy showed him the path to Netherfield. The admiral got lost, not Mr Darcy," Lydia explained incoherently.

"Truly? How brave of Miss Elizabeth," Mr Wickham offered with a smile.

"Not at all." Elizabeth laughed. "I simply showed him the direction. I believe we are giving too much importance to a simple gesture."

Mrs Bennet disagreed with her daughter.

"Well, the admiral was impressed. He is a gentleman. He is so polite and friendly enough. My type of gentleman. Not like others who are silent and aloof. But I suppose those gentlemen possess other qualities that are admired in certain circles. Rich people are very strange at times."

Mr Collins readily interrupted her.

"I beg to differ, my dear madam! I have had the privilege of meeting enough rich people through the benevolence of my noble patroness, and I can testify they are well-educated, gracious, and courteous."

"Mr Collins, we already know Lady Catherine de Bourgh is a woman with no faults. Happily for us, very few are the same, or else we would not have anyone to make sport of," Mr Bennet said.

The officers smiled at the statement, but Mr Collins seemed lost for words once again. Any remark about Lady Catherine that did not contain flattery was obviously hard for him to comprehend.

"Mr Wickham, are you acquainted with the admiral?" Elizabeth asked. "I understand he has some close connection to Mr Darcy's family, but you did not greet each other, did you?"

The officer looked surprised.

"Not really. I did see him a couple of times when I was very young, at Pemberley, but not in the last few years, and I doubt he remembers me."

"Well, you may come to dinner tomorrow and meet him," Lydia cried.

Elizabeth saw Jane's eyes widen at such an improper invitation; fortunately, Mr Wickham immediately declined it.

"Thank you, Miss Lydia, but I already have another engagement. Besides, I am sure my presence would displease Darcy and consequently would ruin your party. I would not want that."

"You are more than welcome to dine with us some other time. All three of you," Mrs Bennet said to the officers.

"You are very kind, Mrs Bennet. It would be our pleasure," Mr Denny answered on everyone's behalf.

"Indeed. I imagine it is more convenient for the officers lower in rank to dine separately. Many titled people prefer to only mingle with those of their own rank. Of course, Lady Catherine is not the same. She often invites me to dine at Rosings Park," Mr Collins said solemnly.

"How fortunate for you," Mrs Bennet replied. "Gentlemen, how do you like Meryton so far? Does it meet your approval, compared with other towns where your regiment has camped before?"

"Meryton is a lovely place, and the company is particularly delightful," Mr Wickham replied, looking at Elizabeth, then back to her mother and sisters. His meaningful glance was not subtle, and Elizabeth did not miss the narrowing of Lydia's and Kitty's eyes as they looked in her direction.

"We hope you will come to the Netherfield ball," Lydia said.

"We have not received an invitation yet, but if Mr Bingley sends one, we shall gladly accept," Mr Denny replied.

"I know Mr Bingley intended to issue an invitation to Colonel Forster for all the officers," Jane admitted warmly, clearly hoping to put Mr Bingley in a favourable light.

"I never doubted him," Mrs Bennet said. "Well, a ball

without officers, especially when they are in the area, has no appeal. Many young men willing to dance are often the most important asset at a ball!"

"Well, I shall comply with my duty and will dance at least one set with all my cousins," Mr Collins promised in earnest.

Elizabeth was already engaged for the opening dances with the irritating parson, and whilst her sisters may somehow manage to escape their cousin's clumsiness, Elizabeth had no chance. She cringed when Mr Collins offered her a broad grin of contentment. Suddenly, the ball became an event to be dreaded, and she wondered how she could avoid it. Not even the presence of the charming Mr Wickham and the prospect of dancing with him was enough compensation.

What was she to do to discourage Mr Collins's preference towards her? Would it be helpful if she were more impertinent towards him? Friendlier towards the officers? Less respectful of Lady Catherine's greatness? Or to simply point out to him — straight and decided — that any possible connection between the two of them was only in his mind? Of course, he had not expressed his intentions yet, so such a response from her would be improper and even ridiculous. Not to mention the damage it would cause her mother's poor nerves, for which she would never be forgiven.

No, there was nothing else to do but wait and hope the upcoming days and the ball would not be as disastrous as she feared.

Seeing Wickham at Longbourn pained and angered Darcy. That scoundrel seemed perfectly at ease, as though he was certain nothing could touch him. And he appeared to visit the Bennets with the familiarity of a close acquaintance.

During all the years since he had discovered Wickham's true character, Darcy had rarely considered exposing him. First, because he wished to avoid hurting his father. Then, because he did not want to reveal his personal problems and bear the rumours and gossip that would arise. And lately, because such a disclosure would hurt Georgiana too, and nothing in the world was worthy of his sister's suffering. In his mind, it was other people's responsibility to see beyond Wickham's charming manners and to discover his true nature for themselves. If they were not able to do so, that would be entirely their problem.

The thought of Elizabeth being deceived by Wickham made him cringe. There was only one sort of friendship Wickham could have with a young lady, and to imagine Elizabeth in such a circumstance disgusted and sickened him. He could not allow it, or he would blame himself for the rest of his life. He had to think of a way to warn her and perhaps Mr Bennet too. It was his duty to at least tell her as little as was required so she could decide for herself whether Wickham was worthy of her consideration. It was a matter he had to ponder carefully to determine how much he trusted her, how much he could say without causing more damage to those dear to him. And such a conversation could not take place in public, in her parents' home. But where else? And when?

He had already decided he would break the connection with Miss Elizabeth Bennet soon. And his judgment told him that the best course would be for Bingley to separate from Miss Jane Bennet too, before it was too late. If things occurred as he imagined, he would soon put his acquaintance with the Bennets among his memories. But his care for Elizabeth would not disappear. He wished her to be safe and happy. It was both his duty and desire to accomplish that goal.

How would he do it, and how much would she allow him to interfere in her life? It was difficult to presume. But telling her the truth about Wickham was the least he could do.

And suddenly, the revelation struck him; he knew when and how.

She often took long walks alone, far enough from her home to assure privacy for a delicate conversation. He would ride twice a day on the grounds between Netherfield and Longbourn for as long as he was still in Hertfordshire until he happened upon her. It was a good plan, and Darcy was quite pleased with it.

∞∞∞

"How did you enjoy your visit to Longbourn, Admiral? Was it entertaining enough?" Miss Bingley asked that evening, during dinner.

"Exceedingly well. Just as I enjoyed the long ride back. The estate is lovely and the neighbours very pleasant. I congratulated Bingley for renting it."

"Netherfield is a good property," Mrs Hurst agreed. "Of course, it is nothing compared with Pemberley but good enough to rent. Charles should think of something of more consequence when he decides to purchase."

"And hopefully in another county," Miss Bingley added.

"It is foolish to compare any estate to Pemberley," Bingley answered. "Just as it would be ridiculous to compare myself with the Darcys. I am very pleased with Netherfield and even more so with its location."

"I do not expect you to compare yourself with the Darcys, nor to find an estate like Pemberley. But I just wish you would be more fastidious in judging people and properties," Miss Bingley said.

"More like Darcy, you mean," Bingley mocked his sister.

"Yes, more like Mr Darcy. You have the tendency to approve of everything and everyone too easily. Such generosity might induce you to make a decision that will affect your life for the worse," Miss Bingley insisted.

Darcy watched the arguments with amusement. If the two ladies knew the admiral as well as he did, they would have noticed that he was at the edge of his patience and likely wished to cease the discussion. Yet, they continued, until the gentleman's politeness was defeated by ire.

"You are rather severe and critical, Miss Bingley. Had I not known better, I would have assumed you had spent your entire life among the most titled families and owned several estates already."

The admiral's statement, although calm and civil, silenced the sisters, who seemed to take offence and be angered by it. Reminding them of their modest origins and scolding their unjustified pretentions was something they both deserved, but nobody — not even Darcy — had the audacity to do it directly.

Bingley looked surprised and sympathetic to his sisters but said nothing to contradict the admiral.

Darcy was aware that the conflict over Bingley's preference for the Bennets despite his sisters' disapproval was apparent and tormenting for the young man. The brief visit to Longbourn had been enough for the admiral to recognise Bingley's admiration for Miss Jane Bennet and the beautiful lady's warm regard for him.

Just as it seemed clear to the admiral that he did not support Bingley's inclination either, Darcy admitted. Furthermore, he feared the admiral would recognise his peculiar interest in Miss Elizabeth — hence his increasing curiosity about her.

"Anyone with even a slight education would easily recognise the lack of manners and faulty behaviour when they saw it," Miss Bingley said, trying to sound composed behind her anger.

"Caroline, you always see faulty behaviour when it comes to the Bennets," Bingley said with unconcealed displeasure. "You deliberately judge them too harshly."

"I pride myself in being fair and realistic in judging people. I do not allow myself to be easily deceived by shallow smiles," Miss Bingley concluded.

"I confess I saw not many flaws in the Bennets. No more than in any of us. If we are to be fair and realistic, each of us should admit to our own faults and misbehaviour at times," the admiral said.

"True," Bingley quickly agreed. "And if we are to be even fairer, Miss Jane Bennet is the most admirable lady I have ever met. Her stunning beauty is completed by gentleness and kindness, and her manners are perfect in every respect. Even Darcy could not find anything to disapprove of in her, except that she smiles too much."

While his sisters again rolled their eyes with mockery, the admiral looked puzzled.

"Since when did charming smiles become flaws? This is a harsh and ungenerous judgment. And rather ungentlemanlike, Darcy."

"It was a mere comment made when I first met Miss Bennet. After knowing them better, I find little wanting in the two eldest Miss Bennets. I already declared that," Darcy replied.

"It is surprising that Mr Darcy changed his opinion on the subject quite drastically in such a short time," Miss Bingley said with sharp mockery. "He turned from being Eliza Bennet's most severe critic to showing admiration for her fine eyes, whatever that means. It is astonishing. I expect him next to call Mrs Bennet a wit, and I shall never trust men's judgment again."

"Let us be serious," Mrs Hurst interjected. "Jane Bennet is a dear, sweet girl, but her family and connections are impossible to overlook. And Charles, your admiration for her is only the latest in a long line of appreciation for many women over the last few years. Just remember the other ladies who have charmed you, and be careful with your behaviour before raising unreasonable expectations. Jane Bennet is nothing like the young ladies of the ton, who are well accustomed to the ways of the world."

"What if I am careful about my behaviour and if I am aware of the expectations I am raising? Stop mentioning me being charmed by other ladies in the past. I know my heart and my mind!"

"How can you know them, Charles, since you have only known Miss Bennet for two months?" Miss Bingley replied angrily.

The admiral sipped some wine, watching his companions.

"Forgive me. I am lost regarding the reason for your debate. I fully understand Bingley admiring Miss Bennet. She is truly one of the most beautiful ladies I have ever met — and I have met so many that I barely remember all of them."

He gulped some more wine, then continued. "I have listened to you criticising the Bennet family, but is Mr Bennet not a gentleman? Is Miss Bennet not a gentleman's daughter? If you were to ask me, a gentleman's daughter with such beauty and sweet nature has every reason to hope she would make an excellent marriage. She only needs to go out more, to attend a few parties and balls during the Season, and she would easily find several eligible men to fight for her attention."

"Yes, but who would take her to those parties, since she has such poor connections? Her father might be a gentleman, but her mother? Her other relatives? One of her uncles is an attorney, and the other one is in trade and lives near Cheapside!" Miss Bingley said maliciously.

Her spiteful tone clearly annoyed the admiral as much as it did Darcy.

"There are many worthy men in trade, such as your father," Darcy replied.

Miss Bingley paled. "Yes, but he made a fortune and fought to improve his family's wealth and situation in life. He was acquainted with some titled families in town, and he provided us with the best education. He did not succeed in purchasing an estate, but he did leave Charles a generous fortune to buy one. Surely he cannot be compared to a country gentleman who cannot ensure a decent dowry for his daughters and whose estate is entailed to a distant cousin! What will happen to them once Mr Bennet dies?"

Miss Bingley's wounded pride seemed to have defeated her reasoning, and her tone, her expression, even her words towards the distinguished guest were unacceptably impolite. Bingley attempted to stop her with no success, while Darcy gazed at the admiral, wondering why he would allow such a conversation to continue, why he carried on a debate with Miss Bingley on a subject of such little significance to him.

Darcy himself had had his share of sharp exchanges with Miss Bingley regarding Elizabeth, but he had done so in complete consciousness. He had expressed his admiration for Elizabeth on more than one occasion, although he knew it would increase Bingley's sister's resentment. But the admiral was not a man to contradict, especially when he was right, and even less so to deliver offensive replies. And Miss Bingley appeared to have lost her composure and manners, proving she lacked dignity just as much as the people she loathed and rebuked.

The admiral, however, continued unruffled.

"My dear Miss Bingley, please believe me that I have the highest appreciation for your father. He has done nothing but admirable things for his family, and nobody could question his merits. However, the comparison with Mr Bennet's situation is a puzzle difficult to solve. If we are to speak in general, with no reference to any acquaintance, who is in a more advantageous position in society? A gentleman with a poor financial situation, or a man making a living in trade who possesses a good sum of money?"

With that, the admiral glanced at Hurst, then back to the Bingley sisters, ruining the last trace of their calmness.

"What is your opinion, if I may ask?" Mrs Hurst asked.

The admiral shrugged with a genuine smile.

"I truly do not know! Most arranged marriages are based on one spouse belonging to an old or titled family with little money and the other being in possession of a considerable fortune but with fewer connections. I have no children, but if I had, I am sure I would have encouraged them to marry following both their hearts and their minds. I do encourage Darcy and my other single nephew, Richard, to do so, but I see not much progress in either case, though for different reasons."

Miss Bingley appeared doubtful, while Mrs Hurst stole a glance at her husband, then paid attention to her plate.

"Would you not have influenced your children's choices of spouses, Admiral?" Miss Bingley enquired. "Not even with some advice, leading them in the right direction? Young people are often deceived by shallow feelings and mistake a mere infatuation for deep love. In such cases, is it not the family and friends' duty to pull them back onto the proper track before making a decision they will regret their entire lives?"

"If that were the case, I might intervene with a bit of advice. But no more."

Miss Bingley appeared more and more anxious; even her face changed under her distress. "Sir...do you mean that you would have allowed your daughter or son to marry someone beneath them? Someone unworthy of your name and position? Someone who met with people's rejection and criticism? Someone with no education but a handsome appearance? Even a peasant, a servant?"

"I advise young people of my acquaintance not to marry without affection and to give their admiration to someone who deserves it. Someone worthy of it, not necessarily by name or position but by character and nature. I would give you the same advice, if you asked me for it, Miss Bingley. I wish with all my heart that you do not come to agree with me only after you marry."

Miss Bingley turned pale; Darcy grew uncomfortable too and interjected.

"It is even more fortunate if one falls in love with someone from their own circle. I know this is the case with most of the acquaintances the admiral and I share."

"That statement sounds like you are mocking me, Darcy," the admiral said. "I do not have many acquaintances who married for love, as you well know. Those who did were perhaps just fortunate to find someone within their circle. I shall not refrain from advising every young lady or gentleman to marry someone that equally pleases their eyes, their ears, their heart, and their mind."

"It was certainly not my intention to be disrespectful,"

Darcy replied. "Quite the contrary. My own parents were equally fortunate in their choice of a spouse. Both came from old, respectable families, and their deep affection and loyalty to each other added to all the other things they had in common. Their marriage was truly to the advantage of both. One to which everyone should look up to."

"What if one cannot find such a person? Or what if one did find such a person but their feelings were not reciprocated? Would it be better to never marry than settle for less?" Mrs Hurst asked.

"That is an excellent question, Mrs Hurst, and I truly do not have an answer. I would say it depends on the individual. What I do know for sure is that one cannot be happy, and marriage might turn into a cage of turmoil, if there is no affection or attraction between spouses," the admiral said.

"I would dare say the marriage might also turn into turmoil if it is based only on a shallow admiration and meaningless attraction that will soon pass, leaving behind only regrets and frustration," Miss Bingley declared.

"True," the admiral admitted. "That is why I mentioned that, in my opinion, one should choose to satisfy all the senses. And, of course, the senses must be stirred all the time, so the pleasure remains longer. There is nothing more satisfying for me than to be able to carry on an interesting conversation with a spirited lady that I admire."

"I agree," Darcy said absently, holding his glass, drawing all eyes upon him. He felt slightly embarrassed by the words that had slipped from his lips, so he tried to keep his composure while he continued. "A lady's beauty is easily enhanced or shadowed by her knowledge, education, and wit."

"We must also be aware that it is the same for men. As handsome as a man is, his manners, his conversation, his amiability will make the ladies admire him or not," the admiral concluded.

Emptying his third glass of brandy, Bingley began to laugh. "That is what happened to Darcy when we appeared at the

Meryton assembly. The first time the ladies saw him, all of them stared at him, whispering about him with interest. Luckily for me, very soon his aloofness and haughtiness made everybody favour me over him."

Darcy and the admiral joined him in his amusement. "Do not be so modest, Bingley. Everybody favours you over me, all the time," Darcy said, and Bingley laughed again.

The admiral's statements distressed Darcy and brought back his previous struggles. He agreed with most of what the admiral had said, although such sensible advice was difficult to follow in real life.

His own parents had often advised him the same way, but since their deaths, life had left him alone, with the responsibilities of everyone whose lives depended on him. Yes, nobody should marry without love, admiration, and attraction. That is why he had been reluctant to take a single step towards any young lady he had met. None of them held his interest and his admiration in any particular way.

However, no responsible gentleman would disregard the demands of duty, either; he had to mind the obligations towards those who depended on him and the expectations forced upon him by society, his family, and his own common sense.

Elizabeth Bennet had stirred his senses in a way no woman ever had before. Although she was a gentleman's daughter and he had never doubted her worthiness, he could not consider her the future Mrs Darcy. Too many obstacles stood in the way of such a notion, and the power of his desire to be with her appeared more a sign of weakness and a childish infatuation than a grounded affection that could be the basis of a lifetime commitment.

Being certain Elizabeth received his attention with pleasure and reciprocated his admiration, Darcy grew worried. He feared that the admiral's attention to the Bennets would arouse new reasons for hope in her and would generate unrealistic expectations, especially if he continued to visit the Bennets and to spend more time in her presence. He feared that

Elizabeth would assume too much from his mere politeness and would suffer when he left and ruined her hopes.

Consequently, he decided to limit the time he was in her company. He could not renege on the dinner invitation without appearing rude and without having to provide the admiral with detailed and awkward explanations. So, he would go, but afterwards, he would only meet her at the ball once more, then he would depart for London.

"Darcy? Darcy!" he heard a loud voice calling.

"Yes, Bingley?"

"The admiral and I are going to have a drink in the library. Will you join us?"

Only then did he notice that Miss Bingley and the Hursts were ready to retire. He nodded and followed the two gentlemen.

"You have seemed quite absent since the last course," Bingley said.

"Yes…I apologise."

"Is something wrong?" the admiral asked once the library door had closed behind them.

"No. I was thinking about my return to London after the ball."

"I must go to London too, but I shall return before Christmas," Bingley declared, seeming slightly uneasy.

Admiral Pembroke was watching him sympathetically. "Surely it must be hard to be torn between your wishes and your sisters'. Sometimes, one must impose one's own will in regard to one's own future."

Bingley looked surprised, his face coloured, then he glanced at Darcy. "Admiral, I was quite impressed with your opinions about marriage," he said. "My only question would be… how can one know the difference between infatuation and true love? How can I be certain that my feelings will last? And how can I be sure that a lady possesses genuine affection for me and is not just accepting my courtship because her family insist upon her doing so? Or because by marrying me she can ensure a safe future for her and her family?"

Bingley seemed so distressed that the admiral looked torn between laughing or pitying him.

"My boy, to such a question I would know the answer in a blink of an eye if it involved a lady and me. If it is about you, you should seek the truth for yourself. You should feel the truth. I have heard that you have been enchanted by lovely young ladies many times. But may I ask — how many women have you loved?"

Bingley was puzzled. "Loved?"

"Yes, loved. That feeling that keeps you awake during the night and anxious during the day and makes your blood run through your veins and sets your heart pounding. That sensation that makes you unaware of the world around you except for one person."

Bingley remained silent, thoughtful, bemused. "Well, I…I shall have to think about that."

"You do so, my boy. As for the lady's feelings, again, a man should know, should feel. From a smile, from a glance, from a shiver, from a mere gesture. You cannot be deceived if you seriously search for the truth."

"And yet, so many men of consequence are misled by ladies' demure appearances and gentle manners, induced to believe themselves in love and loved in return, only to find they were wrong when it was too late," Darcy said severely. "I do know several such cases myself, and I believe a man cannot be cautious enough in this regard."

Bingley's distress increased, and the admiral laughed even louder.

"That is because we men often allow our pride and arrogance and selfishness to guide our judgment. We consider ourselves to be superior to others, we appreciate our assets too much and others' too little, and we see the faults in others but never our own. Therefore, when we like a young lady, we have a tendency to assume she must like us too, and we judge her every action and gesture to support our assumption and to satisfy our vanity. And when we find out we have been wrong, we claim she has deceived us, although in truth we have deceived ourselves."

"Perhaps," Darcy said. "But you cannot deny that there are young ladies who would pretend to have more feelings than they truly possess to secure a husband."

"I fear you have met more such cases than I have, and you seem far more worried by the notion than I am," the admiral replied with amusement. "Or perhaps you are more eligible and more desirable than I was. Darcy, I wonder how many ladies you have been smitten with and how many you have loved — if any."

The question took Darcy by surprise, and he glared at the admiral reproachfully. Until recently, he would have answered such a question lightly. He had been enchanted a few times by some beautiful young ladies, but never more than a distant admiration that passed before it was even acknowledged. Elizabeth's presence in his life had changed that completely.

"It is very late. We should retire for the night before we open another debate. My life is completely uneventful, I assure you," he responded more coldly than he wished to.

"Yes, I feared that would be the case," the admiral said.

Bingley began to laugh loudly, despite Darcy's frown and reproachful expression.

"I am glad you are entertained, Bingley," Darcy said. "At least you do not look worried any longer."

"I am still worried, but the admiral's advice has helped me."

"I am pleased to hear that, my boy. Regarding your concern — even if the lady does not return the same level of affection at the beginning of a marriage, if she is worthy of the effort, and the gentleman's feelings are strong enough, he should pursue her and conquer her. There is nothing more delightful than making a beautiful lady fall in love with you and enjoying your success. Sadly, most gentlemen of the ton enter into arranged marriages and could not care less about their wives. They only comply with their marital duties and put the effort into conquering others."

"I can easily understand your meaning, sir. And I truly

enjoy listening to you. You speak so lightly yet so decidedly of these matters with the ladies," Bingley said admiringly.

Darcy smiled to himself, more comfortable now he had ceased to be the subject of the conversation. The admiral had always been a favourite with the ladies — more than the family would like to admit. He had observed the man garnering much attention on each of the rare occasions they had attended balls and parties together. In that regard, his cousin Colonel Fitzwilliam was very much like the admiral.

"Bingley, one more thing, regarding Miss Bennet."

"Yes?"

The older gentleman emptied his glass, while his younger companions looked at him enquiringly.

"You should be content that Miss Bennet does not have the proper connections to take her out into society. If she did, she would surely have many suitors, and you would have to face stiff competition."

Bingley's eyes widened at such a statement, and even Darcy was stunned. The admiral's sincerity was equally pleasant and disconcerting, and he appeared utterly diverted, while his younger companions found nothing to say in response.

After another glass of brandy, all three agreed it was time to finally retire for the night. The next day, with the dinner at Longbourn, was expected to be at least equally entertaining and challenging.

Chapter 5

T hinking about their discussion kept Darcy awake most of the night. Whilst he was aware that the admiral's conversational skills had been influenced by the numerous drinks he had enjoyed over the day, his reasoning was sound, though hardly applicable in their society.

Yes, it would have been the perfect match for him to marry the only woman who delighted all his senses, as the gentleman stated. He was bewitched while watching Elizabeth supporting her ideas, carrying on teasing conversation, smiling, dancing, walking. And most importantly, she seemed so natural in her manners, as though she was unaware of the effect she had on him.

Perhaps she was unaware, after all; she could not have much experience with men. In their confined society, she could know little about the art of seduction, he mused, smiling to himself. And yet, she had succeeded where many others had failed. If the admiral could hear his thoughts, he would call him arrogant again. No, he was not arrogant, only realistic; he had little doubt about that.

Imagining himself married to Elizabeth, having her by his side day by day — and night by night — caused him an inner thrill that worried him. If he allowed himself to dive into that dream, he might be in real danger of dismissing his reason entirely.

Mostly against his will, he would attend dinner at Longbourn. Since the admiral wished to go, he could not possibly refuse; and even if he could, an evening in Elizabeth's company was almost worth bearing her mother's offensive manners.

The admiral might have been correct in justifying Mrs Bennet's desperate efforts to find eligible husbands for her daughters. In all honesty, most mothers had that goal, even those with less difficult situations than the Bennets. Yet, it was no excuse for the woman's lack of decorum and thoughtless actions. She was obviously pushing Jane Bennet towards Bingley, and — much worse — she supported that clergyman's ridiculous inclination towards Elizabeth.

Darcy shivered, wondering what would be worse: to know Elizabeth was attracted to Wickham or to see her married to a man so beneath her in intelligence and spirit.

Darcy was the last to arrive at breakfast, and he noticed Bingley's sisters were in low spirits, while Bingley was engaged in another conversation with the admiral.

"Darcy, Bingley just told me something intriguing. One of the officers we saw yesterday — I thought he looked familiar. Was that Wickham, whose father managed Pemberley? Who was George's godson?"

"Yes," Darcy replied while taking his seat.

"Did you know he was here? Are you still friends? I remember you were displeased with him at some point."

"No, we are not friends. I never imagined I might meet him here and even less that he would join the militia. It is just an unfortunate coincidence."

"Ah, I see you are still displeased with him."

"That would be an understatement. But truly, this is not a conversation to be carried on during breakfast and certainly not in the presence of ladies," Darcy concluded, concentrating on his plate.

"I have heard — and I have noticed on one or two occasions — that Mr Wickham is a great favourite at Longbourn. He seemed especially close to Eliza Bennet," Miss Bingley interjected.

"Have you? I am rather astonished you know so many things about the Bennets, even though you are reluctant to see them," Bingley intervened. "And speaking of the Bennets, are you certain you will not join us for dinner tonight?"

"Dear Lord, I am absolutely certain!" Miss Bingley said, rolling her eyes.

"As you wish. I am going to call on Colonel Forster this morning and present him with the invitations to the ball. Darcy, Admiral, would you care to keep me company?"

"If you do not mind, I would rather decline, as I have to write several letters today," Darcy answered. He did intend to write to his solicitor, to Mrs Reynolds, and to Georgiana. But even more, he wished to avoid another meeting with Wickham.

"Write one to your uncle, my brother, too. They are waiting for news from me," the admiral requested. "I shall go with Bingley. I intended to meet Colonel Forster regardless."

"And you, Hurst?" Bingley enquired.

"I have no desire to go out in such weather," the man answered. "Lord, it is so dull here. Nothing to be done most of the day. I hope we shall return to London soon."

"We shall. Hopefully immediately after the ball," his wife said, glancing at her brother. Bingley said nothing.

When the other gentlemen left, Darcy chose to write his letters in his room; staying in the library, as he wished to, would expose him to Miss Bingley's company, which was no more pleasant to him than that of Wickham's. Not equally appalling but irritating enough. He wondered how it was possible that the lady continued in her efforts to insinuate herself with him, even though his response to her was always cold and barely polite.

Miss Bingley's attempts to draw his attention made her no better than Mrs Bennet, or his aunt Lady Catherine de Bourgh, if he was to be completely honest. Just as the admiral had stated.

Darcy also expected that the admiral would have much to say — and much to ask — in regard to Wickham; the subject would not be easily dropped, and the admiral was not a man to be easily deceived.

Therefore, he had to carefully decide what to reveal regarding his dealings with the scoundrel. The admiral was also not a man to be easily calmed once his ire had been raised, and while Wickham deserved all possible anger, Darcy had to consider the consequences of a scandal, especially related to Georgiana.

"Upon my word, I knew Mr Darcy was rich, but I did not know he was quite so important," Mrs Bennet said. "My sister Phillips hardly believed me when I told her about his connections. Truth be told, now I better understand why he refused to dance with you, Lizzy. You must not be upset. He is certainly accustomed to much prettier women, not to mention much wealthier."

"You are perfectly right, Mrs Bennet," Mr Collins interjected. "Lady Catherine de Bourgh says Mr Darcy has been blessed with everything a young man could hope for. That is why she says he is a proper match for her daughter."

"Well, Mr Darcy is certainly too rich for us," Mrs Bennet replied. "I mean, for all of us, here in Meryton. Mrs Long complained about him not addressing a single word to her, but why would he, if he is related to earls and admirals?"

"I am not upset with Mr Darcy, but I do not agree with excusing his rudeness based on his connections," Elizabeth said, mostly as a joke. "He might be related to an admiral and an earl, but the admiral himself — who is the son of an earl — behaves amiably and is neither arrogant nor presumptuous."

Elizabeth felt amused by the conversation and exchanged glances with her father, who was reading in a corner, rolling his eyes occasionally.

"That is because you rescued the admiral when he was lost in the woods, Lizzy. I bet if you saved Mr Darcy, he would be more amiable and would dance with you," Mrs Bennet replied, making

Elizabeth laugh.

"I would rather leave Mr Darcy to wander until he became more amiable by himself," she said, receiving an appalled look from Mr Collins, who interjected with apparent distress.

"My dear cousin Elizabeth, please mind your words! I understand you enjoy teasing, but one cannot speak in such a manner about Mr Darcy! Lady Catherine would never approve of it, and she would not easily forget such an offence."

"Mr Collins, I shall try to mind my words when Mr Darcy is present. As for Lady Catherine, fortunately, she cannot hear me speaking, so she has no opportunity to approve or not."

She felt exceedingly diverted, while Mr Collins's displeasure and anxiety were visible.

As the hour for dinner approached, Mrs Bennet sent all her daughters to change into their best gowns to make a good impression 'just in case' the admiral had some nephews or younger friends to whom he might recommend them.

Elizabeth was the first to return, and she noticed her mother's scolding glare for not being elegant enough. She disregarded it and went to the window and gazed out. She had chosen one of the muslin gowns she had worn for dinner at Netherfield; it was fashionable enough for a mere family dinner, even with an admiral and an earl's nephew and grandson in attendance.

Jane and her younger sisters all were received with an approving nod by their mother. Even Mary looked her best, and Jane was simply stunning, as Mrs Bennet repeated.

"Now, girls, one more thing. You know Mr Darcy is upset with Mr Wickham. Since Mr Darcy is related to the admiral and is Mr Bingley's friend, we must be careful not to annoy him by mentioning his enemy. So, no speaking of Mr Wickham tonight, remember?"

"But Mama, why can I not speak of my friend?" Lydia argued, supported by Kitty.

"Because I say so! And do not make me say it twice, young lady!" Mrs Bennet scolded her. "My nerves are not to be challenged further! Now go and sit there. Mr Collins, you may sit next to Lizzy, if you wish."

With such arrangements that made Elizabeth — as well as Jane — blush with mortification, time passed, and the guests arrived. They all gathered together in the drawing room for a little while, and the conversation was slow to begin.

When dinner was served, everybody moved to the table, which barely accommodated so many people, so they were slightly cramped, as Elizabeth observed. Mr Darcy had certainly noticed, especially since Mr Collins kept leaning towards him to say something. The admiral seemed not to care, being too busy debating politics with Mr Bennet and asking for Elizabeth's opinion from time to time.

"Admiral Pembroke, I know you are a hero and spend most of your life at war, fighting for our country," Mrs Bennet interjected solemnly, "but may I ask — do you have no family? A wife or children?"

"No, ma'am, no wife or children. But I do have a family — my sister and brother, my nieces and nephews, as well as some close friends, like this young man Bingley over here. And I would not call myself a hero, by any means."

"Oh, but I am sure you are! You will not return to the sea, will you?"

"No, not again. I am too old for that. My age and an injury caused me to be discharged from the navy," he answered, keeping a light tone.

"Then you still have time to marry and have children! You are certainly not too old for that!" Mrs Bennet concluded, causing her husband and her eldest daughters more embarrassment.

Mr Darcy and Mr Bingley were clearly also uncomfortable, but the admiral laughed.

"You are too kind, ma'am, but my youth is gone. I have been married to the sea for so long that I cannot imagine another wife, even if the first one left me. Or I left it."

"One can hardly imagine what a lifetime in the navy and

on the sea means," Mr Bennet interjected, to silence his wife. "However, it might be easier than some marriages."

The admiral laughed again, and so did Mr Bennet.

"I was talking about marriage last night with these two young men," the admiral added. "I have never been married or even engaged, but I have the audacity to give advice about it. You know what is said: when you cannot do a certain thing, teach others how to do it."

"I have not heard that saying before, but it certainly sounds like a wise one," Mr Bennet agreed, and Elizabeth smiled too. She was pleased to see her father so much at ease with the admiral, and the illustrious guest treating her father as an equal.

"Lady Catherine always advises me on important matters," Mr Collins interjected. "Her ladyship's knowledge and wisdom are valuable on any occasion, even when she is not familiar with a certain issue. I never disobey her requests, and I am proud of that."

"Mr Collins, I do not wish to be rude, but we should make a pact not to mention Lady Catherine so often tonight. She is my sister-in-law and Darcy's aunt, and neither of us mention her in a month as often as you do in a few hours."

Mr Collins took the unexpected censure with an offended air and seemed tempted to reply but remained silent.

"I hear Mr Darcy is engaged to be married to Lady Catherine's daughter," Mrs Bennet said, unaware of the mortification she caused.

"Such a report is not correct, ma'am," Mr Darcy responded. "I am not certain where you heard it from, but I would suggest giving it no credit."

Mrs Bennet looked at Mr Collins, whose expression revealed increasing agitation.

"I must follow the admiral's suggestion of not mentioning Lady Catherine de Bourgh so often, by adding the subject of marriage to the same list," Mr Bennet intervened.

"Mr Bingley, did you give the officers an invitation to the ball?" Lydia asked, changing the subject as requested.

"I did, Miss Lydia. Just earlier today."

"How wonderful! I cannot remember another ball with so many officers! Now we can all dance as much as we like! There is nothing worse than a ball where gentlemen are scarce and some ladies cannot enjoy every set."

"I am ready to dance with all my cousins," Mr Collins declared. "As well as with other young ladies that might be in attendance."

Lydia rolled her eyes in exasperation, and Elizabeth frowned, realising that the gesture had not escaped the notice of anyone at the table.

"Are you sure Lady Catherine would approve of you dancing so much?" the admiral asked. The mere question, although asked obviously in jest, panicked Mr Collins instantly.

"You believe she might not?"

"I can hardly say, but I know Darcy is her favourite nephew, and he barely dances at all, as far as I remember. Unless he has changed his preferences."

"He has not," Elizabeth answered before she had time to consider her words. "He does not like dancing and considers it a diversion popular amongst the less polished societies of the world."

"Yes, that is how I remember it." The admiral laughed.

Elizabeth smiled while wondering why Mr Darcy looked so uncomfortable. She smiled, but he did not.

"I have not changed my preferences," Mr Darcy eventually admitted. "However, to complete my statement to Sir William, I accepted that dancing can be a refinement of polished societies too. I hope you also remember that part, Miss Elizabeth."

"I do, sir. In other words, you admitted that a well-educated gentleman can dance just as well as a savage." She ended with a smile, pleased with her teasing tone. He deserved to be reminded that his arrogant declarations did not go unnoticed.

"I did not say such a thing," Mr Darcy immediately argued somewhat harshly, though Elizabeth kept her smile while their gazes locked. A long moment passed, then he finally averted his eyes.

"In fact, you are right, Miss Elizabeth. I did admit that."

"Well, let us drink to that," the admiral said with amusement. "Seeing Darcy defeated and forced to admit his errors is something rare and utterly entertaining."

"Mr Darcy does not look very entertained, but it is a good opportunity to drink nevertheless," Mr Bennet accepted.

While the two had their glasses filled, Elizabeth and Mr Darcy smiled at each other across the table, though for different reasons.

Chapter 6

The three gentlemen returned to Netherfield close to midnight. The weather was cold, and the wind brought the smell of winter.

All three were in reasonably good spirits, and despite already having enjoyed several drinks, they still stopped in the library to enjoy another one and share their opinions of the evening.

"I was more diverted than I expected," the admiral declared. "What an interesting family the Bennets are! Mr Bennet and his wife could not be more different, and their daughters have inherited a fascinating variety of traits that make them utterly charming."

"I admit Mr Bennet is more pleasant company than I anticipated," Darcy replied.

"Well, considering you had never spoken to him until yesterday, how could you have even formed an opinion?" Bingley enquired.

"True," the admiral said. "I am glad to see you more decided, young man! Good for you. And I must say, Miss Bennet seems to have a nature as pleasant as her appearance."

"I believe Bingley should be more cautious in showing his admiration," Darcy declared. "He has already roused expectations, and it will be difficult to deal with the consequences. In such a small town, people assume much, judge quickly, and rumours are easily spread."

"That is a sound statement, Darcy," the admiral answered.

"I would also recommend any gentleman to show prudence in his manner towards a young woman. Society can be quite unfair in its judgment, whether in a small town or in the city. What is acceptable for a man might ruin a woman's reputation forever."

"I am aware of that," Bingley responded. "Did you notice any flaws in my behaviour towards Miss Bennet? If so, please tell me. I would by no means do anything to harm her."

"Your behaviour was flawless, from what I noticed," the admiral said. "However, you do realise that Mrs Bennet is waiting for a proposal very soon. That is not necessarily your fault, but hers. Mr Bennet seems more reasonable in his expectations."

"Indeed. Mrs Bennet seems determined to understand only what is convenient for her," Darcy uttered.

"Yes, very much like your aunt Lady Catherine!" Admiral Pembroke laughed. "By the way, that clergyman pushed me to the edge of my patience. Dear Lord, could a man be more annoying? Can you imagine him in a conversation with Catherine? He might be a good man, after all, but he is ridiculously irritating."

The admiral was laughing openly, but Darcy was not equally diverted.

"What upsets me the most is that Lady Catherine has seemingly discussed with him matters that should have stayed within the family. Not to mention they are untrue."

"You mean your engagement to Anne? Catherine has been carrying on this nonsense since you were infants — speaking of ridiculously irritating."

"Please forgive my intrusion," Bingley interjected, "but if there is no truth in such an engagement, why would Lady Catherine claim something that might affect her daughter?"

"Because she is very much like Mrs Bennet," the admiral answered in jest. "She understands only what is convenient for her. And sadly, age has not improved her. Poor Anne. I wonder how she bears her mother's obsession."

Each sipped from their glasses, then the admiral

continued, "That clergyman seems inclined towards Miss Elizabeth. I hope he does not propose to her. And if he does, I hope she does not accept him. That would be deeply disappointing for me, since I find Miss Elizabeth absolutely enchanting."

Darcy sipped more brandy; the same matter troubled him, but he did not dare speak openly about it.

The admiral laughed again. "Dear Lord, I just realised I have the same taste in women as the clergyman! That is worrisome and frightening!"

"Sir, I do not feel comfortable making sport at the expense of Miss Elizabeth, after we just dined with her family," Darcy said in earnest.

"Oh, come now, do not be unnecessarily serious, Darcy. I am not making sport of Miss Elizabeth. Quite the opposite. I am declaring my admiration for her. Her wit is just as sparkling as her pretty eyes."

Darcy smiled to himself; he had confessed his admiration for Elizabeth's pretty eyes to Miss Bingley — an error for which he still blamed himself.

"Did I mention Darcy refused to dance with Miss Elizabeth on the first evening they met?" Bingley interjected, clearly induced by the brandy. "We were at an assembly in Meryton. He called her tolerable, and I believe she heard him! I have heard rumours about it. People know you offended her, my friend."

The admiral choked on his drink. "Surely you did not, Darcy!"

"He did!" Bingley insisted. "Every time they have met, they have fought. Over anything! No wonder she despises him."

"Miss Elizabeth most certainly does not despise me, Bingley. We have never fought, only debated over various subjects, as two educated people should do. I called her tolerable at the assembly because you annoyed me, Bingley, and kept insisting on me dancing when I specifically mentioned I did not wish to. The offence was not aimed at her but at you!"

"I must agree with Bingley — it is no wonder she dislikes

you," the admiral uttered. "She might not despise you, but you are certainly not her most favourite man in the world. That is obvious to anyone. I hope you have apologised to her."

"I have not...there has been no such opportunity yet. But I shall."

"Miss Elizabeth stayed at Netherfield for four days, and Darcy did not find an opportunity to apologise," Bingley said, trying to stand up; he was unsteady on his feet, so he resumed his seat but smiled widely, and so did the admiral.

"I am sorry to interrupt your amusement, but it seems we have had too many drinks tonight. We should retire and continue our conversation tomorrow."

"That is a sound suggestion," the admiral admitted. "Darcy always has sound suggestions."

"So, Admiral, will you stay another week, to attend to ball," Bingley asked hopefully.

"I would not miss it for the world."

They left the library together, each walking to their own room.

"Darcy?" the admiral called him.

"Yes, sir?"

"Tomorrow, we should speak more about that Wickham fellow. I met him when we called on Colonel Forster, and there is something that bothers me about him."

"Very well, sir. Good-night for now."

Talk of the dinner lasted long after the three gentlemen had left Longbourn. Mrs Bennet was the most thrilled about the success of the evening, but Mr Bennet also admitted it had been delightful.

Mr Collins still seemed offended after being silenced and scolded; therefore he retired to his chamber as soon as the guests departed.

Elizabeth had enjoyed the dinner exceedingly and felt grateful for the admiral's amiability towards her family and for his apparent support of Mr Bingley's admiration for Jane.

From Mr Darcy, she had still noted signs of disapproval, yet his manners had obviously improved during his two visits at Longbourn. He was still far from the friendly Mr Bingley, and even from the admiral, yet not as arrogant and haughty as he had showed on other occasions.

The detail that had grabbed her attention had been the subject of his engagement to Lady Catherine's daughter. Mr Collins had mentioned it several times, yet Mr Darcy had dismissed it readily. She had not expected Mr Darcy to speak about his engagement — whether it was true or false — in the presence of her family, which she knew he despised.

Even towards her family, Mr Darcy had behaved fairly well. He had hardly spoken to her mother, except for complimenting the meal, but he had participated in conversation with her father and the admiral. She had noticed some disapproving glances when Lydia or Kitty mentioned the officers, or when Mr Collins expressed his opinion on a certain subject, but for that, Elizabeth could not blame him.

After more agitation, the family retired for the night. Once in their room, Elizabeth listened to Jane speak about Mr Bingley for a little longer until both fell asleep.

Two days of rain, cold, and wind followed, and the Bennets did not see the residents of Netherfield. The ball was four days away, and the preparations kept the ladies occupied, despite being trapped inside. On top of everything, they were forced to bear Mr Collins's company, sermons, and long speeches. As the recipient of his particular attention, Elizabeth found each hour spent in the house torture.

On the third day, the rain stopped, and Lydia and Kitty immediately planned a visit to Maria Lucas, while Mrs Bennet decided to take the carriage and call on Mrs Phillips. Mr Collins remembered he had been invited by Sir William to call on him, so he joined the party.

While Mrs Bennet insisted on taking Jane too, Elizabeth decidedly refused, claiming she was not feeling well. Indeed, the prospect of more of Mr Collins's company made her feel nauseous.

She remained at home with her father, wrote to her aunt Gardiner, and since Mr Bennet was reading, she decided to go for a walk. Careful to avoid any possible meeting with her mother and sisters — and especially with Mr Collins — she took the path leading away from Meryton. In truth, she feared she would not be able to avoid Mr Collins for too long, and he seemed determined to disregard all her attempts to reject his attentions. Since he planned to return to Kent after the ball, she dreaded the moment he would propose and the terrible fight which would surely follow when she refused him.

As she walked on higher ground, towards Oakham Mount, she glanced around, enjoying the view. She sat on a tree stump for a little while, putting her thoughts in order and trying to calm herself.

Eventually, she returned following an alternate path, more difficult but significantly shorter. Her attention was suddenly drawn by some whimpers, so weak that she at first missed them. She looked around, and the whimpers increased. It was surely the sound of an animal in pain, and she tried to locate it, not without fear, since it might have been a dangerous situation, and she had nothing with which to protect herself.

Her search was hard, since there were bushes and thorns, and the ground was slippery. She was even tempted to leave, but the whimpers broke her heart. Finally, her eyes alighted on an image that made her gasp in horror and sadness.

Hidden in the hollow of a tree, under some branches full of thorns, seemed to be a den. Near it, a dog and two puppies were lying dead, having obviously been attacked by some wild animals. The whimpers came from inside the hollow, and she tried to reach it, struggling to remove the branches around it. It was a daunting task, as the wood was cold, wet, and dirty. The thorns pricked her hands through her thin gloves, but she continued her efforts. Her gown, her petticoat, and her shoes all became muddy, yet she did not give up until she gained access to the hollow.

With her heart racing, she took off her bonnet, then reached her gloved hands into the hollow. She gasped again when she felt something soft, but the whimpers increased.

Carefully she pulled her hands out, and with them came two puppies, as small as her palm. Their eyes were closed, and they were thin and frozen, as well as dirty with mud and blood. With care, she held them in her arms and used her bonnet to clean them. Soon, the bonnet was wet and dirty, and she discarded it, together with her gloves, then she pulled up the hem of her dress and cleaned the puppies with that.

The whimpers only increased, so she held the animals close to her chest, determined to return home immediately before the wild animal that had killed the others returned.

She walked for a while, but with the puppies in her arms, the path she had taken was even more difficult. A few drops of rain made things even worse, and she was still far away from Longbourn. She walked until she reached a clearer path that led to the road, then the sound of hoofs made her stop. She hoped it was someone she knew and who could take the puppies to Longbourn.

Her hopes turned into distress when the rider stopped near her and dismounted; the last man in the world she wished to see her in such a state approached, calling her name with worry, even panic.

"Miss Bennet? Dear Lord, what happened? You are hurt! Heavens, let me help you! Are you bleeding?"

"Mr Darcy, please…I am not hurt! I know I look miserable, but I found these puppies…they are barely alive, and I need to take them home to warm them as quickly as possible."

She spoke quickly, and he stared at her, lost and bewildered.

"You are not hurt?"

"No, sir," she said, indicating the puppies.

"Oh…" he said. After another moment of confusion, he hastily took off his hat, then he pulled off his neckcloth and put it inside the hat before holding it out to Elizabeth.

"You should put the puppies in here. They will be warmer than in your arms."

She nodded and placed the small burdens into his hat, which he held in one hand. The whimpers increased for a few moments, then soothed.

"Thank you," she whispered.

"You are hurt," he said, taking her right hand in his. Only then did she notice her bare fingers, red from the cold and from bleeding scratches.

"Your face is scratched, too," he whispered.

"Oh…it is nothing, I assure you. Please take the puppies to Longbourn. Hill will take care of them until I arrive."

"You want me to leave you here? In your situation? In the rain?"

"Of course. If you take the puppies, I shall be home in no time."

"That is out of the question. You must ride my horse, or we shall walk together."

She laughed nervously. "Your worry is appreciated, but I cannot ride your horse. I cannot ride any horse."

"Then there are only two choices. We may either ride together or walk together," he said decidedly. She stared at him in disbelief, blushing at the mere thought of riding with him. Surely he could not mean that! Yet, his expression was determined.

"There is no use in arguing further. Let us walk," she eventually said. "We should make haste."

Indeed, she hurried her pace, and he stepped by her side, with his horse following. He was carrying the hat with the puppies, who were still whining at times.

"You look very ill and very cold. You should take my coat," he suggested.

"Absolutely not," she replied. "Please do not insist. We

shall be home soon, and your coat will only delay me."

"As you wish," he agreed, and they continued walking.

Eventually, they arrived. It was raining steadily, and the wind was blowing, but the danger had passed. They hurried to the door and were about to enter when it opened, and in front of them stood the entire Bennet family, Mr Collins, Charlotte and Maria Lucas — all staring at them in complete bewilderment. Mrs Bennet gasped, covering her mouth with her palm, while Lydia cried, "Dear Lord! Lizzy, what happened? Are you hurt?"

"I am not hurt. Forgive me. I must go and change," she said, grabbing the hat from Mr Darcy and running up the stairs.

She heard Jane following her, asking again if she was hurt, and she denied it.

She entered her room and took out the puppies, putting them in a blanket by the fire. Only then did she glance at her reflection in the mirror. She was wearing no bonnet, her hair had escaped from its pins, her face was dirty with mud and traces of blood, and her clothes were dirty and ripped.

"Lizzy, what happened?" Jane whispered, caressing her face. "Oh dear, you are hurt — this is blood!"

"I am not hurt, Jane. Believe me! Help me change, and I shall explain everything. There is really no reason to worry. I merely found two puppies, which I tried to save. Please bring me some milk while I wash myself. And please calm Mama and Papa. I have already made a fool of myself in front of Mr Darcy. We do not need another spectacle."

Chapter 7

Darcy tried to respond to everyone's questions, yet his answers were hesitant. There was little to tell them, except that he had found Elizabeth and escorted her home. He felt so uncomfortable and was looking for an opportunity to escape, yet he felt trapped between Mrs Bennet and Mr Collins and had to bear Mr Bennet's silent, sceptical scrutiny.

"Lizzy was always a wild child! It is not the first time she has brought home a wounded animal. She is so thoughtless, so neglectful of decorum!" Mrs Bennet complained. "That girl will be the death of me. I tell you that!"

"I cannot but agree, Mrs Bennet. Cousin Elizabeth's actions are certainly not what is expected from a young lady. Thank goodness Lady Catherine is not here to witness this!"

"I am sorry you had to see my daughter in such a poor state. I am sure it was appalling to you. I cannot even imagine what the admiral would say. Or Mr Bingley. I hope they will not avoid us because of Lizzy's imprudence."

"I see no lack of decorum in Miss Elizabeth's actions," Darcy intervened. "She is kind-hearted and generous, and she saved some poor souls in need, even at the expense of her own comfort and safety. I find it to be a commendable gesture, and I am quite sure the admiral and Bingley would agree, regardless of other opinions."

"How generous of you, Mr Darcy!" Mrs Bennet said. "But where was she? How did you meet? Where did you find her?"

"Ma'am, I believe Miss Elizabeth would be better placed to answer these questions. I was just taking a ride, following the road between Netherfield and Longbourn, when I saw her. I am not certain of the precise location, but I am sure she will be."

"Regardless, it was very fortunate that you happened to be there at the perfect time, sir," Miss Lucas interjected. "I believe Mr Jones should be fetched to examine Eliza and perhaps provide something to put on her scratches."

"Yes, yes, I shall send for him right away," Mrs Bennet replied impatiently. "But there is no need to make a fuss out of this incident, since Lizzy is not hurt. I hope to keep it private."

Darcy glanced at Charlotte Lucas and at Mr Collins, then at Mr Bennet, who was rolling his eyes. Mr Collins's agitation was a clear indication of his incapacity to keep anything private.

"Let us make sure Lizzy is unharmed," Mr Bennet suggested. "Privacy is the least of my concerns."

"Lizzy is well," Miss Jane Bennet answered, entering the room. "She has some scratches, and she might have caught a cold. I have already asked John to fetch Mr Jones."

"Good," Mr Bennet agreed. "That is my Jane — little talk and more action."

"I shall take her some warm milk, some soup, and some tea and stay with her for the rest of the day," Miss Bennet continued. "Thank you for your assistance, Mr Darcy. Charlotte, Maria, please excuse me."

With that, the young lady left, and Darcy smiled to himself watching her. It was the first time he had seen the eldest Miss Bennet so determined and taking charge in front of her family.

"Mr Darcy, would you care for a drink?" Mr Bennet asked. "It is raining. I can offer you my carriage as soon as John returns."

"A drink would be perfect. Then I must return to Netherfield. I am expected."

"I would gladly join you, but I promised Miss Lucas and Miss Maria that I would escort them home," Mr Collins said.

"Then by all means, do not change your plans, sir," Darcy

immediately replied. "I would not want to cause any discomfort to the ladies for the benefit of a mere drink."

Mr Collins still seemed undecided, but Darcy followed Mr Bennet into the library, where the host closed the door.

"I am glad you can enjoy a drink in peace, Mr Darcy," Mr Bennet said, filling his glass. "I assume you have borne enough bustle and annoyance for today. I am sure you are not accustomed to this sort of din, which is rather usual in our family."

"That is not my concern, sir, I assure you. I hope to hear good news after Mr Jones's examination. Although Miss Elizabeth is not harmed, a cold is a real threat."

"It might be, but nobody dies from a mere cold. Mrs Bennet says so all the time. And certainly not my Lizzy."

"It was brave and kind-hearted of her to save the puppies, though I am not sure they will survive."

"Yes. That is Lizzy. Such small puppies will surely not survive without being nurtured by their mother, and Lizzy will suffer for it, but she will certainly save others again, if the occasion arises. She is stubborn, even headstrong," he ended with loving reproach.

"I would call it determination and kindness. As I said, it is commendable."

"Well, your aunt would certainly not approve, and I am sure Mr Collins will inform her immediately."

"I wonder whether Miss Elizabeth is concerned about my aunt's approval."

"Not at all, I am sure. But Mr Collins intends to... Oh well, I shall not bother you any longer with our family's problems."

"The rain has ceased somewhat. I shall leave you now."

"Please convey my best regards to Mr Bingley and the admiral."

"I shall," Darcy said, and minutes later, after a brief good-bye to the ladies, he left.

The ride was short, but the rain started to pour again, making it unpleasant. He thought of Elizabeth, remembering his fright the moment he saw her and assumed she was injured, then his relief when he understood she was unharmed. Well, almost unharmed, as her hands were covered in scratches, and several marred her pretty face too. Also, her thin gown provided little protection, and she might still fall ill.

He imagined her disappointment if the puppies did not survive. There was little he could do to help her, but the few minutes of riding in the bad weather gave him an idea.

∞∞∞

Elizabeth spent the following hours in her room, with Jane, trying to nurture the puppies. They did not eat, not even a few drops of milk, despite their attempts. They tried with a teaspoon, drop by drop, but the result was discouraging.

The apothecary examined Elizabeth and recommended some tea to prevent a cold and some herbal cream for the scratches. As for the puppies, Mr Jones believed they had no chance of survival.

"Unless you find a female dog to accept and feed them, they are as good as dead. They are too young to eat and drink, as much as you may try."

"I shall ask around tomorrow. Perhaps someone has a dog with puppies," Elizabeth said.

"Well, I do not know of anybody," the apothecary replied. "But I shall let you know if I hear of any."

Discouraged and disappointed, Elizabeth finally joined her family for dinner. She had to bear her mother's scolding and even a lecture from Mr Collins until she lost patience.

"Mama, if I do not look well enough, I shall not attend the ball. It is truly not much of a loss for me. And Mr Collins, please know that I am perfectly aware of your disapproval, which is unfortunate but bearable to me. We all have things we disapprove of in others, and somehow, we survive."

Her outburst did not impress Mrs Bennet but stunned Mr

Collins, who remained bewildered and less talkative for the rest of dinner.

As dessert was being served, a servant informed them that somebody from Netherfield had come, asking for Mr Bennet, and on that gentleman's bewildered nod, he ushered a man inside.

"Mr Darcy sent me with this note, sir," the man said, holding out a piece of paper. Mr Bennet took it, looking at it for just a few seconds before handing it to Elizabeth. She took it tentatively, aware of the curious glances of her family, and read it quickly.

> *Sir,*
>
> *I apologise for interrupting your dinner; however, the reason is a rather urgent one. I hope you might pass the following information to your daughter Miss Elizabeth.*
>
> *I took it upon myself to make some enquiries, and one of the maids has a brother who owns a female dog which had three puppies a month ago. I truly believe the two little souls you found have a better chance this way.*
>
> *If you agree, please give the puppies to the man, and we shall make sure they are united with the mother dog tonight. Have no worries; they will be well taken care of and supervised to be sure they are accepted and fed properly.*
>
> *I hope you will forgive my presumptuousness. If you have found another solution, I wish you good luck with it.*
>
> *F Darcy*

She stared at the letter, then at her family, whose eyes were all focused on her, waiting for an explanation.

"Mr Darcy has found a female dog to nurture the puppies. This is by far their best chance. He said I can send them tonight."

"So, send them," Mrs Bennet said. "We have enough other things to worry about."

"I shall send them," Elizabeth said. "Mr Darcy has promised they will be well taken care of. I shall go and visit them tomorrow."

"You are wasting your time," Mrs Bennet interjected. "You should be concerned by your future, not by some stray puppies."

"Please wait a moment. I shall fetch them now," she told the servant, then hurried and returned with a small bundle wrapped in a blanket.

"Where are you taking them?" she asked while handing it to the servant. "I would like to see them tomorrow."

"To Netherfield, miss. The dog and her puppies have been taken there and will be kept there until they all grow up. Mr Darcy said so, and Janey's brother Tom agreed."

"Thank you," she whispered, and the servant left.

She returned to the table, and the family resumed their dinner.

"How kind of Mr Darcy to take so much trouble," Jane said.

"Well, when one has enough money, one can do whatever he pleases," Mrs Bennet said, annoyed by the interruption. "And when one has not enough money, one should be more guarded with her behaviour," she continued, glaring at Elizabeth.

"Mama, I understand you are upset with me, though I do not know why. Can we please eat, so I can return to my chamber and sleep?"

"Well, Lizzy, you may do whatever you want. You always do, in any case."

The conversation was scarce for the rest of the evening, and as soon as dinner ended, Elizabeth excused herself, claiming she had a headache.

In truth, she felt perfectly well yet bewildered by Mr Darcy's gesture. To make the effort to search for a dog and find one in such a short time only revealed more of his character. Her opinion of him had improved slightly in the last few days, but she would never have expected him to have a tender heart and care so much for anything or anyone outside his circle.

He had been thoughtful with her when they met, offered his company and protection for the puppies, then escorted her home. And then, he had taken his endeavour further to find the best chance of survival for the little ones. Yes, he had all the money he wanted, to do whatever he pleased, and he could pay people for their involvement. But that did not diminish his merit; very few men, if any, would have done that for a woman they did not like well enough to dance with, and for some dying, stray puppies.

She was determined to thank him the next day; if only his effort was not in vain, and the little souls would survive.

∞∞∞

"Miss Elizabeth's habit of wandering in the woods alone is not to be encouraged, though her gesture was admirable," the admiral said, sipping from his glass. "What if she had met another man, with less honourable intentions? If someone attacked her? I might sound ridiculous, but I have heard enough reports about young ladies being attacked, even in Hyde Park, not to mention in secluded woods. And not just women but men too."

"You seem very concerned by this, Admiral," Bingley said.

"I am. As I said, I have lived long enough to see and hear worrisome reports. I am glad Miss Elizabeth is unharmed."

"She is," Darcy said. "I am glad she agreed to allow the puppies to be brought here. Perhaps she will not have to bear a disappointment."

"You seem concerned too, Darcy. About Miss Elizabeth and her feelings," Bingley added.

"I only did what any man of honour would. Nothing more," Darcy said, gulping his wine.

"I am glad you did not mention anything during dinner. Caroline would have surely found more to disapprove of in Miss Elizabeth's actions, and I have no disposition to argue with her again."

"Mrs Bennet disapproved too, and so did the clergyman."

"I imagine as much," Admiral Pembroke. said "Tomorrow,

we should pay them another visit."

"The servant told me Miss Elizabeth would like to see the puppies tomorrow."

"She would? Even better. Bingley, you should send Mr Bennet a note in the morning and invite him for a drink, with all the ladies. You owe him as much after he hosted us for dinner."

"All the Bennet family?" Bingley asked, slightly panicked. "That will surely enrage Louisa and Caroline, especially if they are unaware of it."

"You may inform them at breakfast and tell them the Bennets are my personal guests. If they are displeased, they may retire to their rooms."

Bingley emptied his glass and filled it again. He could not contradict the admiral but was concerned about his sisters' responses too.

For Darcy, the day had been so strange that he needed some more time to reflect upon it. After returning to his room, he assumed another sleepless night was ahead of him.

The previous night he had slept little too, as he had had a long-awaited conversation with the admiral about Wickham. He had revealed all their financial dealings, the offering and refusal of the living, the debts he had covered several times, the disloyalty, the deceptions over the years. Of the incident with Georgiana at Ramsgate, he mentioned nothing, except that Wickham had met Georgiana and tried to take advantage of her friendship too. Except for Colonel Fitzwilliam, nobody knew of his sister's attempted elopement, and he intended to keep it that way.

The narration had angered the admiral so much that his first impulse had been to confront Wickham immediately. That a scoundrel had taken advantage of George Darcy's generosity and attempted to defraud his children challenged the admiral's frail patience. It was quite an effort for Darcy to calm the man, and he expected a rather violent outburst at the gentleman's next encounter with the scoundrel. He knew Elizabeth — and the rest of the Bennets — were friends of Wickham and wondered whose side Elizabeth would take and whom she would trust.

Once Elizabeth filled his mind, her image remained there for a long time. Lying in his bed, he mused on what would have happened if she had agreed to ride with him and he had held her in his arms. Or if he had taken her hands in his and touched her scratches. And perhaps pressed his lips to them.

He tried to dismiss such thoughts, but he failed, and they followed him even when he finally fell asleep, turning into a tormenting and delicious dream, which he would not ever dare to share with anyone.

Chapter 8

Mrs Phillips arrived before breakfast, causing an early upheaval in the family. She came to see her sister, Mrs Bennet, and to enquire after Elizabeth, hardly breathing from panic.

As she had long been awake, Elizabeth noticed her aunt's arrival and ran downstairs, worried that something terrible had occurred. She stopped in the hall, eavesdropping by the door, when she heard Mrs Phillips's cries of despair and her mother's worrisome responses.

"Dear sister, what happened to Lizzy? I barely slept last night. Mr Phillips was told by Sir William that she had been found injured in the wood. Covered in blood! Who did such a thing to her? Will she recover?"

Elizabeth rolled her eyes, ire mixing with annoyance.

"Oh, nonsense, Sister!" Mrs Bennet replied. "Come and sit, and I shall order some tea. Will you stay for breakfast?"

"No, no, I must return home soon. I just came to see what had happened! So, there was nothing?"

"There was something, but you should know Sir William and Lady Lucas know nothing, as much as they claim to be titled people! I wonder who spread such a report! It must have been Charlotte or Maria or Mr Collins. What a tedious man. If I did not know he wishes to marry Lizzy, I would not even speak to him!"

"Do not speak so loudly. He might hear you. Is he not here?"

"No…apparently he had some business in Meryton early

this morning, though I cannot imagine what that might be. He is such a hateful man!"

"So, what happened? Is Lizzy injured?"

"In some way…not much…she wandered through the fields — you know she does that all the time! Even the admiral has scolded her for that silly habit. She found some dead dogs and two barely alive puppies, and she brought them home. She dirtied her gowns and scratched her hands and face rescuing them. Just before the ball! Imagine! How can she appear in such a state at Netherfield? Mr Collins was rather appalled seeing her. I fear he might not propose to her after that."

"So, she is injured? Why did they say she was covered in blood? Was she not?"

"She was. Mr Darcy looked appalled too when he brought her home, although he tried to excuse what he had seen. I can only imagine what he thought, seeing her in such a dreadful state. It is no wonder he refused to dance with her. For some strange reason, he called her adventure 'commendable'. Perhaps because she saved his uncle, the admiral. Do you know Mr Darcy is the grandson and the nephew of earls?"

Mrs Bennet was babbling, and Elizabeth's impulse was to stop the maddening exchange, but she felt tired and was loath to be caught in the middle of it.

"So, Lizzy was in the woods with Mr Darcy? And he brought her home?"

"Yes. He said he found her and escorted her home. Last night he even found a dog to feed the puppies. I cannot imagine what happened to him to show such sudden amiability to Lizzy. It must be because of his uncle, the admiral."

"Mr Darcy walking alone with Lizzy? This is hard to imagine… Very peculiar."

"Well, who knows what is in the mind of a man like Mr Darcy. He either refuses to dance with her or acts like a friend. He seemed very friendly to Mr Bennet too — what do you say? He never spoke a word to Mr Bennet until the admiral came."

"Very strange indeed, Sister. One might say that a man

who walks with a young woman in a secluded place might like her…even more than he should…"

"Oh, that cannot be in Mr Darcy's case. He is cold and haughty and ruins everybody's disposition," Mrs Bennet replied.

"Who knows, Sister. Who can read his mind? Such rich and important people are not like the rest of us, I tell you," Mrs Phillips uttered.

"Speaking of important and rich people, Admiral Pembroke seemed to really like Lizzy. I even thought he might propose to her. He must be in his fifties, but he is still like a young man. Can you imagine what that would mean for me?"

Elizabeth gasped in horror, and she made her presence known by crying, "Mama! How dare you say such things? What is wrong with you? Can you not understand the harm you may cause to our family by spreading such nonsense? What if the admiral hears such reports? I would die of shame!"

Elizabeth was so outraged that she could not even mind her words and had to fight tears of frustration.

"Oh, calm down, Lizzy. You are too sensitive and too careless when it comes to your actions," Mrs Bennet responded. "I can say whatever I want to my sister. You should instead worry about dying of shame when the admiral hears from Mr Darcy about your appearance."

"Lizzy, you look truly terrible! Oh dear!" Mrs Phillips said. "Look — three scratches on your face and two on your neck. They will look dreadful in your ball gown!"

"That is my last concern, Aunt Phillips. For heaven's sake, stop talking such nonsense which will only expose our family to ridicule! I saved two puppies, that is all. I am not intending to marry anyone — clergyman or admiral — and I shall not even attend the ball, so there is no need to worry about my scratches. This is all outrageous and ridiculous!"

Her mother and her aunt looked stunned by such an offensive outburst, but she could not care less.

Mr Bennet and the rest of the family appeared, drawn by the loud voices, their confusion apparent.

"What on earth is this scandal before breakfast?" Mr Bennet asked. "Sister Phillips, what brought you here at this early hour?"

"Nothing is happening, Papa. Only nonsense, as usual," Elizabeth replied. "I shall be in my room. I do not feel well enough for company." She tried to leave the room when she almost bumped into John, the manservant, who was holding a note. In the hall, she spotted another man waiting.

"This was brought for Mr Bennet," John said. "From the admiral and Mr Bingley, I was told."

Mrs Bennet gasped with apparent joy, while Mr Bennet took the note. Although curious, Elizabeth left hastily and slammed the door of her chamber so hard that she was sure it resounded throughout the entire house.

She felt the need to cry in frustration, but she resisted. Her mother was driving her to the edge of her patience, and regardless of her efforts, Mrs Bennet followed her impulses, disregarding common sense and decorum. There was nothing to be done. Unlike other times, she found she was bothered by the notion that either the admiral or Mr Darcy thought ill of her or of her family.

Her mother's ridiculous assumption that the admiral might have an interest in her was completely outrageous and could damage even Jane's relationship with Mr Bingley. Yet, Mrs Bennet refused to see reality, and her father was content to make sport of his wife instead of censuring the breaches of decorum.

"Lizzy, may I come in?" she heard Jane's timid voice.

"Yes, of course." Elizabeth tried to compose herself so her sister would not see how disquieted she was.

"I am sorry you are upset, Lizzy. Please do not mind Mama. You know she wishes the best for us."

"She might, Jane, but wishing the best might cause us the worst. I cannot remain silent to such nonsense! I hope you do not mind, but I have a headache and would rather rest."

"Oh…I am so sorry to hear that. Papa has received a letter from the admiral. He has invited all of us for tea at Netherfield."

Elizabeth arched her eyebrow. "All of us? Today? All of a sudden? What is the occasion?"

"We do not know...the note only mentions drinks. Mama is thrilled beyond reason, and she assumes more than there is. And the note mentioned that you are welcome to see the puppies if you want."

"Oh yes, I would like that very much! What did Papa say? Shall we go? Though I wonder how much Mr Bingley's sisters approve of such an invitation. Or Mr Darcy..."

"Please come and speak to Papa. He will decide. And please try not to argue with Mama any further."

"I shall try. Has Aunt Phillips left?"

"Yes. Come, I shall meet you in the drawing room."

A few minutes later, after changing her gown, arranging her hair, and placing a scarf to cover her throat, Elizabeth went to join her family.

Mr Bennet glanced at her while speaking to his wife and his other daughters.

"I see no reason to all go for a short, sudden visit. I cannot refuse the admiral, but I shall not stay more than an hour. Lizzy should come too, to see the puppies, since she was mentioned in the note, and her presence is likely desired. I cannot take her alone, so another one of you should come. Three of us will be more than enough."

"Well, I shall not insist on this visit," Mrs Bennet said. "Mr Bingley's sisters are not pleasant company, and I do not wish to see them. Since you are determined to take Lizzy, Jane should go. I am sure her presence is the most desired."

"Then it is settled," Mr Bennet approved. "To Netherfield we shall go and return soon. If Mr Collins returns, do not tell him where we are!"

An hour later, the three of them arrived at Netherfield and

were received by a happy and nervous Mr Bingley. His sisters — much to Elizabeth's surprise — were there too, and they offered a polite, though distant, welcome.

"My dear Eliza, what happened to you?" Miss Bingley exclaimed. "Oh dear, what are those marks on your face? You look truly ill!"

"I had a small accident, Miss Bingley. It is nothing to worry about, but I thank you for your concern."

"Scratches or not, I believe Miss Elizabeth looks lovely," the admiral interjected. "In fact, you all look lovely, ladies. I understand Miss Elizabeth's marks are proof of her bravery."

"Bravery is too strong a word." Elizabeth smiled. "If you do not mind, could I see the puppies now?"

"Darcy's servant should know about them," the admiral answered.

"I would be glad to escort you, Miss Elizabeth," Mr Darcy unexpectedly offered. "The quickest way would be through the servants' wing."

"What puppies?" Miss Bingley asked. "Where is Mr Darcy going with Eliza? To the servants' wing? Why?"

"I shall explain it to you," Mr Bingley offered, while Elizabeth followed Mr Darcy along the hall. She felt slightly disconcerted by the idea of going somewhere with only Mr Darcy.

At the stairs, he stopped, looking at her. "I shall lead the way."

"Very well, sir. Have you seen the puppies yourself?"

"Yes...I admit I was curious...and worried."

"You are very kind, sir," she said, and he turned to glance at her.

"Since you do not approve of the word bravery, I do not approve of kindness in regard to the same matter," he said with a little smile. She found nothing to reply, only noticing how much the smile changed his countenance.

Once they were downstairs, Darcy led her to a room with several windows and filled with various supplies. In a corner, there was a shelter filled with straw. Elizabeth approached carefully and saw a mother dog lying down with three puppies gambolling around her. She leant closer and recognised the two little puppies she had rescued, tucked against the mother dog's belly, struggling to suckle a little milk.

"This is Dolly. She had three puppies of her own and she seems to have adopted these two. The moment she was given the puppies, she was also offered good food, which I think eased her acceptance."

"Dolly is such a pretty girl," Elizabeth said. "Would it help if I took all of them to Longbourn and took care of them?"

"Not at all. Dolly's owner works at the stables, and his wife is a maid. They check on the dogs regularly. They are taken care of in the best possible way, I assure you."

"Thank you, sir," she repeated. "You are very kind indeed."

"Then I dare say you were brave," he jested, and she laughed.

"Let us not argue over whose behaviour was more heroic. It is fortunate the puppies are alive and were provided with the best care in order to survive. And that was your doing, sir, as much as you wish to deny it."

They were in a room of supplies, in the servants' wing, with lots of voices around them, but still, they were alone, talking over a subject of mutual interest, even teasing each other.

A maid entered, gasped at seeing them, and quickly excused herself, disappearing into another room.

"We should leave before we disturb the household's activity," Mr Darcy suggested. "I promise to let you know if there is any news. As soon as they grow stronger, you should come and visit again," he offered.

"Thank you, Mr Darcy. I trust they will be well taken care of, under your supervision."

"Do not thank me, Miss Bennet. After all, I feel they belong to me as much as they belong to you. We could say we share the puppies," he said, attempting a joke.

For some reason, both of their countenances changed colour, as if touched by the same sort of feeling aroused by his mere statement.

"The scratches are still visible," he said, and she felt his gaze on her face, on her throat, and lowering to her hands. She felt more anxiety and tried to conceal it with jest.

"I know they are visible. And I know I look very ill — my mother mentions it at least twenty times a day."

"I did not say you looked ill. Quite the opposite," he said, then paused while she watched him in confusion. His voice was hoarse and serious, and his expression was different in a way she could not define.

"I just hope they are not painful," he continued.

"Oh no, not really. Mr Jones's cream was helpful," she replied, feeling herself flush.

"I am glad to hear that. You did not catch a cold, I hope?"

"No. Thank you for asking. You are very kind to enquire. I hope your hat and neckcloth were cleaned?"

"No...they are in the shelter. Look. I allowed the puppies to use them."

He smiled, and dimples appeared in his cheeks. She stared at him for another moment, troubled by a sudden quivering; then she leant forwards to take a better look at the dogs and finally turned her eyes back to him.

"That was very kind of you, Mr Darcy. You must allow the person with whom you share the puppies to show you some gratitude," she joked, and he replied with another smile.

"I would gladly allow you to do whatever you want, Miss Bennet, since I doubt that I could win any argument with you."

He was joking — teasing her — and his friendly countenance was just as disquieting as his proud and arrogant one, though in a different way.

"We should return to the others. I hope you approve of how the puppies are being cared for," Mr Darcy said.

"Very much so, sir. Yes, you must return before others wonder about our absence."

Chapter 9

For two days following the call at Netherfield, it rained constantly. No activities out of doors were possible, and another visit to the puppies was out of the question.

Elizabeth felt at peace that the little souls were being taken care of in the best way. There was not much she could do for the time being. She had decided she would take the puppies the moment they were weaned, but until then, the solution offered by Mr Darcy was the best.

Besides the bad weather, there was another reason that kept Elizabeth in the house; she felt a strange thrill and anxiety at the notion of seeing Mr Darcy again, one she could not explain but that disquieted her. Kitty and Lydia, together with Jane, went to Meryton one day, and they returned with the joy of having met the officers and told Elizabeth Mr Wickham had particularly enquired about her.

"Lizzy, I hope you will not dance more than two sets at the most with Wickham. We want to dance with him too," Lydia said.

While assuring her sister she must not worry, Elizabeth realised that she had been so absorbed in other things lately, that she had almost forgotten about Mr Wickham and the distress he had suffered at the hands of Mr Darcy. Seeing more of the latter's character, she was even more intrigued by the notion that he had purposely disregarded his father's wish and consigned his childhood companion to poverty out of jealousy and malice.

Being trapped in the house, Mr Collins's company became

more tedious, but — to Elizabeth's relief — his attentions to her seemed to have diminished.

"Thank God the scratches on your face look better, Lizzy," her mother said on the morning of the ball. "You do not look as pretty as you used to, and I doubt anyone will want to dance with you, except perhaps for Mr Collins. But at least you do not look as ill as a few days ago."

"How comforting to hear you say that, Mama," Elizabeth said. Arguing with her mother was pointless, just as Jane had said.

The Bennet ladies prepared themselves with extra care. Mrs Bennet insisted that Jane must look her best, since she claimed the ball had been thrown in her eldest daughter's honour by Mr Bingley. As much as Jane tried to convince her it was not true, Mrs Bennet insisted.

Although Elizabeth had been unsure whether she wished to attend, once she decided she would, she was more concerned with her image than she had been on other similar occasions, for no apparent reason.

The rain was still pouring, but an hour prior to their departure, it stopped. Despite being already dark, the sky could be seen clearing, the moon and the stars showing their faces timidly. At the same time, the temperature dropped considerably.

The Bennets — together with Mr Collins — were among the first guests to arrive.

They were greeted with joy by Mr Bingley and with cold politeness by his sisters. Moments later, the admiral appeared with an expression of genuine delight. Behind him, Mr Darcy bowed his head, welcoming them with much more restraint.

"Oh look! Denny is here!" Lydia suddenly cried. "And Pratt and Wickham! Let us go and speak to them."

Before they could be stopped, Lydia and Kitty ran down the hall, with everybody staring after them. Elizabeth looked at Jane — who was blushing with shame under Miss Bingley and Mrs Hurst's appalled glares — then at her father, who seemed vaguely amused by the scene. Her mother had already chosen a seat by the wall in the ballroom and had saved another one for Mrs Phillips.

While Mr Bingley offered his arm to Jane and her father spoke to the admiral, Elizabeth found herself alone with Mary. The ball had not even started yet, and her family was already embarrassing themselves. And to complete her mortification, she saw Mr Collins approaching Mr Darcy again. She could see that they were talking, and she observed Mr Collins's bowed head and Mr Darcy's stern expression — clear signs that the conversation was not going well.

Shortly afterwards, more guests arrived, including the Lucases. Elizabeth was pleased to see Charlotte and found some comfort in talking to her, while Maria sat with Mary.

Mr Collins greeted Sir William, and Mr Darcy immediately departed, causing Elizabeth to smile. The poor man seemed relieved to escape Mr Collins's insistence, and Elizabeth could sympathise with him.

Slowly, the ballroom became so crowded with people that some gentlemen preferred to stay in the hall. The musicians prepared their instruments, and some couples moved into the centre of the room, ready for the first set. With delight, Elizabeth noticed Mr Bingley and Jane engaged in conversation, and she expected — and hoped — they would open the ball together.

"My dear cousin Elizabeth, my dear Miss Lucas," Mr Collins said, approaching them with a large grin on his face. Elizabeth was not certain whether she should laugh or roll her eyes.

"Miss Lucas, may I have the honour of dancing a set with you," the unctuous parson asked.

Charlotte smiled, and Elizabeth saw an opportunity to improve her own evening.

"If Charlotte does not oppose it, I suggest you dance the first set with her. I should like to discuss a certain matter with my father."

"I do not oppose it at all," Charlotte replied.

"That sounds like an excellent arrangement," Mr Collins

said. "And then I shall dance the second set with you, Cousin Elizabeth. You must not feel slighted."

"Mr Collins, I can safely say I do not feel slighted at all," she answered in all honesty, walking towards the chairs. She watched Jane beaming at Mr Bingley's side, leading the row of dancers. Neither Miss Bingley nor Mrs Hurst were dancing, only talking to each other.

Lydia and Kitty, as well as several other young women, were dancing with officers.

Elizabeth remembered the assembly when she had also sat out for a few sets, causing Mr Darcy to call her 'slighted by other men'. This time, as she had just told Mr Collins, she did not feel slighted at all.

The music had already begun when Mr Wickham — who was apparently without a partner too — walked towards Elizabeth. He smiled and she smiled back. Out of the corner of her eye, she saw Mr Darcy walking in her direction too; she had the feeling he intended to come to her, but seeing Mr Wickham, he stopped. Moments later, he joined the group with the admiral, Mr Bennet, Colonel Forster, and Sir William.

"Miss Bennet, I am sorry for not coming to speak to you earlier. I was exceedingly happy to see you, but you were in company I preferred to avoid."

"It is good to see you, Mr Wickham. At a ball, one has to bear all sorts of company, some less pleasant than others. It is a good thing we have enough people to choose from."

"True and wise, Miss Bennet. Would you do me the honour choosing me as your partner for this set?" His manner was teasing, and she answered in the same tone.

"I would say you have chosen me for this set, and I am pleased with your choice."

"Excellent." He took her hand and escorted her to the floor, joining the row of other couples. As she followed the steps, she cast a look at Mr Darcy and noticed — and also felt — his dark stare upon her. Or perhaps upon her dance partner.

"I heard you were caught in some rather traumatic

circumstances," Mr Wickham said. "Please forgive my insolence, but I have to say some of the marks of it are still visible. I hope you feel well?"

"It is not insolence if it is honest. I do feel well. There was no trauma, only a little bit of adventure caused by some puppies. I hope you did not hear an exaggerated report."

"I admit I was very worried and intended to call at Longbourn. But I feared I might happen upon Darcy there. The rumours said he was also involved in your little adventure…"

Elizabeth felt her cheeks burning.

"Mr Darcy was only involved in escorting me home, as any gentleman would have done, I suppose."

"Yes, of course. I was a little surprised to hear Darcy had become a friend of your family and a regular visitor."

"Mr Darcy has visited us a few times, together with Mr Bingley and the admiral. We would be proud to call him a friend, but I am not certain that is the case."

"Yes, Darcy is capable of making people like him when he wishes to. However, even as a child he did not have many friends. That might be yet another reason why he is jealous of me," Mr Wickham said meaningfully, and Elizabeth felt uncomfortable.

"Jealousy implies Mr Darcy would like to have as many friends as you have. I am not sure that is the case," she said.

Mr Wickham's grin grew broader. "You must be correct. On careful consideration, I am not even sure why he is jealous of me and denied me what was rightfully mine, given by my godfather."

Elizabeth was still curious about the conflict between the two men but not desirous of hearing the story of the living once again.

"Perhaps we should ask Mr Darcy when the opportunity arises. That would be the fairest approach. Ask him directly, and perhaps the clarification will lead to a new understanding between you."

"You are as lovely as you are kind-hearted, Miss Bennet.

The bridge between the two of us has been long burnt, and Darcy started the fire. There is nothing to be done."

"If that is your belief, we had better not even speak of this matter again. Would you not agree?" Elizabeth concluded.

"As you wish. I only mentioned my past misfortune with Darcy because I was told he had offended you too. In fact, he has a habit of offending people everywhere he goes."

"Again, I am sure the report you heard was exaggerated. If there was an offence, it has long been forgotten. Mr Darcy — as well as the admiral — has been nothing but polite to everyone lately, as far as I know."

"Perhaps Darcy has changed a little, though I know he is too proud of himself to even consider he might have to modify his behaviour."

"I can neither support nor contradict your claim, Mr Wickham, but I am not comfortable speaking of a gentleman without giving him the chance to defend himself."

"I perfectly understand you. I am sure that seeing Darcy more often, and since he has become a friend of your father, you have the tendency to forgive some of his flaws. Generally speaking, rich people are more easily forgiven than the rest of us."

At that moment, his voice contained a trace of insolence, which irritated Elizabeth.

"Mr Darcy's wealth is of no concern to me, and it certainly does not influence my reason. However, I am sure many men of your age have flaws that need to be forgotten and forgiven. Mr Darcy deserves no more or less forgiveness than you or any other."

Before Mr Wickham had time to reply, the music stopped, and only then did Elizabeth realise half an hour had already passed.

"Thank you, Miss Bennet. Your company was absolutely enchanting, as always," Mr Wickham said without any reply to her last statement.

"It was my pleasure, Mr Wickham," she replied. She

reunited with her sisters while Mr Wickham withdrew immediately. Mr Collins was also walking their way with Charlotte, the pair still talking together. His grin irritated Elizabeth, and she was ready to leave the stifling ballroom when she found herself face-to-face with Mr Darcy. She startled, and her cheeks burned as he was so close that he was almost touching her. He realised too and took a step back.

"Miss Bennet, if you are not otherwise engaged, would you do me the honour of dancing the next set with me?"

Mr Collins and Charlotte approached, and Elizabeth considered declining that particular set, since it was tentatively promised. But instead, she said, "Thank you, yes. Mr Collins has asked for a set too, but I am sure he will agree to choose another one. Will you not, Mr Collins? I cannot possibly refuse Mr Darcy."

Mr Darcy looked puzzled and Mr Collins displeased, and the latter struggled to maintain a formal, polite countenance while answering.

"Of course not, my dear cousin! I would not dare refuse Mr Darcy anything he would do me the honour of asking for."

"I promise to never ask anything from you, Mr Collins," Mr Darcy uttered. "If I ever do, please consider refusing it, without concern. Thank you, Miss Bennet. I shall return for your hand when the music starts."

Elizabeth gazed after Mr Darcy's departing figure in a state of disquiet. She had been surprised by his offer; he had not danced the first, and she had expected he would not dance at all. Why would he single her out? Because he wished to compensate for his rudeness at the assembly? Or because he was on friendly terms with her father?

"My dear cousin Elizabeth, will you then save the third set for me?" Mr Collins asked. "It would be an honour to dance with you after Mr Darcy. And I hope you realise the honour he is giving you by dancing with you. I believe it is out of consideration for my close bond to Lady Catherine de Bourgh."

Elizabeth looked at her cousin, astounded. Could he be serious? There were times when she wondered whether he was in his right mind — and this was one of those times.

"The next set is certainly secured for you, Mr Collins," she answered briefly, but he continued to speak of Lady Catherine until fortunately the music began, and the pairs lined up. She saw Mr Darcy approaching, and in order to escape from Mr Collins, she walked towards him and met him halfway.

"Miss Bennet…"

"Mr Darcy…"

He stretched out his hand, and she placed hers in his palm. His fingers closed around hers — a simple gesture, one that occurred every time, with each set, with each partner. And yet, she felt more distress than ever before, and as she walked by his side, she questioned the strange sensation that made her quiver.

Chapter 10

"I thank you for finally dancing with me, Miss Bennet," Mr Darcy said. His voice was light, and there was mirth in his gaze, which she doubted she had seen before.

"Finally, sir? If I remember correctly, it was you who refused to dance before. With me or anyone else," she answered in the same manner.

"True. But you also refused me twice."

A little smile was on his lips, and she arched her eyebrow in doubt.

"Surely you are joking. Or perhaps your memories are confused."

"Not at all. I first asked you at Sir William's party."

"At Lucas Lodge? When? Oh, on the occasion you claimed that every savage could dance? Yes, we all heard about that statement," she teased him.

"Yes, that was the occasion. And you cannot deny it was a refusal."

"If it was, it was surely well-deserved, considering the request was not a serious one. Neither the music nor the occasion was proper for dancing."

"I cannot argue with you."

"And the second time?" Elizabeth asked, amused and growing more at ease with him.

"The second time was at Netherfield, when I asked you to dance a reel."

Elizabeth's confusion increased. Was he mocking her?

Was he attempting to make a joke or to make her feel uncomfortable?

"You cannot be serious about that one, Mr Darcy. We both know you only asked for the pleasure of despising my taste! You must admit it."

"Not at all. You expect me to admit a reason which you choose to call mine, but which I have never acknowledged and have had no opportunity to deny."

His tone was teasing, and so was hers, but there was also some determination in it.

"Is that true? Even if you did not disapprove of me — which we both know you do — would you, who never dance, not even at St James's, have danced a reel with me, while Miss Bingley and Mrs Hurst played?"

"If I asked, I certainly expected either an acceptance or a rejection, and I was prepared for both," he said with a little smile. "And the reason you assume I asked was as far from my intention as possible."

"What other reason might you have had, Mr Darcy? If my recollection is accurate, it was the same evening you criticised Mr Bingley's careless writing and his quickness in doing certain things which led to the imperfection of his performance."

"Your recollections are similar to mine, yet your assumption is still in error. And your rejection can still be counted," Mr Darcy insisted. Their eyes met and locked; his smile, as small as it was, revealed his dimples and caused her to quiver again, almost missing a step.

"Very well. I shall not argue with you any longer. Let us call it a truce and enjoy this dance. I confess I did not expect you to be such a skilful dancer, considering how much you dislike the activity."

"I have learnt, Miss Bennet. There are many things I dislike and still perform reasonably well. But tonight, I am enjoying myself exceedingly. I am glad you are not disappointed with my company."

"Not at all, Mr Darcy. It is fortunate we are only dancing

for the first time now, when the other's company is not as unpleasant for each of us as it used to be." Elizabeth smiled.

Mr Darcy seemed undecided about how to reply, and after a long pause, he finally said, "Yes, very fortunate."

For a while, they followed the music in silence, then a little later, Elizabeth started a conversation about the number of pairs on the dance floor and afterwards about the weather, and finally about the puppies they shared. The subject brought smiles to both and dissipated most of the tension, though the notion of sharing something with Mr Darcy was disquieting enough for Elizabeth.

She noticed many intrigued gazes on them — and even mentioned it to Mr Darcy. People were obviously surprised to see the gentleman dancing, and particularly with her out of all the ladies in attendance. He had not asked Mr Bingley's sisters, as was expected, but her. Even her father and the admiral, who were talking and drinking in a corner with Sir William and Mr Phillips, seemed to be discussing them and probably making sport at their expense.

Elizabeth was aware of the stares and whispers and could even guess what they might be saying, since everyone knew of Mr Darcy's offence against her at the assembly.

She did not feel perfectly comfortable during the dance, though she did enjoy every minute of it. Mr Darcy's company, as pleasant as it had become, was never comfortable to her and probably never would be.

$\infty\infty\infty$

Darcy escorted Elizabeth back to her sister Jane, then joined the admiral, Mr Bennet, and Bingley. He had felt the curious stares upon them during their dance but chose to disregard them. He was accustomed to people staring at him, but it had seemed to bother Elizabeth, despite her statement that she was enjoying the dance.

Their dialogue enchanted but also puzzled him, and there were words that he would have to recollect and reflect on later. Her feelings were still unclear to him, and his were not perfectly clear to himself, either.

However, he could hardly remember another time when a dance and a conversation had been so delightful to him. Being the recipient of Elizabeth's attention and teasing was enchanting. And the feeling of teasing a bright woman with a sharp mind and sparkling eyes, even in a room full of people and music, was absolutely charming in an intimate way. Something he had never experienced before.

The musicians were taking a longer break, and some of the gentlemen left the ballroom, including Colonel Forster and most of the officers. In the hall, a crowd of men were smoking cigars, talking, and laughing, while the ladies remained inside, taking seats to rest. Only a few men remained in the ballroom, Darcy's little group among them.

"Well, Darcy, what a delight to see you dancing! I wonder if I have had this pleasure before," the admiral teased him.

"And with my Lizzy, of all ladies," Mr Bennet added. "You have certainly compensated for your previous sins, sir. At least in the eyes of my wife and her friends."

"I believe it is the third time I have seen Darcy dance," Bingley added.

"Now, you must invite other ladies to dance too, Darcy. It is only gentlemanly," the admiral said. "Since you gave such a lovely performance, you cannot refuse other ladies the pleasure of your skills."

"I am glad I provided you with such an excellent source of amusement, Admiral," Darcy answered, causing the gentleman to laugh.

"I am glad too," the admiral said. "One should amuse himself as much as he can at such parties."

"Darcy is rather fastidious. As I have told him many times," Bingley uttered. "He rarely amuses himself at any parties."

"He seemed to be amusing himself quite well tonight. Am I wrong, Darcy?" the admiral insisted.

"I enjoyed my witty conversation with Miss Bennet," Darcy said. "Though I could have enjoyed it just as much with no music and no crowd. A library or a peaceful drawing room would have been ideal."

Admiral Pembroke laughed again, joined by Bingley.

"I understand Mr Darcy's dislike of balls," Mr Bennet interjected. "All the noise, people, and music is really giving me a headache. I would give anything for a little bit of peace and quiet, a book, and perhaps a glass of wine."

"I would not reject such a suggestion," the admiral replied. "While I by no means dislike balls or parties, they can become tiresome at times. I would enjoy a little bit of rest too, and I believe the library would be the perfect place."

Darcy was momentarily confused, but Mr Bennet nodded energetically.

"Will you go to the library now?" Bingley asked, puzzled too.

"Yes, and as soon as possible, while Mr Collins and Sir William are still occupied with each other. Will you join us?"

"I would like to," Bingley said, "but as the host, I cannot abandon my guests. I shall happily escort you there, though."

"That is not necessary. We shall easily find both the library and the drinks," the admiral jested. "Darcy, will you join us?"

Darcy hesitated only a moment. "Gladly, sir."

The three of them exited, and Darcy turned to see Elizabeth watching them. He smiled at her, but she seemed rather uneasy and averted her eyes, confusing him.

On their way to the library, they walked through the crowded hall, full of the smoke of cigars and clamour of voices. Entering the peaceful room, lit only by the fire crackling in the hearth, was relieving and comforting.

Mr Bennet sighed and immediately made himself comfortable, while the admiral did the same. Darcy lit two more candles and filled three glasses of wine.

"Thank you, Mr Darcy," Mr Bennet said. "Having you serve me a drink is something I never imagined. I would tell Mr Collins and my wife about it if I did not fear hearing it repeated till the end of my days."

His tone seemed serious, but there was a twinkle in his eye, and the admiral laughed. Darcy did not know how to take the statement and chose to say nothing.

"Darcy is among the best men I have ever met, and I have met quite a few," the admiral said. "Not always pleasant in behaviour nor amiable in manners, especially with strangers, but excellent in character. As well as kind and generous. So, serving us a drink I could well imagine, especially since he is the youngest of us."

"I dare say Mr Darcy is the only subject about which Mr Collins's praises seem justified," Mr Bennet said.

"True," the admiral replied. "Equally annoying but justified. Darcy, would you be so kind as to pass us a cigar, too? I hope you do not mind."

"Not at all, sir." Darcy hurried to oblige, offering each a cigar and keeping one for himself.

"I am not sure whether I should light this," Mr Bennet said. "I have quite a bad headache. Perhaps some peace and quiet will be good medicine."

"Mr Bennet, I can ring for a servant and ask for some herbal tea for your headache," Darcy suggested.

"That will not be necessary, sir. Please do not trouble yourself further over me. It will be gone soon."

"Perhaps some fresh air will help. I shall open the window," the admiral said.

"Please, allow me to do it," Darcy offered, hurrying to the window. Spending time with the admiral had always been a delight to him, but Elizabeth's father was an equally pleasant companion. And, despite his attempt to sound light, Darcy had noticed the gentleman's pale countenance displaying a trace of some discomfort.

When he opened the window, the first thing that hit Darcy

was the cold air, as one would expect on a winter's night. Some clouds had gathered again, but the moon and a few stars were still visible.

The second thing, and one that froze Darcy in place, was the sound of voices, amongst which he recognised Wickham's. He had no desire to listen, but he was stunned to hear the name Lizzy Bennet followed by laughter. He struggled to understand what was being said and so closed the window and locked it.

"Darcy, what happened? Why did you close the window? Leave it open a little. We need more fresh air," the admiral said, frowning at him.

Darcy glanced at him, silently indicating towards Mr Bennet, but the admiral continued, heedless.

"Open the window wide, Darcy."

"There is noise out there...people drinking and smoking and talking..."

"That is expected, for sure. Why would we care about them? We shall refresh the room for a couple of minutes."

Before Darcy had time to protest, the admiral strode towards him and threw open the window.

"There!" he said with satisfaction. Cold air burst into the room, together with words that carried dreadful, unthinkable meanings.

Chapter 11

"I must say, I did not believe you when you first told us, Wickham," a male voice said. "Everybody says Miss Elizabeth despises Darcy! Lydia and Kitty have said so a hundred times!"

"She might have despised him once, but money always changes a woman's opinion. Especially one with no dowry and no connections."

"But she is charming. Even you said as much, Wickham. And if her sister marries Bingley…"

"*If* her sister marries Bingley. If! I understand Bingley will leave soon, and I have heard of no engagement."

"True…"

"As for Elizabeth, she is pretty, charming, and delightful. I would not mind spending more time with her. Yet, she cannot expect a decent marriage proposal, so Darcy's offer might have been the best she could hope for," Wickham's voice claimed.

Darcy glanced at his companions, panicked, horrified, hurrying to close the window, but Mr Bennet grabbed his coat sleeve and indicated that he should keep silent. Furthermore, Mr Bennet moved to another chair nearer the window, so he could better hear. The admiral seemed shocked and ready to leap into action, so Mr Bennet repeated his gesture for him.

"Still, Wickham, why would Darcy expose himself in such a manner by meeting her in the woods and now dancing with her? And visiting her father? And what about the admiral? He has spent the evening with Mr Bennet. They seem to be friends."

"That is strange, I admit. The admiral is a navy man and a man of the world. He knows how these things are settled. As for Darcy, he is not acting like himself. The witty Miss Lizzy might have something special that Darcy likes. I wonder what it is…"

"Some puppies, I heard," another voice said, followed by a peal of laughter.

"Perhaps Darcy will marry her, after all!"

"Do not be an idiot, Denny. I have known Darcy all his life. He would never marry into that poor and ridiculous family! Can you imagine taking his mother-in-law and sisters to Pemberley? Or to his box at the theatre with Lord Matlock? He would be the laughingstock of London! Besides, he is engaged to his sickly cousin Anne."

"True…"

"I know only too well what I speak of. Nobody knows Darcy better than I do," Wickham concluded.

"I shall rip him apart," Darcy said and burst out of the library. Looking back briefly, he saw Mr Bennet looking pale, breathing irregularly, his hands grasping his glass as he stared at the rug.

Enraged, Darcy disregarded the people staring at him as he strode along the hall. His head was spinning, and he was trembling with anger, disgust, shame, and resentment that he did not even try to suppress; his entire being screamed for revenge. Once out of doors, he hesitated for a moment, wondering where the group of scoundrels were, and he moved around the house until he heard voices and laughter. He did not even dare imagine what further horrible things were being said and heard by Mr Bennet, but he would stop it all in a few moments.

As he approached, he saw Wickham, Denny, and Pratt. They were smoking and drinking, still laughing. Seeing him, surprise silenced them, and they looked momentarily bewildered, glancing at each other, then at Darcy.

Wickham took a step back, while Darcy stepped forwards. He took a deep breath, his fists clenched, his reason warning him against any imprudence. He dismissed the voice of reason, but not another voice, loud, deep, shattering the night, falling like thunder from the window.

"Darcy, bring those vulgar miscreants to the library now! Discreetly, if possible, so as not to ruin the ball. Tell them not to make me hunt them down, which I am willing to do at this very moment."

If at first the three men had looked dumbfounded, panic now fell over their faces at the admiral's voice, as they realised they had been heard.

"You heard Admiral Pembroke. He is expecting you," Darcy said, his anger palliated by the expectation of revenge. "Except for you, Wickham. I shall deal with you myself, this very instant."

He stepped forwards, and Wickham stepped back, disbelief and fright written on his face. The other two still looked bewildered, standing together as though in a poor attempt at defending themselves, abandoning the one who had caused the trouble.

"Darcy, first bring that useless wretch to look Mr Bennet in the eye and explain himself. Then, you may kill him if you like. I wonder why it has taken you so long."

Darcy needed another breath to cool his temper; the admiral was at the window, leaning through it, as if he was ready to jump out.

"Into the library! Now!" Darcy shouted, grabbing Wickham's arm. The man struggled to free himself but in vain.

"But...Mr Darcy...you cannot treat us in such a way!" Denny attempted to say. "I am not sure what is happening. We have done nothing wrong. We were talking and—"

"Mr Denny, do not make a fool of yourself," Darcy said coldly, disgusted by the man who suddenly seemed weak and frightened. "Admiral Pembroke and I were in the library with Mr Bennet. We heard everything you said. You may either go to the library now or bear more severe consequences."

"I must speak to Colonel Forster," Pratt said. "We cannot

be threatened and forced. We are officers. I am going back to the regiment now."

"But the admiral!" Denny said. "We cannot disobey him!"

"You do as you please, Denny. I am not going."

They continued to argue while walking towards the door. Darcy was still holding Wickham, but he realised he had to make a decision before they entered the house. He could not pull Wickham along the hall, in full view of the guests, nor could he hold all three officers to prevent them from leaving. The situation was dreadful, ridiculous, and dangerous in many ways, and anger still prevented him from thinking clearly and reasonably.

"Darcy, this is absurd," Wickham finally said. "Are you going to make a spectacle in your friend's house? For a joke? I do not know what you heard, but—"

"What on earth is happening here? Where have you been? What are you doing?"

Near the door, holding his glass and cigar, Colonel Forster was staring at the men, dumbfounded. Behind him, the admiral waited.

"We were having an argument," Darcy explained. "Denny and Pratt were desirous of your presence, Colonel. I suggest we all settle this matter in the library, discreetly, as gentlemen and officers should."

"Let us go," Colonel Forster said. "Whatever is happening, I shall not have my name and my regiment polluted by scandal."

A few minutes later, eight men were gathered in the library. One of them was Bingley, bewildered, incredulous, stunned, wondering what had happened in the short time between the sets. The rest of the party continued, the music could be heard, and the pairs of dancers were on the floor.

Outside the library, people were enjoying what they called

one of the best balls in the neighbourhood. Inside, there was anger, resentment, hate, and threats, and the only agreement was to call that night one of their worst ever.

"I am ashamed, appalled, disgusted, and disappointed," Colonel Forster said. "I could never imagine my officers behaving in such a repellent way. I do not even know what to say...how to act... This is undoubtedly a matter of honour. But I hope we all agree that duels are illegal, and such a solution should be dismissed entirely."

"Nobody wants to duel with these worthless nothings," the admiral replied. "I was considering shooting them, but not in a duel, only for the fun of hunting them down."

The officers stared at him, then looked at their colonel, begging for support. Nobody doubted that the admiral was speaking in earnest.

"Let us hope that will not be necessary, Admiral," the colonel answered.

"Why not? So many better men than these have been lost in battle. You will easily replace them with better ones."

"I am sure I am not wrong in presuming that just one man is guilty of starting the rumours and engaging the others in this loathsome situation," Darcy interjected. "It is not the first time Wickham has acted in this despicable manner, and I blame myself for not taking proper measures a long time ago."

"Come, Darcy, you cannot put all the blame on me! You have always hated me, even when your father loved me," Wickham responded.

"You must kill him. There cannot be any other way," Admiral Pembroke said coldly with an unreadable expression on his face. "And if these other idiots allow themselves to be so easily influenced by him, they are not worth anything either. Shoot them, I say. Or send them to war tomorrow. I can easily arrange that."

The officers tried to defend themselves again, their voices affected by alcohol and fear, now sounding pathetic.

"What I would like to know," Mr Bennet finally said

weakly, distress and grief apparent on his pale face, "is why gentlemen and officers who have been welcomed into my home would think so ill and speak in such an awful manner about my family, who have been nothing but kind and friendly to them."

"Mr Bennet, we…" Denny began to mumble. "We were fools…we drank too much…there were rumours and…we were only joking. Wickham said—"

"Do not dare put the blame on me!" Wickham yelled, and an argument between the officers started.

"Silence!" the colonel shouted. "Mr Bennet, I can safely say they do not think ill of your family, but they did not think at all. I have heard nothing but praise of your family since we arrived in Meryton. Whatever caused this dreadful situation, these men will find ways to remedy the wrong. They will offer apologies and compensation to your family, of any sort you wish, Mr Bennet. Including of a financial nature! You must state your demands, and I shall ensure they are carried out."

"Nothing can remedy such a wrong, and no compensation can mend a father's aggrieved heart, Colonel. I was a fool to allow these worthless men near my family. You may choose their punishment. What worries me is that such abominable rumours have likely been spread about Meryton and are hurting my family, especially my daughter Elizabeth."

"If that is true, I assure you it will be immediately corrected!" the colonel said. "I shall make sure of it! This conversation will not end tonight."

"Damn right it will not!" the admiral shouted. "The consequences must be equal to the damage to the name of a remarkable young woman. If Miss Elizabeth was my daughter, you would all be dead by now!"

"Since my name has been polluted too, I also demand satisfaction," Darcy interjected. "To begin with, I request that you keep Wickham imprisoned at your barracks until I decide what to do with him. He owes me a significant amount of money, which I want to be paid by the end of this week."

"What? You cannot do that, Darcy! By the end of the week?

How can you do this to me? We discussed this last summer when we had another disagreement, remember?" Wickham replied, fear obvious in his insinuating tone, which Darcy understood. It was nothing but a hidden threat to reveal the planned elopement and to hurt Georgiana too. He struggled to keep his composure, staring at Wickham until the man lowered his eyes. Then, calmly, he addressed the admiral.

"I should follow your advice and kill Wickham. After all, it would be presumptuous of me to contradict an admiral."

Nothing else was added until the door opened, and Caroline Bingley appeared.

"Charles, what on earth are you doing here? Mr Darcy? Admiral? Why are you all here? Supper is being served, and everyone is asking about you! Charles, this is not the way to host a ball!"

"We beg your forgiveness, Miss Bingley. I take full blame," Colonel Forster replied. "Unfortunately, my men and I must return to barracks immediately, and we shall not be able to enjoy the meal. I shall return to retrieve my wife later. Come, let us leave."

The three men followed their colonel; Miss Bingley rolled her eyes with obvious frustration and disapproval, demanding her brother return to their guests immediately. Bingley obeyed after a brief hesitation, and soon enough, the three men found themselves alone again, as they had been an hour ago.

The room was the same, yet it felt utterly different, and Darcy barely dared to look at Mr Bennet. Guilt replaced his previous ire, and he was as furious with Wickham as he was with himself. He began to understand his imprudence, from escorting Elizabeth home with the puppies to dancing with her — only with her — and exposing her to speculation, as absurd as it was. Mr Bennet was rightfully grieved, but how would Elizabeth feel when she found out? How would she respond? How would he ever look at her again? How would he be able to right the wrong he had caused, although unwillingly?

"I would rather go home too," Mr Bennet whispered. "I feel

rather unwell. I certainly do not wish to return to the party."

"Would you not be better to rest a little? Perhaps sleep a little? Please consider having some herbal tea...you may rest in my room," Darcy said.

"No, thank you. If you could only ask for my carriage. Do not say anything to my family, please, only that I was tired and went home. I shall send the carriage back for them."

"As you wish...but if you are unwell, it would not be wise to be home alone."

"I shall not be alone. The servants will be there. Hill has some herbal remedies too. She will make me some tea."

"Perhaps Mr Jones should be fetched?" Darcy insisted as Mr Bennet was looking worse by the minute. He knew he had no right to impose on the man; Mr Bennet was almost a stranger to him, but he was genuinely worried, and the fear for Mr Bennet's safety induced his actions.

"No...please do not make more of all this than is necessary, Mr Darcy. I need nothing more than to be home alone, in my bed."

"Very well, sir. Forgive my insistence. But I shall escort you home in my carriage, just to be sure you have arrived safely. Then I shall return immediately."

"You should accept Darcy's offer, sir," the admiral interjected. "Please do so. In the meantime, I shall go and speak to your family, to calm them."

"Very well, Mr Darcy, call your carriage. And Admiral, please do not worry my daughters. Allow them to enjoy this night. It might be the last before a dark period of tormenting times."

"Mr Bennet, we shall speak more about this tomorrow. Until then, please rest and try to calm yourself. Darcy and I shall call on you tomorrow," the admiral said.

"You will be welcomed, but the situation will not change."

"No, but we shall see it in a better light. My anger was justified, and I would have readily shot those idiots. But in truth, no real tragedy occurred, thank God. Drunken fools always say ridiculous things, but nobody in their right mind would believe them. To suggest that Darcy might have an illicit relationship with Miss Elizabeth is as absurd as saying I am Napoleon."

"Indeed, sir, I hope you do not—" Darcy attempted to say, but Mr Bennet silenced him with a gesture of his hand.

"Of course I do not give an instant of consideration to that nonsense. Not just because I trust my daughter Elizabeth with my life, but because she and Mr Darcy only began speaking civilly to each other a few days ago. I would no more suspect she was engaged in an illicit relationship with Mr Darcy than with my cousin," Mr Bennet tried to jest.

Not long after, Darcy's carriage took two silent, embarrassed men to Longbourn and returned one to the party.

Chapter 12

As soon as she woke up, Elizabeth hurried to her father's room. She was deeply worried since she had heard he had left in the middle of the ball, although her mother had claimed it must have been a scheme to escape the party.

The second part of the ball had been strange. She had danced the third set with Mr Collins, while her father, Mr Darcy, the admiral, and several officers had been missing from the ballroom for a long period of time.

The fact was puzzling, but when she had asked Mr Bingley, he had told her that her father was in the library in the company of Mr Darcy and the admiral. That had put her mind at rest; however, time had passed with no sign of them. By the supper set, none of the party had appeared, and there was much perturbation among the guests, until Mr Bingley returned with news about Colonel Forster and a few of his officers being called away on urgent business.

The absence of the officers was disappointing to many of the ladies and raised more questions for Elizabeth. Somehow, in her mind, the absences of Mr Wickham and Mr Darcy, at the same time, were connected, as unlikely as it seemed.

And then, the news of her father returning home — with Mr Darcy no less, in his carriage —stunned her. Yet, the admiral spoke of it lightly and assured her she had no reason to worry. For the first time since she had met him, she doubted the man's sincerity.

Upon their return to Longbourn, her mother and sisters

chatted endlessly, Mr Collins expressed his opinions about the party that nobody wanted to hear, but Elizabeth could think of little else but Mr Darcy and her father. She visited the latter and found him peacefully asleep, with a glass of brandy and a cup of tea near his bed.

Feeling distressed, Elizabeth only slept for a few hours. The rest of the house was soundly asleep when she rose, and she found Mr Bennet in the library, sitting in his favourite chair.

"Papa, how are you feeling? Have you rested well? You look so pale. Should I fetch Mr Jones?"

"I slept, Lizzy. Please do not worry about me, child. There is enough you have to worry about."

"What do you mean, Papa?" she asked with a surge of anxiety.

"We shall discuss it later. My head is still fuzzy, probably from Hill's herbal tea. I have sent John to fetch me some coffee."

"Papa, you are scaring me," she said, taking a seat, but he said nothing. The door opened, and they expected John with the coffee; instead, Mr Collins entered, clasping his hands together.

"My dear Mr Bennet, Cousin Elizabeth, how fortunate to find you here! There is something I want to tell you—"

"Mr Collins, please forgive my rudeness, but I am in no disposition for conversation," Mr Bennet interrupted him. "I just told my daughter the same. I felt quite ill last night, and I still am not completely well. I need some time to recover, in silence and solitude."

Mr Collins seemed stuck between offence and astonishment and in need of air. Despite her concern and curiosity, Elizabeth supported her father and immediately stood up.

"Come, Mr Collins, we must leave my father to rest. If you need help with any matter, I shall be happy to assist you."

Mr Collins reluctantly agreed to follow Elizabeth. In the hall, he seemed tempted to speak again, but she addressed him first.

"I know you plan to return to Kent tomorrow. I hope you

will not postpone it. I am sure you will be thrilled to see Lady Catherine, and she will be happy with your company."

"I would never dare postpone a plan approved by her ladyship. She highly disapproves of that! However, I still have to complete my assignment before I leave Hertfordshire. This is what I intended to speak to Mr Bennet about…and you. I spoke to Mrs Bennet last night, and I fear I might have raised some expectations that I cannot fulfill…"

"Mr Collins," Elizabeth said decidedly, "I am in the position of being able to speak on my father's behalf as well as my own, and I assure you there are no expectations that you need be concerned about. It was a pleasure to have you as a guest, and we wish you a safe journey home. I am sure my father will be pleased to receive a letter from you."

"Are you sure? I intend to call on Sir William…to speak to him. We agreed last night…"

Elizabeth watched the clergyman trying to keep his composure, and she pitied him for the disappointment he was about to suffer.

She understood his meaning very well; after he had arrived in Hertfordshire, he had spoken to her mother and made plans to propose to her. However, the events of the last few days, as well as Elizabeth's lack of encouragement and harsh manners, had likely changed his mind. He probably doubted Lady Catherine de Bourgh would approve of her — which she knew to be true.

Apparently, the poor clueless man had taken Sir William and Charlotte's politeness as encouragement, and he intended to propose to her instead. Elizabeth had no doubt that Charlotte would refuse him; after all, they had known each other for less than a fortnight and had scarcely been in company. No reasonable man would propose under such circumstances, and no woman would accept.

"I believe you are entitled to call upon anyone you wish to whenever you want, sir. You need not ask anyone's opinion on your plans. Except for Lady Catherine's, of course."

"Cousin Elizabeth, your wisdom is much appreciated. Miss Lucas speaks highly of you, and now I can see why. I hope Mrs Bennet will not mind if I have breakfast with Sir William."

"As I said, a gentleman in your position should make his own decisions," she replied. She was certain her mother would be devastated and angered by the notion he might propose to Charlotte and would do anything to prevent it. Luckily, Mrs Bennet and her other daughters were still sleeping after the ball. Mr Collins would likely return disappointed from Lucas Lodge, and they would have to bear his whining for another day and a half.

After Mr Collins left, Elizabeth returned to her own torment. Her father was not in good health and, more importantly, not in good spirits. Her intuition had not betrayed her — something had happened the previous night, and assuming what it could have been, she feared the worst.

Restless, she counted the minutes until her father would wake up, to resume their conversation. However, her mother and sisters woke up first, and breakfast was prepared. Mrs Bennet asked about her husband and Mr Collins and was displeased with the news about both.

When they gathered around the table, Lydia and Kitty started a discussion about the ball. Mr Bennet joined them, and the food was served. He was silent, while his daughters were chatting.

"My dear, is it true that you came home in Mr Darcy's carriage?" Mrs Bennet asked.

"Yes."

"I imagine it is large and elegant!"

"I cannot say. It was dark and cold, and I had a horrible headache."

"Something strange happened at that ball," Lydia interjected. "You left, and then Colonel Forster left with all the officers! I mean — the most handsome of them. Harriet Forster did not know that her husband had left. We all wanted to dance with Wickham, and he suddenly disappeared too! What bad luck that was! There must be another ball soon. I shall ask Harriet to host one."

"Lydia, I shall hear not another word about the officers, especially not about that Wickham fellow! Not now, nor ever! From any of you! Is that clear?"

Mr Bennet's voice shook the room, and all the ladies stared at him, dumbfounded. Elizabeth had never heard her father shout at them or scold them with such severity.

"But Papa—"

"Not a word, Lydia!" he repeated, his voice lower but demanding.

"But why? You cannot just forbid us from speaking to somebody. That is not fair!" Lydia whined, supported by Kitty.

"Mr Bennet, the girl is right. You must tell us why. Such a demand is unheard of!"

"Why, Mrs Bennet? Because you and I and our daughters are a laughingstock among the officers and probably the entire town! Your favourite, Mr Wickham, calls you ridiculous and silly and laughs at you with the other officers. He speaks of your daughter in the most despicable manner. Is that enough reason? Fortunately, I hope the colonel will make sure we do not see him too often from this day forward!"

The silence that fell in the room allowed Elizabeth to hear her own heart beating. She noticed Hill and John watching from behind the door, obviously drawn by the raised voices. Her sisters and mother were all breathing irregularly, still in shock.

Mr Bennet put down his fork and left the table without another word. After a brief hesitation, Elizabeth ran after him. None of her sisters dared follow her.

"Papa?" she whispered from the door, watching her father rubbing his temples, his eyes closed.

"Come in, Lizzy. Sit down and close the door."

"Papa, I do not know what happened, but you look very ill. I shall fetch Mr Jones."

"Sit down, Lizzy! I am sure I look better than I feel. I shall tell you what happened, although I would give anything not to have to do so."

He poured himself a drink, and Elizabeth frowned.

"Papa, you have barely slept or eaten. You should not drink at this early hour."

"I shall need more than one glass to tell you what I must, Lizzy."

"You may tell me anything, Papa. Whatever happened, we shall face it together."

"I fear you will have to face it by yourself, Lizzy. As much as I would like to, there is not much I can do."

Several minutes later, the short yet dreadful narration ended, without Elizabeth having said a word to interrupt it. She needed a while to comprehend what her father had said. Astonishment, disbelief, and shame made her hands tremble, and she clasped them together.

"Why would they say such horrible things, Papa? They must know it cannot be true! I thought they were friends…"

"Why? Mr Darcy claims that Wickham spread malicious falsehoods on purpose to blacken his good name and did not care whether he hurt you too. The others engaged in this atrocity because they are vulgar miscreants, as the admiral said. I am not sure whether they believed it or not, but they found it amusing."

"What do you mean, Papa? Could they possibly believe such a dreadful story? Am I so despicable in their eyes? Why?"

"Lizzy dear, I cannot answer that question. I have no doubt you are as good as a young lady can be. There is no reason for anybody to think ill of you."

"And Mr Darcy — what will he think of me? For someone to imagine that Mr Darcy could… And I could… There can be nothing more appalling! And the admiral? What is he thinking? I shall never dare to see any of them again!"

"Mr Darcy and the admiral were equally shocked and

enraged. Mr Darcy marched out to confront the officers, and the admiral seriously suggested he shoot them. I would certainly not have opposed it."

"But Papa, where did all this occur? Who else was there?"

"Nobody else was around at that moment. Do not worry. Mr Darcy held his temper well enough to avoid a bigger scandal. And the admiral called in Colonel Forster, who took charge and sent the scoundrels away. Mr Darcy seemingly has proof that Mr Wickham owes him a large amount of money. He has decided to throw the man in debtors' prison, and I shall insist on him doing so!"

"Dear Lord, I cannot believe all this... Have I done something to cause it? Poor Mr Darcy. He was so thoughtful to escort me home and to take care of the poor puppies. That was all! And instead of being praised, he is laughed at and his honour doubted!"

"Strangely enough, Mr Darcy blames himself for not being more careful with his actions and exposing you to such rumours."

"Surely that is not true, Papa! Was there something wrong in our behaviour?"

"Of course not, my dear. I am so sorry, Lizzy…I feel it is my fault! I never took good care of any of you, never censured Lydia and Kitty, never corrected your mother's breaches of decorum… and now you must suffer…"

"Papa, please," Elizabeth said, embracing him. "Do not blame yourself for the actions of some horrible men! I am upset, but it will soon pass, and so will these rumours. Nobody in their right mind would believe such falsehoods."

"I believe the same, Lizzy. You are loved and admired by everyone who knows you. Such gossip cannot ruin the good reputation you have held in this community all your life. I must go and speak to Colonel Forster now."

"Papa, you look unwell. Please rest a little longer. Your health is more important than anything else. I shall bring you something to eat, and you must sleep a little more."

"Very well, Lizzy. Besides, Mr Darcy and the admiral promised to call and bring news…"

"Let me help you to your room now, Papa. We shall see what happens later."

"Wake me up when they arrive, Lizzy."

"I shall, Papa," she answered, secretly wishing the ground would open up and swallow her so she would not be forced to ever see Mr Darcy again.

She helped her father into bed, then returned to the library alone. Her mind tried to make sense of everything her father had related to her, word by word.

The notion that anybody could imagine she was Mr Darcy's mistress was astonishing, appalling, and mortifying. She felt ashamed just thinking about it. And such an insinuation had come from the man she had considered a friend, the man whose claims against Mr Darcy she had at first believed. The man whose attentions once pleased her. How could she have been such a simpleton?

Perhaps she deserved Mr Wickham's lack of consideration, since she had granted him her trust so carelessly. Also, she had always found Mr Denny and Mr Pratt pleasant and friendly and had never doubted their integrity. Instead, she had doubted Mr Darcy's character because of his cold manners. While she had easily admired the appearance of goodness, for a while she had failed miserably to recognise the goodness itself. Yes, she had been a complete fool, and she was now suffering the consequences.

As much as she had tried to reject her father's concerns, the more she reflected upon it, the more she feared the false reports were spread wider and would be more difficult to dismiss. She did not care much about it for herself, but she felt offended, hurt, and ashamed for Mr Darcy and the admiral.

But she was not alone in the danger. Such reports could affect and ruin her sisters' futures, too.

The Netherfield party was expected to depart for London in a few days. Mr Darcy would certainly want to distance himself from the scandal; that was understandable. Elizabeth felt a tightness in her chest at the thought, but she refused to acknowledge the reason for it. Yes, she had enjoyed Mr Darcy's company and the set they had shared; the dance and the conversation had truly been a delight. And the quiver she felt every time he touched her hand was pleasant and disturbing beyond her understanding. But she expected nothing from him except perhaps to see him again from time to time and maintain a friendly acquaintance, especially if Mr Bingley proposed to Jane.

But would he, now that he was involved in the scandal? What was he thinking? Would he even return to Hertfordshire, to Jane, or would he rather keep his distance, just like his friend?

Had Jane's happiness been wasted and her future ruined too? Elizabeth did not care much for herself, but for her sister and her father, she prayed to see those men punished and suffering too. Especially Mr Wickham, who had forced her to see the flaws in her character and lose faith in her wit and judgment.

Chapter 13

With the ball ending late and the servants moving around until dawn, some of the Netherfield residents kept to their rooms until late in the morning. Two of them had had no sleep, though, and they were talking in Darcy's room, drinking at an hour inappropriate for brandy.

"There is not much we can do with the other two idiots," Darcy said. "As much as I share your anger, we cannot just kill them for spreading malicious reports."

"I know. If we could, there would be more people dead than alive," the admiral agreed. "But they must pay, and Mr Bennet must receive satisfaction. And Miss Elizabeth, of course."

"We must be careful not to cause more harm, instead of satisfaction. I wished to rip Wickham apart, but I still wonder how I controlled myself not to beat him. But the scandal would have only aggravated the rumours and spread them further."

"This is the worst part. Even if we kill Wickham and the other miscreants, it will not stop the gossip nor repair the damage."

"I have the biggest share of the blame, Admiral. It was my responsibility, and I failed in it."

"What blame? What responsibility, Darcy?"

"Of keeping Wickham from hurting more innocent people. And of considering my actions more carefully. Of anticipating such consequences and preventing them."

"That is ridiculous. You have done nothing wrong. Or

have you?" the admiral enquired.

Darcy averted his eyes before he met the scrutinising gaze again.

"Wickham...this past summer he attempted to elope with Georgiana."

"What?"

"Please keep calm, Admiral. Except for Richard, nobody else knows, and I trust you to keep the secret."

"Certainly! But...what happened? When? Where?"

"In Ramsgate. Fortunately, Georgiana told me, and I intervened in time. No real damage was done, except for the grief inflicted on my sister. That is why I hesitated to confront Wickham in public — I think him capable of attacking Georgiana too if he feels trapped and in danger."

"I see. Then you should have killed him. Or thrown him in prison or sent him to the colonies!"

"I should have. I was thinking of my father and what he would want. You must know he was very fond of the scoundrel, despite my attempts to reveal his true character. My memories kept me from taking more severe measures...exposing him when I first saw he had befriended the Bennet family. I should have expected him to say and do anything to harm my reputation."

Darcy felt anger overwhelming him again, as well as remorse and guilt. He felt the admiral's stare on him and poured himself another drink. He was tired, his mind perturbed, and the brandy made him dizzy.

"Darcy, I have something to ask you, but you may choose not to answer me. Is there any truth to these rumours? Even a little bit?"

"Dear Lord, of course not!" he replied with indignation.

"Wait, wait! I did not mean you would ever ask Miss Elizabeth to be your mistress as that scoundrel suggested. Nor that you would be engaged in any improper conduct with her in the woods. But still, I have noticed..."

"Noticed what, Admiral?"

"I do not want to upset you, but I have observed you showing more attention to Miss Elizabeth than to any other woman. I mean small gestures, glances, conversation…that sort of thing."

The admiral paused, but Darcy remained silent, gulping more brandy.

"I might be wrong, Darcy, yet… Escorting Miss Elizabeth home when you found her in distress is something any honourable man would do. But taking so much care of the puppies? By yourself? And the little things you say about her… and singling her out by dancing only with her? The way you two spoke during that set drew my attention too, although it was perfectly proper. Something in your countenance was different, though."

Another pause followed, and Darcy still could not form a reply.

"Am I wrong, Darcy?"

"You are not wrong, sir," he finally admitted. "I have admired Miss Elizabeth almost from the beginning of our acquaintance. Her spirit, her wit, her open manners and confidence, her kind and affectionate heart — I have never found all these traits together in any woman."

"Well, now we are in agreement. And I have to say, I am not surprised by your admiration — I agree with everything you said. I am just stunned that you moved from refusing to dance with her and offending her to admiring her in such a short time."

"I hoped I had already cleared up that misunderstanding at the assembly with you, Mr Bennet, and Miss Elizabeth herself. She was kind enough to forgive me."

"So, what did you intend to do? Before this scandal occurred?"

"Do, sir? In regard to what?"

"To Miss Elizabeth, of course."

The admiral's stare grew more intense, and Darcy became uncomfortable.

"Nothing, of course. Miss Elizabeth is an exceptional, honourable young lady, the daughter of a gentleman. She has my admiration and consideration. I have never bothered her with an improper word or gesture."

"I do not doubt that. That was not my meaning. You are eight-and-twenty and reluctant to marry Anne or any other woman, to my knowledge. You are acquainted with the most eligible young ladies in town, but none have held your particular interest. Am I wrong so far?"

"You are not wrong, sir, and I believe I can guess the direction of your reasoning but—"

"Let me finish. You met a young woman who impressed you with rare traits and admirable accomplishments. As you said, she is the honourable daughter of a gentleman. Unlike many others, including myself many years ago, you have the liberty of making decisions for your present and your future as you wish."

"I shall not deny any of it, nor my struggle for some time now. While I do have the liberty, I also have the responsibility of making decisions not only according to my wishes but also for the benefit of my sister and my name. I cannot neglect the expectations that I have to fulfil, especially in choosing the future Mrs Darcy. Would you not agree?"

"I would and I do. Utterly and completely. So, you do not deny you have considered Miss Elizabeth as the future Mrs Darcy?"

"How could I deny the truth? But there are many other obstacles that might become stronger than my desire."

"I see no obstacle, except her lack of dowry and poor connections and some need for improvement in her mother and younger sisters' manners. I remember you expressed these objections when we first spoke of the Bennets. Back then they were meant to temper Bingley's admiration for the eldest sister."

"Yes, I remember too."

"Darcy, I shall insist no further. I also remember declaring I would not force anyone I know to marry against their wishes, and I shall certainly not break that principle with you. Besides, you are known for always fulfilling your responsibilities perfectly, so you must know best."

"I do not deserve to be mocked, Admiral. I have already confessed my struggle and admitted my failure in making a decision. I thought of little else last night. I know the best solution to remedy my wrong and to protect Miss Elizabeth and her family would be to marry her, despite the other scandal that would arise amongst my family and friends. I am sure you realise that."

"Of course I realise it, Darcy. The scandal you will have to face if you marry Miss Elizabeth might be even greater than if you do not marry her."

"Regardless, I am seriously considering discussing the matter with Mr Bennet and then Miss Elizabeth."

"Darcy, I hope you do not intend to marry the lady because of gossip. That is insufficient reason for a permanent commitment, and the obstacles would remain. Even worse, they might grow and make you both miserable."

"Admiral, I am completely dumbfounded. Only moments ago, you insisted on me marrying Miss Elizabeth. Did I misunderstand you?"

"Not at all."

"And now, when I am tempted to do so, you suggest the opposite. May I have your honest opinion? Do I have your approval?"

"Do you need my approval, Darcy?"

"No, but I would like to have it, nevertheless. I value your opinion more than anyone else's."

"Then I shall express it clearly. I recognised Miss Elizabeth's admirable qualities from the day I met her. I had no doubt that any man would be fortunate to have her as his wife, but I never imagined that man might be you. After this conversation, there is no question in my mind that your marriage to Miss Elizabeth would be to the advantage of both! If…"

"If?"

"If you marry her because your heart desires it and your mind is willing, not because of the fear of ruined reputations caused by stupid rumours."

"Yet, the consequences of the scandal cannot be neglected."

"True. But even Mr Bennet dismissed the rumours. He was hurt and aggrieved on behalf of his daughter, but he did not hold you responsible in any way."

"Yes, he told me as much. Thank you for this honest conversation, Admiral. I value it more than you might know."

"I want to see you happy, Darcy. And Miss Elizabeth."

"So do I, Admiral."

"However," Darcy continued, "to be happy — or at least at peace — Wickham must be removed from the neighbourhood. The sooner the better. The longer he stays here — even under the colonel's supervision — the greater the chance he may hurt either the Bennet family or Georgiana. I know I am being selfish, and I am hardly acting in a gentlemanlike manner, but I want him gone, no matter what."

Admiral Pembroke arched his eyebrow, and Darcy gave a nervous laugh.

"Please do not tell me again to kill him, Admiral. You sound very much like Richard when I told him about the elopement."

"What can I say, Darcy? Richard is my nephew and an army man too. We have similar ways of thinking and acting."

Darcy smiled bitterly. "I must consider everything carefully. In the event of a trial, even if Wickham ends up in prison, our name would be mentioned, considering he was my father's godson. Wickham can say things that would hurt Georgiana too, as well as Miss Elizabeth. Have I already said that? I am so tired that I can hardly think."

"I cannot dismiss your concerns, Darcy. We agree that he must be sent away immediately. What do you propose?"

"I am not certain. Perhaps an active regiment? Would that

be possible?"

The admiral frowned. "It is possible, Darcy, if you pay for the commission. But I do not agree with putting the burden of his cowardice and lack of honour on someone else, especially if his comrades must rely on him. Why must other officers suffer because we want to rid ourselves of the scoundrel?"

"You are right, of course, Admiral. Forgive me. I was being selfish and thoughtless. I must give it further consideration."

"If you will allow me a suggestion, I believe transportation would be the best choice for Wickham."

"Transportation?"

"Yes. You may send him to one of the prisons abroad and be done with him. Or, put him on a ship, give him some money, and pray he has learnt his lesson and will start anew — which I very much doubt."

Darcy needed only a moment of reflection until the burden felt like it had been lifted from his chest.

"That is the perfect solution, indeed. I shall provide him with the means for a new beginning — I am sure my father would not want to see him die in prison. After that, I shall consider myself discharged of any responsibility and hopefully not see him again."

"If you ask me, you have long fulfilled any responsibilities, Darcy, but do as your conscience requires."

"Admiral, you knew my father longer than I did. You know what an extraordinary man he was. How honest and generous, dedicated to his family and to his responsibilities. A man who despised deception and disguise."

"I did know him very well. We grew up together. He was my best friend, and nobody could take his place in my heart after he died. He was a remarkable man and a great friend."

"Then how was it possible that such a man remained ignorant of Wickham's character? Or perhaps not ignorant, but he chose to dismiss the evidence and still hold the scoundrel in affection. Wickham was always lazy with his studies, disregarded his father's demands, and wasted his money and his time in deception. He even left a maid at Pemberley with child while my father was still alive."

"I cannot explain it either. But Darcy, we men are far from perfect. Even the best of us. We have weaknesses that we hide, we have buried secrets, we do things we are ashamed of. Among so many praiseworthy accomplishments, your father had some failures too. Like any other man."

"I find it hard to believe. I cannot remember anything to condemn in regard to my father. Not even the smallest thing."

"Just because you do not remember, Darcy, does not mean those failures did not exist, just as it does not mean they diminish your father's generally excellent character. As for Wickham, I cannot be certain why George favoured him against the evidence. However, I am sure he would have requested harsh punishment if he had known what the scoundrel attempted with Georgiana! Have no regrets about following through with our plan!"

"You must not worry about that. I shall speak to the colonel and Wickham immediately."

"Would you like me to join you?"

"If you wish. I would appreciate your support. Afterwards, we should call on Mr Bennet. I hope he is feeling better. He looked truly ill last night. I feared heart failure."

"Let us hope that is not the case. I have grown truly fond of that country gentleman."

"So have I," Darcy admitted.

Chapter 14

Elizabeth did not manage to soothe her torment despite sobbing for a while. Jane came to her and, as much as Elizabeth tried to spare her sister pain, she could not resist Jane's pleas and revealed the secret.

The sorrow which shadowed Jane's handsome face only deepened Elizabeth's misery, and they embraced each other in a desperate attempt at comfort.

"I cannot believe Mr Wickham is such a vicious man!" Jane whispered. "Vicious, hateful, spiteful man! How did we allow him to deceive us all?"

Jane's outburst of anger — never heard before — made Elizabeth embrace her tighter.

"Dearest, you warned me not to trust strangers so readily. I am the only one who allowed herself to be so easily deceived. I was flattered by his attentions and upset by Mr Darcy's arrogance, so I chose to confide in the one who flattered me. I was an utter and complete fool."

"Nonsense, Lizzy! I shall never forgive Mr Wickham. I shall tell all our relatives and friends to ask Colonel Forster to remove him from the regiment. He cannot be allowed to stay in Meryton."

"Jane, let us calm down. I am reluctant to tell anyone. In truth, I hope such reports remain unknown in Meryton, though I doubt it very much."

"Then what can we do, Lizzy?"

"I do not know, Jane. I do not want to see anyone. My only

concern is Papa. If he does not feel better later, I shall fetch the apothecary."

Despite her desire for solitude, Elizabeth was soon invaded by her sisters and mother, asking for details about the officers. Since she had spent the longest time with her father, they assumed she had more information, which she was not prepared to share, so she denied it. It took another hour until they all departed and she was left alone. She went to see her father, but he was still asleep, so she returned to her chamber and fell asleep too.

A knock on the door and Jane's worried voice awakened Elizabeth sometime later. Her head was spinning, and she felt worse than before the nap, with a terrible headache.

"Lizzy, Papa is asking for you. He is in the library. Oh, dear! Have you been crying? You look so pale, and your eyes are swollen."

"A little. But do not worry. I cannot remember crying in years. Perhaps it was time."

"Dear Lizzy..."

"I shall go to Papa now," she said, wiping her eyes. "He is feeling better, I hope?"

"I believe so. He is with Mr Darcy and the admiral. Mr Bingley is in the drawing room."

The response kept Elizabeth still, staring at her sister. She could not possibly face the two men, especially Mr Darcy. Not so soon after the dreadful events. To know they had heard the horrendous claims about her and Mr Darcy and the meaning behind them was mortifying.

"Jane, I cannot. Tell Papa I am unwell. I do not wish to see Mr Darcy and the admiral."

"As you wish, Lizzy. But Papa insisted. He said it was a matter of great importance. I shall tell him you are ill. Do not worry. Try to sleep a little more. I shall take care of it..."

"No, wait!" Elizabeth said after a brief hesitation, while Jane was at the door. "If you tell Papa I am ill, it will worry and distress him even more. I shall go."

She glanced at her reflection in the mirror. She looked as bad as she felt, and she arranged some pins in her hair before leaving the room.

"Shall I come with you, Lizzy?"

"No, my dear. If Papa asked for me, he must need me alone. Mr Bingley...how is he? I imagine he is distressed, too."

"A little bit...but he is very much his usual self."

"Then go and keep him company, Jane. We shall speak more later."

At the library door, Elizabeth stopped again. She heard low voices, and her first temptation was to run. Instead, she knocked and entered.

The three men were gathered around the desk. At her appearance, Mr Darcy stood up, while the others remained sitting.

Elizabeth quivered as she looked at him; his expression was dark and troubled, as she had never seen it before. His gaze was so intense that she did not wish to hold it or avert her eyes.

"Miss Bennet, I..."

"Mr Darcy I..."

They spoke at the same time; she stopped, feeling her knees would not support her. She looked for a chair; he seemed to read her mind and immediately brought one for her. She sat, and then he was the only one standing, tall, moving awkwardly from one foot to another.

"Mr Darcy, Lizzy, I beg you not to start another argument with each of you taking the blame," Mr Bennet interjected. "I cannot bear it any longer. I am exhausted, and my head is burning."

"Papa, you look ill," Elizabeth said. "You should be in bed, resting."

"You look ill too, Lizzy. But neither of us can rest for now. Lizzy, the admiral and I have something to discuss — we shall be in my old office. Mr Darcy has something to say to you. Please listen to him carefully and do not hurry to answer."

"But Papa—"

"Please, my child. Just listen, and we may discuss it afterwards. Please know that, whatever you decide, I shall support you. And nobody will know of this conversation unless you want them to."

Elizabeth's confusion was beyond words; she felt lost, dumbfounded, and frightened, wondering what else had occurred and what the three men had planned.

"On second thoughts, you should go with Mr Darcy into the other room, Lizzy, so you can speak undisturbed. Somebody might come into the library and interrupt you, but you will be safe there."

"But Papa, can we not discuss it here? I have no secrets to keep from you."

"Mr Darcy has already asked my permission, so it is not a secret to me. You must listen to him."

"Miss Bennet, I promise I shall not trouble you long," Mr Darcy said. "I only need a few minutes of your time, and your decision will be yours entirely."

"Very well," she agreed against her will. She led Mr Darcy to her father's old office — the one he rarely used, preferring the desk in the library. The fire was not lit, so the moment she entered, she felt cold and wrapped her arms around herself.

"Please allow me to offer you my coat," Mr Darcy immediately suggested.

"No, thank you. Please tell me what the matter is. The entire situation is so dreadful that every moment I fear it might get worse."

"I understand your feelings, Miss Bennet. Since last night, I have had no rest considering the circumstances and trying to find a way to reach a reasonable resolution, and I could not find one. I am well aware that my poor decisions in regard to Wickham, as well as my imprudent behaviour towards you — although it was well meant and with the most honourable intentions — caused you harm and torment that cannot be forgiven nor easily forgotten. I deeply apologise to you, but I know my excuses are worth nothing."

"Mr Darcy, I do not understand…what imprudence? What sort of behaviour do you mean? You should know that your excuses do have value, but they are neither necessary nor appropriate!"

"I have known for a long time that Wickham had no scruples in seeking revenge against me in any possible way, with no regard to whomever he might hurt in the process. You have been an innocent victim of a conflict that I should have handled better in the past. My enjoyment in being in your company induced me to do things that could be seen in a bad light…"

"I am still lost to your meaning. We have barely spoken a few times. You escorted me back home and you danced one set with me. That was after Mr Wickham asked me for the first set, and I have danced with many other men in the last year. I see nothing to blame you for."

"Perhaps. However, I shall admit that my attention to you was due to my admiration that, at the beginning of our acquaintance, I tried to disguise. My struggle was in vain, as apparently Wickham, as well as the admiral, noticed my feelings, and one of them acted with malice and a lack of honour."

Elizabeth watched him in utter puzzlement. She sat in a chair — which was cold and uncomfortable. He sat too, then stood up and sat again. She heard some words, barely coherent. He spoke of admiration and feelings in a way that only deepened her confusion.

"Mr Darcy, I beg you to speak more clearly, sir. I am tired, and I confess I am freezing. Please rest assured that I do not blame you at all, and I only hesitated to see you because of embarrassment. Your apologies are not needed, and you have done nothing that I might forgive. The only thing I would expect of you is to punish the men, especially Mr Wickham. I understand you have the power and the means to do that."

"I shall. That, you must not doubt. But your forgiveness was not the only thing that I wanted to ask from you. There is something more important that induced me to address you and to expose you to more distress."

He paused, staring at her. She held his gaze until it became too intense.

"What is it you want to ask from me, Mr Darcy?"

"Your hand in marriage," he said in a tone heavy with emotions.

Their gazes locked again, and she put her hand over her mouth. She could not reply, nor could she understand well enough to offer an answer.

"Excuse me?"

"I am asking you to do me the honour of marrying me, Miss Bennet," he continued, somehow less uncomfortable, though still agitated. "I imagine this request is rather shocking for you. Yesterday, it would have been impossible for me to even consider having this conversation with you. But due to the latest circumstances, I dare say it would be the best solution to remedy the wrong — to protect you and your family from more harm. Also—"

"Mr Darcy, I beg you to stop, sir," she interrupted him. She finally comprehended him, and the astonishment and mortification overwhelmed her. He had chosen to address the rumours of her being his mistress by asking her to become his wife. Had he lost his mind?

"Sir, please do not make this dreadful situation worse than it is. As I said, I have nothing to blame you for. You are as innocent as I am, and it is not your duty to protect me or my family from harm caused by others."

"But, Miss Bennet—"

"Mr Darcy, I do not know how serious you are in your proposal but—"

"Very serious, I assure you! I could not possibly trifle with you on such a matter! I have never spoken more in earnest."

"My answer is equally serious and heartfelt. Your suggestion is unacceptable, and I understand you made it from a deep sense of honour and responsibility, which is simply too much!"

"That is not the only reason…" he tried to intervene. She felt tears threatening to spill from her eyes and did not trust herself to fight them for long, nor could she bear to cry in his presence. So, she continued in haste, turning her back to him.

"I shall not trap you and me in a forced marriage, nor shall I condemn both of us to a life of misery, only to dismiss some malicious gossip that will pass soon. I shall not marry for such reasons, Mr Darcy."

With that, tears defeated her, and she whispered an excuse, then left the room in haste without another glance at him. As she passed the library, she heard the door open and her father call her name, but she pretended not to hear it, returning to her room. She struggled not to cry — it was the second time in one day — but she could not control her emotions any longer. Things were going from bad to worse, like a storm that had swept her up and trapped her in its midst, with no escape. She wiped her eyes, but the tears continued to fall, and she balled her fists in anger and frustration.

Only moments passed before she heard a knock on the door — which she both expected and feared.

Chapter 15

"Lizzy? May I enter?"

"Yes, Papa."

Her father sat down on the bed next to her and patted her hand.

"It pains me to see you crying, my child. Be sure that I shall not force you into any decision. I know you always disliked Mr Darcy, just as I know you liked that Wickham fellow and are probably hurt by his betrayal. I should not have let Mr Darcy speak to you so soon, but he seemed worried about the consequences and confident about talking to you. I knew you would not marry a man you cannot respect and love, regardless of his good character, fortune, and connections."

Elizabeth looked at her father dumbfounded, wiping her eyes.

"Papa, what are you talking about? I was hurt by Mr Wickham — not because I liked him but because I was a fool to trust him! I am as angry with him as I am with myself! As for Mr Darcy, I have long changed my opinion of him, but it is ridiculous to even consider his proposal. What was he thinking? What were you thinking to allow it?"

"Lizzy—"

"Should any man who helps a woman or dances with her be forced to marry her because some scoundrels gossip about them? This is outrageous, absurd! Mr Darcy should challenge them to a duel instead of proposing! I would have done so if I were a man!"

Frustration combined with anger, adding to the feelings that had confused and troubled her for the last few days in regard to Mr Darcy, made her raise her voice and lose her temper. She could see her father still looked unwell, but she still spoke further.

"I do not want to upset you, Papa, nor to offend Mr Darcy. I do respect him and appreciate him, but we barely know each other. How can I accept a proposal he had not considered himself until today?"

"You are not upsetting me, Lizzy. As I said, the decision is yours, and you should ponder it carefully, especially if your feelings for Mr Darcy and Mr Wickham are not as I assumed."

"Papa, I know that marrying Mr Darcy would mean salvation for our family. And I know he is a good man — probably one of the best. But to know that he married me out of charity, out of guilt he wrongly assumed, out of a sense of duty which is exaggerated, would be unbearable. He will come to regret his decision soon and will despise me, even if he would provide protection for our family."

"Marrying a man like Mr Darcy is truly something I never imagined for any of my daughters. As much as I love and value you, I never considered you might even meet such a man, and if you did, he would certainly overlook you as he did at the assembly."

"I shall not argue with that, Papa. I do not know what happened to make him change his opinion and improve his manners so much. I have done the same, I admit."

"It might be the admiral's influence over both of you perhaps. But Darcy is not a man to whom I could refuse anything he did me the favour of asking for. Dear Lord, I am speaking like Mr Collins now…"

"I would not refuse Mr Darcy's request either if he asked for my help in any way. But I shall not accept a forced proposal."

"My dear, we should put aside this matter for now. We all need rest, as neither of us slept much, if any, last night. We shall speak about it again tomorrow, after a good night's sleep."

"There is nothing to speak of, Papa. I already told Mr Darcy that I would not accept a proposal made for such reasons."

"Let us speak again tomorrow, Lizzy," her father repeated, walking to the door.

"Papa, where is Mr Darcy? And the admiral?"

"They are finishing their drinks in the library."

"Did they have any other news?"

"Apparently, they spoke to Colonel Forster. That Wickham fellow is expected to find other employment soon. As for the others, it is not settled yet. The admiral insists they all should come and apologise to us."

"Oh, no, Papa! They might beg your forgiveness, but I shall never grant them mine. I never want to see them again!"

"I assumed you would say that. I am going back to my guests. I shall not attend dinner tonight. I only want to sleep."

"Papa, I hope you will not mention the conversation with Mr Darcy to Mama. Please!"

"Not if I want to have another single moment of peace for the rest of my life, Lizzy."

Once her father left, Elizabeth sat by the window, waiting for the guests' departure. As time passed with no sign of them, her turmoil increased.

She could not recollect Mr Darcy's exact words when he had proposed. She remembered his repeated attempts to interrupt her refusal and some mention of his feelings that Mr Wickham and the admiral had recognised. What feelings he meant, she could not guess, since he had also admitted that he had only considered proposing after the scandal had broken out.

Lost in her thoughts, she observed Mr Darcy departing on his horse — alone. He must have been offended, and rightfully so. But he would thank her in the future; she was certain of that.

She waited a few more minutes, but neither the admiral nor Mr Bingley appeared. Mr Bingley was probably in the drawing room and the admiral still with her father.

She was curious to know whether Admiral Pembroke supported or disapproved of Mr Darcy's decision to propose. He must have known of it, since he had been present when Mr Darcy had discussed it with her father.

The admiral was the brother-in-law of Lord Matlock and the late Mr Darcy's friend. They surely wanted the current master of Pemberley to marry into a titled family with wealth and connections, if he did not marry his cousin Anne. Despite his friendship with her and her father, the admiral knew they moved in different circles, so he was probably relieved by her refusal.

Half an hour later, Jane entered again, and Elizabeth felt almost irritated by the interruption. She did not want to see or speak to anybody.

"Lizzy? Admiral Pembroke and Mr Bingley are ready to leave. Will you not come and say good-bye? Mr Darcy left earlier as he had some business to attend to."

"I do not feel well, Jane."

"I see… The admiral said he would like to say a few words to you. I believe he wants to comfort you. He was so kind and considerate. He explained that he heard the officers making some improper jokes, as most men do when they are drunk. He said Mr Wickham said some impolite things but that we should not allow him to upset us. I know the truth, Lizzy, and I realise it was more than jokes. But for Mama, it was a real comfort, as she has been truly devasted all day."

"The admiral is a kind and considerate man," Elizabeth said.

"Will you not speak to him, then? He is having a drink in the library…"

"I am in no disposition for more conversation, Jane."

"I know, dearest, but he is there alone…he is not a man to be treated disrespectfully."

"Alone? Is Papa not there?"

"No, Lizzy. Papa retired some time ago."

"Oh…very well. I shall speak to the admiral and say good-bye," she reluctantly agreed.

For the second time that day in front of the library door,

Elizabeth felt a surge of panic. Eventually, she pushed open the door and entered; the admiral was holding a drink and a cigar. He stood up and invited her to sit.

"Miss Elizabeth, how are you feeling?"

"As poorly as I must look, sir. I pray for this day to finally come to an end."

"That is understandable. You do not seem happy about talking to me."

"I am not. I beg your forgiveness for being so blunt, but you are already well aware of the truth."

"I have always admired your open manners and blunt sincerity, Miss Elizabeth. Would you allow me to speak in the same manner?"

"Of course. The circumstances require no false politeness."

"Agreed. Then I shall ask directly — why did you refuse Darcy's proposal?"

She had expected the question, but not in such a manner.

"Have you not been informed by Mr Darcy? Or by my father?"

"I dared to insist on having your response directly, Miss Elizabeth."

"Then you will have it. I refused it because it was not the type of proposal to be accepted."

"Marrying Darcy is not acceptable to you? That sounds rather harsh. He is an excellent man, in character and situation in life. Half of the young women in London dream of such an opportunity."

"I must be in the other half, Admiral. I do not deny Mr Darcy's qualities or the advantages of marrying him. I just said that this proposal, induced by unfortunate circumstances, is unacceptable to me."

"Are you aware of the tremendous benefits such a marriage would bring to you and your family?"

"Of course."

"Have you considered that this could be your salvation,

in case you lost your father and your home at the same time? I know your cousin Mr Collins intended to propose to you. You would probably have refused him, but is Darcy's proposal no better? Do you not have more respect and consideration for him?"

Elizabeth felt suddenly drained, exhausted — from tiredness, from emotions, from answering questions that should not have even existed, from doubts, and from the fear of losing control and having her life ruined by others.

"Admiral Pembroke, with all due respect and consideration, please give me enough credit to see that I am not a complete simpleton. I certainly know all this, and it is my respect and consideration for Mr Darcy that induced me to refuse something that he offered out of misplaced guilt. I shall apologise to him if he felt offended, but I am sure he will realise I was right, no later than tomorrow, when we all have clearer minds. We all need rest, as my father said."

"Very well. I shall leave you to rest. However, I shall just ask one more thing. You have mentioned several times that Darcy was forced to propose to you. Am I correct?"

"You are. I told my father the same. How is it possible for a man to be forced into a marriage because he helped a woman and danced with her once? Absurd!"

"It is absurd, indeed. However, I am asking for only one favour. Would you consider a few things by tomorrow? No, do not answer now, just reflect upon them with calm, using your wit and reason."

She breathed deeply, trying to gather a little more composure.

"What things would those be, Admiral?"

"Do you believe, Miss Elizabeth, that Darcy would have proposed marriage to any woman, if they were in your place? Do you think he would take so much trouble to please any other woman with small attentions? Did you ask yourself why he danced with you alone at the ball? Do you remember your conversation during the dance?"

The admiral's words stirred Elizabeth's mind, leaving her more confused. She was too troubled to answer, too troubled to even comprehend the questions properly.

"I shall leave you now, Miss Elizabeth. We shall speak more tomorrow. Please know that you have all my admiration and consideration. I wish all the best for you. That is why I took some liberties in addressing you."

"Thank you, sir. Then, may I ask…am I wrong in assuming that you approved of Mr Darcy's decision to propose to me? Were you ready to support such a marriage?"

"Yes." The answer, so straight and quick, disconcerted her, shattering the last remnant of her composure.

"But sir…may I ask why? What do you gain from such a union which, if it happened, would be only to the advantage of me and my family?"

He gently took her hand and gave her a smile.

"My dear Miss Elizabeth, I shall tell you what I told Darcy this morning. I was charmed by you the moment I met you in the woods. I immediately recognised your admirable qualities. I envy your father for having such a bright daughter, and I envy the younger men who can compete for your favours."

She laughed for the first time since her heart had been pained by the unfair accusations.

"Sir, now you are joking at my expense."

"Not at all, I assure you. At that time, I heard you despised Darcy, and it disappointed me. In time, I was pleased to see some reconciliation between the two of you. Till very recently, I did not suspect a possible connection between you. But the more I think about it, the more I am convinced you would be well suited, and that a union in marriage, regardless of how it started, would be to the advantage of both."

While Elizabeth was stunned by his statement, the admiral bowed his head, placed a polite kiss on the back of her hand, and then exited.

Chapter 16

As tired as he was after the previous day and night, Darcy barely slept, and he woke up in a poor state of mind. He should have returned to London two days ago, but his plans had been completely ruined by Wickham, once again.

The confrontation had been difficult at first, as Wickham had the audacity to mention his father, as well as Georgiana, and it was only the presence of Colonel Forster that kept Darcy from unleashing his resentment. However, when he gave him three choices — debtors' prison, active duty, or passage overseas, after several pathetic attempts at complaining and begging, the scoundrel had accepted the third choice, probably enchanted by the offer of having a comfortable ticket purchased for him and two thousand pounds to begin a new life. Darcy's offer was undeservingly generous, he knew that; even the colonel and the admiral had looked at him with surprise. But he felt it was a reasonable way of removing Wickham from his life while still honouring his father's dying wish, as ill-conceived as it had been.

If he was to count the money he and his father had spent on Wickham, Darcy admitted it had been a huge waste of money which could have supported several worthy families to enjoy a decent life. With Wickham, nothing was decent. Darcy had no expectation that the scoundrel would use the money he gave him in any proper way; he would probably lose it all playing cards on the ship, without even reaching his destination. But that was not Darcy's concern any longer. He arranged that

Wickham would be taken from Meryton and placed in an inn in London, under supervision, until the time of his departure.

The other miscreants involved in the scandal were left to the mercy of Colonel Forster. It was the colonel who insisted that all of them would go and apologise to the Bennets, but Darcy believed it to be a pointless punishment. Those men could not be trusted to even be honest or realise the extent of the damage they had caused.

Above everything else, Darcy's main concern was Elizabeth, whose image and words were painfully vivid in his mind. He had struggled for weeks to conceal his feelings for her but had finally made the decision that he felt would enhance his life, even though it was somehow forced by misfortune. He had gone to propose to her, being certain of his reception, expecting her to be surprised and grateful for the opportunity. Instead, she had not even allowed him time to complete his statement. She had rejected him instantly. Not even the threat of having her family ruined had induced her to show some prudence in her response. She simply would not have him. He had been a fool the entire time; his arrogant estimation of her feelings had been completely wrong. She might have accepted him as a friend, but no more.

Late that night, lying in his bed, with sleep evading him, he recollected their conversation — their argument. First with anxiety, disappointment, and a little bit of resentment for having his feelings hurt. As the hours passed, the recollections returned, and, despite his tiredness, he considered them with more calm, more reason, more carefulness.

Her rejection, though quick, was by no means offensive. At least he should not consider it so. She even mentioned several good things about him but insisted on the unfavourable circumstances and about being trapped together in misery. That was rather hurtful; this was her estimation of a life as his wife? Misery?

He was hurt and disappointed to have lost a dream that had only seemed possible for a few hours. But he knew he had no right to be upset with Elizabeth. If he truly valued her, he had to respect her decision.

The proposal had been sudden, the time distressing, and she had been clearly surprised. One thing was certain, though, and his vanity was not strong enough to defy it: Elizabeth Bennet neither returned nor welcomed his love. Because yes, love must be the feeling that made him lose reason, peace, and rest and induced him to act imprudently, even foolishly. In the end, it was better — more honest, fairer — that she had rejected his proposal than accepted it and given him the satisfaction of a false affection.

He doubted he would speak to her again before his departure. He would maintain the acquaintance with Mr Bennet but would not renew a proposal that displeased her. And yet, the effect of the gossip was still a threat, since there were already questions in regard to the sudden departure of the officers from the ball. He dared not speak of it, out of respect for Colonel Forster, but his young wife did not appear to be someone who could keep a secret. She seemed to be a good friend to Lydia and Kitty Bennet, two girls whose manners showed imprudence and carelessness. A single word slipped by the colonel to his wife was likely to be spread throughout Meryton.

With little sleep and a troubled mind, Darcy decided to go for an early morning ride. He dressed properly and, before he left for the stables, he went down to check the puppies.

They had grown stronger in only two days, but their eyes were still closed, and they were curled up with their adoptive mother. The mother dog and her other puppies also looked better, due to the warm shelter and good food, and Darcy mused on how pleased Elizabeth would be when she saw them. If and when she would come to see them.

He smiled bitterly to himself; he had succeeded in convincing Elizabeth to share the puppies with him, but he had failed when it came to sharing his life.

"Darcy? Where are you going so early?"

Admiral's Pembroke s voice made him stop reluctantly; he

expected a conversation for which he had no disposition.

"For a ride."

"A ride? At this hour? It is raining."

"Yes, I know…" He did not; lost in his thoughts, he had not even looked at the weather.

"I shall walk you to the stables."

"As you wish, Admiral."

"So, what are your plans for today?"

"I have no fixed plans. I have written to my solicitor to prepare the papers for Wickham. And I sent the letter to that acquaintance of yours, as you suggested. Now we must wait for their replies and conclude this business."

"I shall call on Colonel Forster. I want to see what he has decided in regard to the other officers. Then I shall call on Mr Bennet. We agreed to discuss the matter again today, with more calm and less distress."

"As you wish," Darcy repeated. "However, I doubt there is any more calm and any less distress today than yesterday."

"You will join me, I hope?"

"I shall not, Admiral. There is nothing for me to discuss at this moment. If there is something Mr Bennet requests from me, I shall be happy to oblige. But I shall not impose my presence on Miss Elizabeth again. Now excuse me. The rain has stopped. I really need some exercise and fresh air before breakfast."

Darcy hastened his steps before the admiral had time to voice further opposition. The rain had indeed stopped, but the sun was barely visible through the clouds. Regardless, he asked for his horse and patted the stallion, who seemed as eager for exercise as its master. The last time Darcy had enjoyed a ride was the day when he had found Elizabeth with the puppies. He still remembered how frightened he had been to see her with blood on her clothes, and her reluctance when he had offered to escort her home. That was perhaps one of his errors, which had exposed her to gossip and speculation.

He held the reins loosely, and his horse took the path he was used to. When he was close enough, Darcy could not resist the temptation and directed his horse to the very spot he had last seen Elizabeth. He needed only a few moments to reach the place, where he dismounted and tied his horse to a tree, then sat on a stump, looking around. On one side was Netherfield, on the other side Longbourn. He knew he would leave soon, but he did not know if or when he would ever return.

The wind blew, it was cold, and the ground was soaking wet. In places, the water had frozen, and walking was difficult. After a while, Darcy took the reins and led his horse towards the road. He stepped carefully to avoid him or his horse falling and hurting themselves. It took quite some time to reach the road, and only then did he mount again. Longbourn was close, and he could see light in the windows. He wondered whether Elizabeth was awake, how she had slept, and what her thoughts were on that new day. He could find the answer to all those questions if he only called there, but he decided not to. Instead, he turned his horse towards Netherfield and kicked him into a gallop. The ride lasted only moments, as after a bend in the road, a small cry startled him, and he pulled on the reins so hard that his horse reared up.

He saw a silhouette slip and fall, and his heart seemed to stop, then it raced wildly as he realised — even without seeing her face — that it was Elizabeth.

The night was almost worse for Elizabeth than the previous day. After the admiral had left, she remained caught in her turmoil and fell even deeper into it. The admiral's claims about the advantages of the marriage and the questions he had asked that she ponder had kept her awake until midnight. Repeated remembrances of her discussion with Mr Darcy distressed her, pained her, and made her doubt herself and her decisions.

Mr Bennet was still unwell, so before dinner, despite his

opposition, she sent John to fetch Mr Jones, the apothecary. The examination was brief, followed by some bleeding, some suggestions of rest, and some more herbs. None of those put Elizabeth at ease, although Mr Jones assured her there was nothing of immediate concern.

Mr Collins also returned in time for dinner, but he prepared his luggage for departure; he was less voluble than usual, distracted, and with little appetite. Elizabeth assumed he had proposed, and Charlotte had refused him, but she did not question him. Mrs Bennet expressed her disappointment that he was leaving so soon and asked when he would return. Mr Collins appeared somewhat abashed, then he retired to his room soon after, planning to leave Longbourn the next day, immediately after breakfast.

Elizabeth had to listen for several hours to her mother and younger sisters whining about the ban of the officers. All three of them were ready to forgive the indiscretion, calling it nothing but a silly joke. To Elizabeth's pain, they seemed more upset about not having the officers around than about Mr Bennet's illness.

She was relieved to finally retire to her room, even though she did not sleep much. The dawn came with more exhaustion and concerns for the day ahead, and before her family woke, she checked on her father briefly, then went for a stroll.

As she left the house, she briefly pondered that there was a chance — a risk — of meeting Mr Darcy, as had happened in the past. The thought made her apprehensive but did not deter her from her plan. The weather was unpleasant, as expected for the time of year. It rained, then it stopped, but the sky was still cloudy. It was cold and windy, and the slippery ground was unsuitable for walking.

She stayed on the road, walking to the crossroads where one could turn towards Netherfield, where she rested for a moment, then walked back home. Vivid recollections of Mr Darcy taking the puppies and placing them in his hat made her quiver, and her heart became heavier. She would like to see the puppies but did not dare. What would happen to the little souls when he returned to London? She did not want to abandon them, but she could not take all the dogs to Longbourn.

The turmoil built again inside her, and a tear which she wiped furiously burnt the corner of her eye.

Walking home, with the wind now blowing in her face, stepping careful to avoid the puddles, the road back seemed longer.

She only had to go round one bend and she would be at Longbourn's gate. She crossed to the other side of the road, but in the middle of it, she halted at the sound of hoofs. She hurried to step away to avoid the galloping horse, but in doing so, her feet slipped, and she almost lost her balance. Almost. She managed to grab a tree and stay upright, while the rider approached.

She knew it was him. She felt it inside her, moments before her eyes proved it to her. He dismounted, took a step forwards, then stopped, looking at her. Waiting.

"Mr Darcy!"

"Miss Bennet...forgive me for disturbing you. I only wish to know if you are hurt, and then I shall leave you immediately."

"I am not hurt..."

"Very well, then," he replied, turning to his horse.

"Were you visiting my father?" she continued.

"No...merely out for a ride. Please do not worry, I shall not bother you again. Send your father my best regards."

"Mr Darcy!" she called him, and he looked at her, waiting again. She took a step towards him.

"You are not bothering me, sir...I am glad I met you...I want to apologise if I offended you yesterday. It was certainly not my intention."

"I have no right to be offended by a genuine refusal Of an unwanted proposal, Miss Bennet. In fact, your honesty is laudable."

"You are very kind."

"No, I am not. We both know that. I am perhaps arrogant, as you claimed a while ago, and resentful, as I admitted on the same occasion. I am trying to correct these flaws, but my success is still far away."

"Mr Darcy, I can feel your resentment," she said, taking another step. "And I can feel you are upset with me...perhaps offended too. I expected you to not conceal your feelings."

"I am sorry not to fulfil your expectations, Miss Bennet. The truth is, I have concealed my feelings for quite some time now. Another thing I am ashamed of."

"You have nothing to be ashamed of, Mr Darcy. You are too severe on yourself. You are too ready to assume blame that does not belong to you and too ready to sacrifice yourself for the benefit of others."

"I cannot understand what sacrifice you mean, but my actions are not worthy of such a word. It is less hurtful to know your opinion of me is poor and you dislike me than to hear you expressing praise I do not deserve."

"No sacrifice? You were ready to change your life for the mere desire of righting a wrong which was not yours to remedy. You allowed Mr Wickham's deceptions to force you to offer for a woman you did not even like enough to dance with and whom you have only just begun to know. A woman with whom you can hardly agree on anything and of whom your entire family would disapprove."

"You are wrong, Miss Bennet. You are assuming the reason behind my proposal and my feelings in regard to it. But you are far from the truth, I assure you."

She became anxious, and her voice trembled, while he remained frowning, unmoved.

"You are wrong too, Mr Darcy. My opinion of you is not low. If I once disliked you, that changed long ago. It was not my dislike that caused me to refuse you. In fact, it was quite the opposite."

With that, she stopped, as her wildly racing heart warned her that she had said too much.

It was a moment too late, though, as he was staring at her intently, as though struggling to understand her declaration.

And he finally took a step towards her.

Chapter 17

"Miss Bennet, may I ask... We both claim the other is wrong. I wonder which of us is right?"

He sounded timid, and a lump in her throat kept her from replying.

"I do not know, Mr Darcy..."

"I know this conversation may become even more tiresome for you, and I do not want to force you to continue it... but perhaps we could...it would be a pity to..."

He seemed uncertain of his words and his gestures. He looked at her but did not lock eyes. He looked nothing like the arrogant Mr Darcy — the confident gentleman capable of solving problems.

Their tentative conversation sounded silly, and under different circumstances, they would have been amused to listen to it. But at that moment, the tension and the strain of doing and saying what was right became a burden that affected their wit.

"You are not forcing me, sir...I believe we should discuss... and I have not thanked you for taking care of my father and bringing him home after the ball..."

"No thanks are needed. He feels better, I hope?"

"He is still sleeping. At least he was when I left home."

"Has the apothecary been called?"

"Yes. Last night. He said there is no reason for immediate concern."

"I fear my hastiness in...presenting my proposal upset him...distressed him...I should have been more considerate..."

"You are doing it again, Mr Darcy," she said.

"I am doing what?" he asked with concern.

"You are blaming yourself. My father felt unwell a few days ago. I cannot deny that the dreadful circumstances added to his anxiety. And probably after talking to you, and to me, his discomfort increased last night."

"May I be of some help?" he asked, still timid.

"No, but your concern is appreciated."

Elizabeth felt nervous and eager to open the subject that had caused their torment — the one over which both claimed the other was wrong. She hoped he would do it, but he seemed equally lost as to how to continue. She gulped a few times and breathed deeply, hoping he could not hear the beating of her heart.

"Mr Darcy, we still do not know which of us was right or wrong, do we? Should we not clarify it?"

"I hoped we would..."

"You said earlier that I was wrong in assuming the reason for your proposal."

"Yes...and you said I was wrong in presuming why you refused it."

"I am sorry for interrupting you yesterday. I know I should have kept my calm and allowed you to present your reasons. I am aware you were only trying to resolve a dreadful situation in the best possible way. But I am sure you realise that forced marriage is an error and will cause more damage than help."

As she spoke, her voice became stronger and more decided. She found the power to express herself and continued to do so.

"I said you were wrong because I have the best opinion of you, and I value your friendship. I rejected your proposal because I knew it was not what you wanted. And I wish you all the best, truly."

He looked somehow more at ease; his countenance brightened, his eyes locked with hers, and his voice was warmer when he replied.

"Miss Bennet, I shall take the liberty of asking a question which is highly improper and might make me lose your good opinion again. But, as hard as that might be, I cannot allow myself not to address it."

"Please ask," she said, curious and anxious.

"If the scandal did not exist…if there was nothing to force your decision, would you still reject my proposal?"

She was stunned, gazing at him, her eyes captured by his.

"But…if not for the scandal, would the proposal have taken place? You said you had not even considered it until yesterday," she finally whispered.

"It was an unfortunate choice of words. What I meant — and I intended to say — was that, if not for the scandal and the need to protect you, I would not have considered proposing to you yesterday…in such haste and in such an improper manner."

More warmth added to his hoarse voice, and her strength betrayed her again. She blinked a few times, her eyes suddenly clouded, breathing irregularly as she needed more air.

"I do not understand… You considered proposing to me? Asking me to marry you?"

"Yes. Surely you did not believe I would have made such a proposal easily, carelessly, without proper reflection?"

"But…why? How? I never imagined you would… We were barely friends…"

She felt the need for support and leant against a tree, then looked back at him. He was still gazing at her, and she allowed her eyes to lock with his again.

"We were barely friends because your opinion of me was so ill for a long time, Miss Bennet. Deservedly so. I shall not deny it. And because…"

"Yes?"

"Because for a while I struggled with my own feelings. I tried to disguise them from everyone, and I barely allowed myself to acknowledge them." He looked uneasy again, pacing around.

"Despite my admiration for you, I felt it was my responsibility to marry someone…closer to my circle."

"I understand…and I agree. I am sure that is the expectation from a gentleman like you."

"It might be. However, after many years of being out in society, I have never considered marrying anyone…until now," he concluded.

She felt her face burning, while chills ran through her body.

"I can hardly believe it, sir. I do not doubt your sincerity, but it seems impossible."

"Have you not noticed my attention to you?" he enquired, his voice as low as a whisper.

"I have. But I believed it to be an expression of amiability, brought about by the admiral's friendship with me and my father."

"Then, you did not notice my admiration before the admiral arrived at Netherfield?"

He sounded shy, disconcerted, and she was even more confused and doubtful.

"Before the admiral arrived? But we barely spoke to each other at that time…I always felt you were looking at me to find fault…"

"Now I can tell you again that you were wrong," he said with a little smile. "My admiration began almost at the beginning of our acquaintance."

"Surely you are joking!" she cried. "I cannot believe such a claim!"

"I am certainly not joking. As proof, you may ask Miss Bingley. The evening you refused to dance with me, at Sir William's, I unwittingly confessed to her my admiration for your fine eyes. She was just as incredulous as you are now."

"This cannot be!" she repeated, astounded.

"And yet, it is. And your response of complete astonishment is just further proof of how utterly and completely I have misjudged your feelings, Miss Bennet."

"What do you mean, sir?"

"I was convinced that you recognised my admiration and welcomed it. That you returned my partiality. I never doubted your answer to my proposal. What will you say now of my pride and arrogance?" he ended in a humble voice.

"And what will you say of my foolishness, since I never suspected anything of the sort?" she responded, flushed and nervous. "Though…"

"Though?"

She lowered her eyes, shivering again. How could she say what was on her mind? Should she? But how could she not, since he had already done so?

"I confess I have come to enjoy your company since you joined the admiral in visiting my family. I felt touched by your care when you helped me with the puppies…and I was flattered by your asking me to dance at the ball. But I took it as amiability, friendship, generosity. I did not dare assume more. Nobody would."

"You see?" he replied, the little smile broadening on his lips. "We were both wrong, after all. You assumed less, and I presumed more than there was."

"True…and this is what you meant by saying the admiral and Mr Wickham recognised your feelings?"

"It is. Sadly, Wickham knows me well enough to notice any change in my behaviour. He guessed my partiality, but he misjudged it and used it to hurt me. He harmed you and your family too, which was truly my fault, as I said."

"It is certainly not your fault," she responded, confused, quivering as she realised the significance of this latest knowledge.

The rain was about to start again, and she knew she should return home. She had lost track of the time she had spent with him, but she could not possibly leave.

Everything she knew and believed had changed, but the turmoil was still inside her, equally strong. He had proved her wrong, and she had accepted it, but she did not know what to do with that acceptance.

"What should we do now?" He asked the question which was also spinning in her head.

"What is to be done?" she replied shyly. She had already rejected his proposal with determination.

"I would be grateful if you would answer my question, as difficult and improper as it might be, Miss Bennet."

"What question, sir?"

"The question that started our conversation. Would you still have refused my proposal if it was not shadowed by this scandal?"

"Oh..." She bit her lower lip, struggling to respond, not being certain of the answer herself, fearing to give one but wishing to be honest with him.

"I would probably not have done, sir. If the circumstances were different, or if I had known as much as I do now...and if I was sure that you had addressed me willingly."

Neither spoke for a few moments, the silence interrupted by the wind and some thunder from afar.

"Miss Bennet, only an hour ago I told the admiral I would never impose my presence on you again, and I was determined not to bother you again with a proposal that troubled you. Now I am standing in front of you, saying that my proposal is still here — open to you, waiting for you. I shall not force an answer, just as I did not force one yesterday. I am begging you to consider it and let me know what you decide. One word from you, and I shall be forever silenced on this subject."

Her mind was in such a perturbed state that she could not trust her understanding, nor could she form a coherent answer.

"But...sir, are you sure? Do you truly wish to marry me? All of a sudden? There are so many things to consider..."

"Miss Bennet, I have considered them all, and my decision is made. I have never been more certain of anything. And I still believe that a short engagement and a marriage by licence will silence the rumours. I strongly believe it will prevent your family from suffering further distress. And yet, the scandal is not the reason for my proposal, but love, affection, admiration, which now I do not fear to admit."

"Oh…" she whispered.

"I hope my confession has not made you uncomfortable. Please be sure that I am willing to wait for your decision as long as necessary if you are not ready to make it yet."

"Thank you. Please know I am not indifferent to the honour of your proposal. I imagine there is enormous responsibility attached to the position of your wife, and I am flattered that you trust me to be able to fulfil it. I am also aware that such a marriage would be beneficial to my family and to myself. I shall not pretend otherwise."

"And yet, you still seem undecided."

"I am undecided, sir, because I wish to be honest with you. I have the highest opinion of you, and I admire your character, your education, your understanding of the world, and I am sure you are an excellent man. What I still doubt is the nature of my feelings for you. You speak of love, affection, and admiration, while I still struggle to name my sentiments."

"I thank you for your honesty, Miss Bennet. As I said, I can wait, and I would rather have you certain of your wishes. We shall deal with the scandal in some way. If Wickham is removed from the town, things might settle down. If not, we shall find a way to limit the damage, I assure you."

"Perhaps a wedding will provide the comfort all of us deserve. And my father would be at peace, with no further reason for torment. But would you agree to marry a woman who has no dowry, no connections, whose reputation might be damaged? A woman who cannot declare her own love and admiration? A woman who was ignorant of your feelings for months and is still confused about hers?"

Her voice was strangled by tears, and she failed in fighting them. She turned her back to him, trying to compose herself. The importance of that moment overwhelmed her, and while she had expressed doubts in accepting his proposal, she realised the tremendous loss she would suffer if he withdrew it.

"I could and I would, Miss Bennet. My only hope is that one day this woman will come to love me as I do her. That she will become certain of her feelings and have no restraint in voicing them. And even if she agrees to marry me now, I shall call her my companion and my friend until the day she is ready to become my wife in every sense."

Elizabeth's astonishment was now complete, as she fully comprehended the significance of his statement. For the third time in less than two days, she allowed herself to sob again. He took out his handkerchief and gently wiped her face. She did not oppose it, although his closeness and his touch made her dizzy.

"I am ready to marry you, Mr Darcy. And I promise I shall prove myself worthy of your generosity and your trust."

"I do not doubt that, Miss Bennet," he said, gently lifting her hand to his lips, letting it linger there momentarily.

He then held her hands in his for another moment and said, "You should return home now, Miss Bennet. If you approve, I shall come and speak to your father after breakfast."

"I shall look forward to seeing you again, Mr Darcy."

Chapter 18

The walk home was too short for Elizabeth to realise what had happened. She knew, of course, but she could not properly feel the significance of what had transpired between her and Mr Darcy. In a brief conversation, they had agreed to bind themselves to each other and take a step which would change their lives forever.

The renewed proposal had been no closer to how Elizabeth had imagined the moment of her engagement than the harsh proposal a day prior. But his sincerity, the way he had opened his heart to her and confessed his secret admiration was as touching as a romantic proposal after a long courtship. At least she believed it was, since she had no experience with either. That he had loved her for such a long time and considered marrying her, while she was completely ignorant and had misjudged his behaviour entirely, was a revelation that needed time to be properly comprehended.

Of two things she was certain. One, that he truly wanted to marry her and had even promised they would not consummate the marriage until she felt comfortable becoming his wife. Such a vow was generous and puzzling, as she had not imagined a man might do such a thing. The second was that the news of her betrothal would certainly cause more rumours and speculation than any other gossip and would certainly shatter the peace at Longbourn — as little as there was — from that day to the wedding.

She was also sure that she wished to marry Mr Darcy. She

was still slightly frightened by how quickly and easily she had sealed her future, connecting herself to a man she admired and appreciated but barely knew, whose true nature and character were still puzzling to her.

It was raining lightly when Elizabeth entered the house, and she went directly to her father. She was happy to see him awake, already reading, but his face was still pale and altered.

"Papa, how are you feeling?"

"A little better. How are you feeling, Lizzy? I hope you had a good night's sleep, as I see you are in a better disposition than yesterday."

"I have barely slept at all, but I am more at peace than yesterday. Papa, there is something I must tell you," she said, sitting near him.

"What is it, my child?"

"I saw My Darcy just now. By pure chance…"

"Did you?"

"Yes. So we talked. We discussed everything again. He was considerate and patient and…I decided to accept his proposal, Papa."

The gentleman seemed to hold his breath, then he frowned.

"So suddenly? Yesterday you seemed determined to reject it!"

"I know…but it seems I was wrong. Mr Darcy said that he has admired me for a long time…since before the scandal. He said he did not propose to me due to the scandal alone."

"I see… It is unexpected, I grant you that. And you, Lizzy? Have you accepted his proposal for the scandal alone? Perhaps for his wealth and connections? You will be rich, for sure. Even if Jane marries Bingley, your situation will be far better. I have been thinking about this all night. Are you sure you could be happy in this marriage? And that Darcy will be happy too? I love you, my dear, and I want only the best for you."

He was obviously concerned and unsettled, and Elizabeth embraced him.

"Papa, I made this decision, and I accept full responsibility. I shall do everything in my power to turn this marriage into a happy one. I have been honest with Mr Darcy and confessed I am not certain of my feelings. But I know I admire and respect him — I told you that even yesterday. My only concern is whether we are suited for each other."

"You seem sure of your decision, Lizzy."

"I am sure enough, Papa. I know it would be better to take this step than not to take it. As for Mr Darcy's wealth and connections, they are more of a reason to question my decision. Mr Bingley's situation is a comfortable one. Mr Darcy's situation in life implies responsibilities that I know I shall struggle to fulfil, as I am not prepared for them."

"You sound wise and reasonable, my Lizzy. I cannot believe how your life has been forcibly changed in only two days."

"Nor can I, Papa," she said, embracing him again.

"So…Mr Darcy has been in love with you for some time now?"

"Yes, Papa."

"To be honest, I have noticed him staring at you, and the way he acts when you are around. And at the ball, he singled you out, did he not?"

"Yes." She smiled.

"Poor fellow. This must be his punishment for refusing to dance with you at the assembly and calling you tolerable. Fate has a peculiar sense of humour and takes revenge when you least expect it."

"I am happy to see you joking, Papa. Mr Darcy said he will call on you after breakfast."

"Good for him. Have you decided on a wedding date?"

"No…but considering the circumstances and the fact that we have a clear agreement, he suggested a quick marriage. By licence."

"That is to be expected. Which will not make it easier for me to accept it. Now I must become accustomed to the fact I shall lose you soon."

"Papa, you will surely not lose me! Please do not worry. I want you to calm yourself and trust me that all will be well. My only concern is for you to be well, Papa! You must promise me!"

"I shall do my best, Lizzy. Now, I only need a favour: to not say a word to your mother until after breakfast. I am a little hungry, and I hope to eat in peace. Speaking of peace, I am thrilled that I must bear my cousin for the last time today."

Shortly afterwards, they joined the family and found Mr Collins there, making plans for his departure and expressing his eagerness to see Lady Catherine de Bourgh soon. Mrs Bennet looked disconcerted and disappointed, enquiring when he would return.

Elizabeth smiled to herself. She knew her mother was devastated that Mr Collins would leave without proposing to her, and she would probably have to bear some scolding for not encouraging him more. She imagined her mother's response when she found out about the engagement to Mr Darcy, and her smile broadened.

They all began eating, and Elizabeth tried to imagine how the Netherfield residents would respond to Mr Darcy's news. The main object of her curiosity was Miss Caroline Bingley, who apparently had known about Mr Darcy's admiration for her longer than anyone else. It was no wonder that the lady despised her and had attempted to discredit her so many times.

While the notion of her mother and Miss Bingley's shock was diverting, Elizabeth could not help worrying about Mr Darcy's family: his sister, Lord Matlock's family, as well as Lady Catherine de Bourgh. There was no reason for amusement there.

As soon as he returned to Netherfield, Darcy was told breakfast was ready and the family was expecting him. He knew he would find Admiral Pembroke in the library, and he went there first.

"It seemed the ride was beneficial to you, Darcy. You look much better, I must say."

"I feel much better, sir."

"I am glad to hear that. Have you changed your mind about joining me to call on Colonel Forster and then Mr Bennet?"

"In fact, I have, sir. But I wish to call on Mr Bennet first, as soon as we finish breakfast."

"Truly? This is quite a change of mind, indeed. May I ask what has caused it?"

"It is surprising, but I met Miss Elizabeth earlier. A fortuitous meeting."

"Surprising indeed! And?"

"And we spoke. Calmly and at length. And she agreed to marry me." He ended with a smile on his lips, but the admiral was so stunned that he sat down heavily.

"All of a sudden?"

"Not quite. First we argued and disagreed. Then we spoke, and I confessed the truth about my feelings. I also admitted my struggle in regard to proposing to her. I mentioned the expectations placed on me when choosing my wife. She surprisingly agreed they are justified and expected opposition from my family."

"Miss Bennet is a special sort of young woman," the admiral said. "I observed it from the first moment I saw her."

"She is, indeed. She was honest and open and admitted to worrying about the success of such a marriage. She seemed as concerned for my happiness as I was for hers. I needed more persuasion to convince her to accept me. In truth, I humbled myself properly," Darcy said, keeping his smile.

The admiral laughed loudly.

"Seeing the proud and arrogant Darcy humbled must have been quite an image. Then again, humbleness is often appealing to women. On the other hand, most women I know would have been thrilled by your proposal and would have accepted it in the blink of an eye."

"Miss Elizabeth is not like any woman I know. She has taught me how difficult it is to please a woman worthy of being pleased."

Admiral Pembroke laughed again.

"Well, young man, if you keep that in mind and comply with it every day and every night, I have no doubts that your marriage will be exceedingly happy."

Darcy stared at him for a moment, then understood the meaning and felt his cheeks burning.

"I trust your sense of honour and respectability has not prevented you from learning by this age how to reach that goal."

"You should not worry in that regard," Darcy replied hesitantly, feeling embarrassed.

"Good. I once told you that one should marry someone who pleases all your senses. Most men do not understand that is applicable to women too. But then again, most men I know marry for the wrong reasons and do not know how nor bother to please their wives. Neither during the day nor during the night."

"Admiral, I appreciate your advice, but I beg you to change the subject. I do not feel comfortable speaking of this matter, as it involves Miss Elizabeth."

"I respect that, young man. Protecting one's wife is also something most men do not know how to do properly. So, how will you proceed? Have you set a date? Will you still return to London the day after tomorrow?"

"Going to London is even more necessary now. I shall ask for Mr Bennet's blessing today, and I shall take care of the rest of the business whilst I am in town. The sooner this marriage takes place, the sooner all gossip will be buried. I must purchase a licence, and I also have to discuss the wedding with Georgiana, then with Uncle and Aunt Fitzwilliam, and inform Lady Catherine. That will be the most daunting task."

"Agreed. But Georgiana is your main concern. I shall speak to my sister and brother-in-law the moment we arrive, if you approve of it. That way they will be prepared by the time you approach them."

"As you wish, sir. I would not mind if you spoke to them, but I have no concerns about telling them directly. I am ready and capable of defending my choice and my future wife."

"I do not doubt you. Please know you may count on me to be a faithful supporter of your decision and your marriage, even though you surely do not need such support."

"I might not need it, but I certainly appreciate it. I cannot help but wonder whether my father would have approved of it."

The admiral hesitated for a moment, then stood, taking a few steps. Darcy gazed after him.

"I have no doubt that George would have admired Miss Elizabeth as much as I do and would have been pleased to have such a woman by your side. I am almost certain that he would have supported your decision to marry her, too. I hope you can sense the distinction between the two."

"I can, sir. And I thank you again."

"Well now, it seems we have a busy day ahead of us. Let us eat and then call on Mr Bennet. By the by, when do you plan to tell Bingley?"

"As soon as I have Mr Bennet's blessing. For now, only you know, Admiral."

"Thank you. I anticipate no obstacle to Mr Bennet's approval. In truth, I look forward to seeing everyone's response to the news of your betrothal. And please do me a favour and tell that miscreant Wickham, too. Knowing you are happy will surely help me enjoy his miserable future life."

"I shall have the scoundrel removed from Meryton and shipped abroad and then forget about him. But yes, I intend to give him the good news." Darcy smiled mischievously.

"Excellent. Speaking of Wickham, even if you purchase a comfortable cabin for him, I would suggest requesting the ship's captain keep him locked up until they are out on the sea. Just to be certain he has left the country for good."

"I intended to do so, but it is pleasant to realise we think alike, sir," Darcy replied.

∞∞∞

Elizabeth struggled to eat; she had lost her appetite entirely. She was anxious, glancing at the window repeatedly, under her father's insistent scrutiny. She had not had time to even tell the news to Jane, so she nervously awaited Mr Darcy's arrival.

Immediately after breakfast, Mr Collins departed, but not before another long and annoying farewell and best wishes repeatedly expressed. When his carriage finally disappeared from view, a deep sigh of relief was heard from everyone, except for Mrs Bennet, who wondered aloud about the change in the clergyman's plans. Mr Bennet immediately withdrew to the library.

Shortly after Mr Collins's carriage left, the carriage from Netherfield arrived and calmed some of Mrs Bennet's anxiety. Mr Bingley and the admiral engaged in conversation with the ladies, while Mr Darcy enquired after Mr Bennet. He only exchanged a brief glance with Elizabeth before he left the room.

The admiral's expression of satisfaction and his large grin, as well as his gaze on her, revealed to Elizabeth that he had been informed of the news and approved of it. She was thrilled and nervous, could hardly listen to the discussion around her, and barely engaged in it.

Mr Bennet and Mr Darcy came to join them rather quickly, and from one look at them, Elizabeth knew the matter had been settled. The visitors remained less than half an hour, claiming other engagements.

"But you must come to dinner tomorrow before you leave!" Mrs Bennet demanded. "You cannot possibly refuse. It might be our last chance to dine with the admiral!"

"I hope that will not be the case, ma'am," the admiral answered, "but I shall surely come for dinner, and I hope my young friends will accompany me," he concluded, much to Mrs

TO THE ADVANTAGE OF BOTH

Bennet's satisfaction.

With no strangers around, the house became more peaceful. Elizabeth was desirous to finally share the news with Jane and went to ask Mr Bennet when he intended to make the announcement. Once there, Mr Bennet asked her several more questions, to be sure of her decision.

"Mr Darcy is determined to send his physician to examine me, which I find absolutely ridiculous," Mr Bennet said.

"Is he? How generous and kind of him!"

"It is ridiculous and silly to send a man from London for nothing! But apparently, the moment I agreed on his engagement to you, he believed he could impose his will on me."

"Papa, please! Do not be unfair." Elizabeth smiled, embracing him. "If I am to marry and leave you, I need to know you are in good health."

While they talked, a din could be heard from the drawing room, and Mrs Bennet's voice was loud and whining. Mr Bennet rolled his eyes, and with Elizabeth's help, he went to the drawing room to see the reason for such uproar.

Mrs Bennet had collapsed in a chair, with Hill holding her salts and four daughters around her; nearby was Mrs Phillips, in an agitated state of mind. The lady of the house seemed to revive somewhat upon seeing her husband and most wayward daughter.

"Oh, Mr Bennet, you cannot imagine what disaster has befallen us! We are lost forever! My sister just told me there is some gossip about our family. About Lizzy and her habit of wandering like a lunatic across the fields, which is bad enough. But it seems the reports prevented Mr Collins from proposing to Lizzy! He has proposed to Charlotte Lucas instead, and she has accepted! They will be married in two months! We are lost, I tell you! You will die, and we shall be thrown out of the house, and Charlotte Lucas will become the mistress of Longbourn!" she cried hysterically.

Elizabeth hesitated to say or do anything. She glanced at her father, who looked suspiciously serious.

166

"So, Mrs Bennet, you are so desperate and upset because Lizzy did not marry Mr Collins?"

"Of course I am! If she was a better daughter, she would have encouraged him, and he would have proposed to her, as he intended!"

"He? Who?" Mr Bennet asked, and his wife stared at him, a look of bewilderment on her face.

"What do you mean who? Mr Collins, of course! It is all Lizzy's fault, and I shall never speak to her again. I shall never forgive her!"

"I see. I am sorry to hear that, Mrs Bennet. If you were to speak to Lizzy, she would tell you that she is engaged to Mr Darcy. I just gave him my blessing. They will marry likely sooner than Mr Collins, who I understand is your favourite of the two, which will surely pain Mr Darcy."

Elizabeth watched her father speaking, his deep satisfaction brightening his face; her mother stared in shock that increased with every word, transfixed, struggling for air. By the time her father concluded his statement, Mrs Bennet gulped repeatedly, tried to stand up, then went to collapse back into the chair again but missed it and fell to the floor, landing on her buttocks.

Mr Bennet slowly returned to his library, while the ladies tried to pull Mrs Bennet back to her feet — or to her chair.

Chapter 19

The moment they entered the carriage, Darcy gave Bingley the news of his engagement. His young friend's response was at first one of complete disbelief, then of utter puzzlement.

"Marry Miss Elizabeth? How is it possible? You despise her, and she hates you!" he exclaimed.

"That is rather inaccurate, Bingley."

"Inaccurate? You advised me to be prudent and patient in regard to Jane, even though I confessed my admiration for her from the first day we met! You refused to even dance with her sister! You said she was tolerable but not handsome enough to tempt you!"

He paused for a moment, then continued before Darcy could respond.

"You have always expressed your disapproval of the Bennet family! You did not even want to dine with them, until the admiral almost forced you to!"

"Now that is accurate," the admiral interjected, obviously amused.

"Are you marrying because of this scandal? Is Miss Elizabeth forced to marry you?"

"Bingley, I assure you I have long come to admire Miss Elizabeth, and I proposed to her because I wished to. And Miss Elizabeth accepted me without anyone forcing her to do so."

"So…so you are determined to marry?"

"Yes. I shall procure a licence, and I hope to marry seven

days after I obtain it."

"So soon? You mean now, before Christmas?"

"Hopefully, yes. I just wished to inform you as soon as I had Mr Bennet's blessing."

"I cannot believe this," Bingley whispered, as they entered the colonel's house.

Colonel Forster was expecting them and welcomed them with apparent embarrassment, apologising again for his men's despicable actions.

Denny and Pratt asked for the favour of speaking to Darcy and begging his forgiveness again. However, it was Admiral Pembroke who spoke first.

"I am not sure what punishment would be suitable for these miscreants," he said sharply. "I am still talking to Darcy about it. I want to see them crawl in front of the Bennets. I want to see them on their knees, begging for forgiveness. Of course, Mr Bennet does not care about them, and Miss Elizabeth cannot bear to see them ever again. So, I must think of something else, something that will affect them for the rest of their lives."

Denny attempted to interject, but Darcy intervened and silenced him.

"The problem is, your error was more serious than you know, and the offence you caused much greater than you are aware of. There may not be a legal punishment for being a fool, but I must have my satisfaction."

He watched them for a moment, enjoying the expression of distress on their faces.

"You see, I have long admired Miss Elizabeth, but until recently she did not return my affection. I proposed to her, but I needed time to court her and to persuade her into accepting me. You have not only harmed an honourable young woman, the daughter of a gentleman, but also my future wife, since we are to be married very soon."

The news seems to petrify the two guilty, dumbstruck officers; even the colonel looked incredulous, staring at Darcy with a frown and apparent doubtfulness.

"So put yourself in my place. I seek revenge, and I have the means to obtain it. I am in no hurry. I have plenty of time to plan it properly."

A deep silence fell over them; the colonel seemed willing to speak, but no words were heard.

"Mr Darcy, we did not know...we did not mean...it was a poor joke," Pratt mumbled.

"We were fools," Denny admitted in a low voice. "We have no real excuse for it."

"Well, this must be a truth universally acknowledged," the admiral concluded.

"I believe this conversation has come to an end for now," Darcy said. "There is still another one we must have, though. One that will be even more disagreeable."

With that, the pair were dismissed. The colonel offered his guests a drink, and then Wickham was sent for. When he entered, Darcy noticed that the insolent expression on his face had returned.

Darcy informed him that he would have to sign a settlement, then he would receive a ticket and a fair amount of money for him to settle into a new life. But Wickham raised an objection. With disgust, Darcy heard the scoundrel complain that moving to the other side of the world was an extreme decision which required much preparation and extensive expense.

Darcy silenced him instantly.

"Wickham, let us be clear. These are my conditions, for which you should kiss my boots. I am giving you more than you deserve, when you should be rotting in prison or facing transportation."

"Yes, but—"

"The ship will depart in eight days. My men will wait for you on the dock. You will sign the settlement and will be handed the ticket and the money the moment you set foot on the ship, not a moment sooner. The captain will supervise you until the ship is out on the sea."

"But Darcy, eight days? I cannot leave in eight days! I must prepare—"

"There is no negotiation, Wickham. If you are not there on the precise date, you will be arrested and sent to prison. Until then, you are free to go where you want and do what you want."

"But could we not—"

"No!" Darcy interrupted him. "This is my proposal. The choice is yours. Colonel, we shall leave now. I believe we have wasted enough time on this matter."

While Wickham's insolence and confidence seemed gone, Darcy turned to him one more time.

"Speaking of proposals, you will be pleased to hear that I have proposed to Miss Elizabeth Bennet, and we shall marry very soon. Just as soon as you leave England forever. I now have two reasons for joy and celebration."

The expression of dismay, shock, and panic as understanding struck Wickham was so satisfying for Darcy that it almost made all the distress worth it. Almost. He was eager to tell Elizabeth about it and hoped she would be equally amused. Or at least content.

After all, even though he had disturbed the Darcys' lives so many times and abused their trust and their affection, in the end, Wickham had apparently contributed to Darcy's future happiness.

Finally returning to Netherfield, Darcy hoped for a little rest, since he had had two sleepless nights in a row, as well as many restless others since Elizabeth Bennet had invaded his mind.

"Darcy, I appreciated the way you worded the news of your engagement," Admiral Pembroke said as they walked together to their rooms in the guest wing. "It sounded like you had long pursued Miss Elizabeth, and it was a mere coincidence that the engagement happened to occur now. This will surely be helpful for Miss Elizabeth's reputation."

"If we look at the situation from a certain point of view, it is the truth," Darcy said.

"Seeing things from the right point of view is always important," the admiral joked. "You should rest now. I have to say you look very tired. It is no wonder, considering how much you have accomplished in less than a day."

"I shall not deny that," Darcy admitted, allowing a smile. "This morning, I was despondent over my rejected proposal, and now I am betrothed, with my engagement approved and announced. Quite a day, indeed. I only hope Miss Elizabeth is not already regretting it."

"Speaking of the announcement, you still have an important one to make here at Netherfield, and you will need all your strength to do it. I look forward to seeing how Miss Bingley takes the news."

"I am not looking forward to it at all, sir. Especially since I must remain polite, out of consideration for Bingley. But I shall consider it good preparation for the confrontation with the Fitzwilliams and Lady Catherine."

The admiral laughed, but Darcy was too tired to be amused. He found solace in his room and lay in bed, thinking of Elizabeth. He was still incredulous that she had accepted his marriage proposal, and a slight worry that she might change her mind lingered in his head. No, not that she might change her mind; she had made a promise and entered into an agreement that he trusted she would keep. The worry was in regard to her feelings — that she might regret her decision. He would do everything in his power to avoid that. He would not have much time to court her properly, since he would be gone for most of the brief engagement and would barely see her till the wedding.

But afterwards, he would make up for everything she had missed out on due to the haste of their nuptials. As he had already told her, he had no intention of consummating their marriage, not before he was certain of her complete acceptance, of her complete willingness to be his wife. He would be patient, regardless of the time needed.

What he had not confessed to her, and barely dared to acknowledge to himself, was how strong his feelings for her were, how powerful his love was, and how it made him lose control over his heart, mind, and body. A love for which he found no better word than ardent.

Being patient would be a sweet torture, but she was worth waiting for. He did not allow himself to think about the moment when she would truly be his wife; it was too soon to even consider it. But he had the right to at least dream of it, which he did in the short yet restful sleep that claimed him soon afterwards.

His preparations for a confrontation with the Bingley sisters at dinner proved to be unnecessary. Apparently, Bingley had already informed them, and their response had been as Darcy anticipated, but Bingley had forbidden it from being publicly displayed. Therefore, the sisters chose to have dinner on a tray in their rooms, as well as the following morning's breakfast.

A dinner with just four gentlemen — with Hurst more voluble and involved in the conversation than usual — was a pleasure they all shared. Hurst even congratulated Darcy on his engagement and mentioned that Miss Elizabeth seemed like a delightful and charming young woman. He sounded genuine, and Darcy thanked him while hoping Mrs Hurst did not hear him say so, or else the poor man would not hear the end of it.

"Miss Elizabeth is charming and delightful, but I would not dare marry her," Bingley said after his third glass of brandy. "She is too clever, even scarily clever at times. I remember her debates with Darcy when she stayed at Netherfield. Upon my word, I barely understood what they said and what they were arguing about. She even took my side one evening, when Darcy criticised my handwriting and haste in doing things. Even then I barely understood their fight."

"I remember that argument too," Hurst interjected. Darcy smiled again, while the admiral's eyebrow arched enquiringly.

"By the by, Darcy," Bingley continued, raising his voice. "You criticised the haste of my actions, and here you are, proposing and marrying in the blink of an eye! You have no right to ever criticise me again!"

"I shall not, Bingley," Darcy admitted, amused by his friend's disposition enhanced by the drink.

"You are perfectly right about my handwriting, of course. I cannot compare it with your neat and tidy writing. Then again, I cannot compare myself with you in anything. Except that I am more likeable and more amiable than you. Everybody says so. And more pleasant company."

"I support that statement," the admiral said. "Let us have one final drink to that and then go to bed."

"I am sorry for my sisters, Darcy. Caroline had some absurd expectation that you would marry her. I am lost as to why she would even imagine that."

"I have told Louisa the same many times," Mr Hurst interjected. "But women have their own minds, and their imaginations cannot be controlled."

"Let us drink to that too!" Bingley approved, filling their glasses again.

It was close to midnight when the small party finally separated. As they walked to their chambers, the admiral mentioned to Darcy that it had certainly been the most entertaining dinner he had enjoyed at Netherfield — a statement with which Darcy fully agreed.

"I have changed my opinion about Hurst," the admiral said. "He is a pleasant enough fellow. I pity him, for his wife seems to have sucked all the joy out of him. I wonder if this marriage, which clearly brings him little pleasure, is advantageous enough for him."

"Admiral, I have long wanted to ask…how did it happen that you never married?" Darcy enquired.

"You did ask. And others have too. As I said, I have been married to the sea for the last thirty years. Or, better said, the sea has been a demanding mistress, leaving me with no energy and no desire for anyone else."

"Perhaps you have not yet met the woman to stir your desire and your energy, Admiral. I do not dare presume that I could advise you, but I speak from my own experience."

"Perhaps. Or perhaps I met her long ago, and fate was not as good to me as it was to you this morning."

"I am grateful for it, as I am for your friendship, Admiral."

"So am I, Darcy. I shall see you tomorrow morning."

"I might go for a ride before breakfast," Darcy said, slightly uneasy. The admiral laughed.

"An excellent habit that has brought you nothing but joy. It is wise of you to continue it."

"I intend to do so, Admiral. Good-night."

∞∞∞

The first day of her engagement passed in a haze of noise and activity for Elizabeth, which she mostly observed silently, torn between embarrassment and relief that Mr Darcy and the admiral were not there to witness it.

After her father made the announcement, her mother moved from elation to fainting and back several times. She cried for the Lord, then for Hill, then kissed Elizabeth, then fainted again. When Mrs Phillips arrived, the sisters shared in the exultation.

"My dear sister, what a fool I have been! How could I have even imagined Lizzy would marry that clergyman? All this time, she knew Mr Darcy would propose! Of course she rejected Mr Collins and would have nothing to do with him! She knew too well that Mr Darcy was interested in her! What a bright girl my Lizzy is!"

"Mama, a few days ago you said the admiral should propose to Lizzy," Lydia interjected, and Mrs Bennet became crimson with ire.

"I never said such a thing! How could you say something so stupid, child? You never pay attention to anything! The admiral was so friendly with Mr Bennet and with Lizzy because he knew Mr Darcy would propose! Stop talking nonsense, Lydia!"

"My dear sister, the rumours said Mr Darcy and Lizzy...you know...that he would not marry her."

"Who said such a stupid thing? Tell me who! Mr Darcy will surely call them out and shoot them! He and Lizzy were engaged all the time — why else would he dance with her and only her at the ball? And they will marry before Christmas. Surely that is proof it was a long arrangement between them! But Lizzy was so sly and did not say a word!"

"I do not know who, Sister! I told you that. I heard there were some officers..." Mrs Phillips replied while Elizabeth watched from afar, too dismayed to even intervene in what had turned into an irrational argument. Jane only glanced at her apologetically, in a failed attempt to comfort her.

"I bet it was that Wickham who started the rumours," Mrs Bennet guessed, much to Elizabeth's astonishment. "He courted Lizzy too, and he asked her to dance the first set with him! I am sure he was jealous of Mr Darcy. Like Mr Darcy was not ten times better than him! Taller and more handsome! Who cares about his red coat? Mr Darcy has ten thousand a year!" she concluded in a loud and exultant statement, to which Mrs Phillips nodded approvingly.

Elizabeth was too astonished by her mother's correct assumption and too embarrassed by the way she had expressed it, and she could not choose if and how to reply.

"It might well be, Sister!" Mrs Phillips said.

"Would you ever have imagined, Sister, that of all my daughters, the stubborn headstrong Lizzy would be the most courted one? And she will make the best of marriages! I cannot imagine how she charmed the proud Mr Darcy, but I thank the Lord for that! I thought Jane would make the best match marrying Mr Bingley, but we all must admit that Mr Bingley is nothing to Mr Darcy!"

Elizabeth and Jane looked at each other, but neither spoke. Eventually, Mrs Phillips returned home, taking the extraordinary news to Meryton and spreading it around the town that afternoon.

Mrs Bennet turned her attention and distress towards the following day's dinner, asking what Mr Darcy's favourite dish might be and asking Hill to prepare a lavish feast.

Mr Bennet did not leave his library till dinner time. Elizabeth was the only one who asked about his health, and he claimed he was feeling better.

Dinner was just as maddening to Elizabeth as the rest of the day had been, and when it was time to retire for the night, it came as a blessing. However, Mrs Bennet came to speak to Elizabeth twice more before she finally fell asleep.

Elizabeth and Jane had time to exchange a few words, but not many. Elizabeth was exhausted, still wondering whether the events of the day had been real. So much had happened since morning, it could have easily filled a month. She still had so many things to think about, but it was too soon for proper reasoning.

Chapter 20

Elizabeth had started the previous day with torment, and she had ended it with torment too, but of an utterly different kind. The recollection of the fortunate encounter that had changed her life — their lives — was too fresh, too vivid, and her senses too stirred to allow rest, and Mr Darcy's words resounded in her mind countless times.

Restless the entire night, she slept poorly and was relieved when the morning came.

Jane was still soundly asleep, and Elizabeth decided that nothing would make her feel better than another early morning walk. She carefully prepared herself, checking her reflection in the mirror, and left the house in a state of agitation that could not be soothed.

She walked away from the house to the spot that had now become so meaningful to her. Although she had enjoyed morning walks since she was a child, Elizabeth could not remember one that had given her more pleasure. She admitted that she was nervous but delighted at the prospect of meeting Mr Darcy, as unlikely as it seemed.

There had been no agreement, not even a hint of such an encounter, and she knew he was preparing for his return to London; yet she hoped. She was still somehow concerned that he might change his mind, and after all the uproar her mother had created, a broken engagement would have been truly hurtful to her reputation. Furthermore, it would have been hurtful to her; with her feelings still torn, still uncertain, she discovered new sentiments every other moment, as had never happened to her before.

As soon as she passed through the gates, Elizabeth saw Mr Darcy sitting on a stump, his horse tied under the trees, waiting. He stood up and approached her. His countenance did not appear quite comfortable, but a smile brightened his face, and she noticed that smiling suited him very well and made him look even more handsome. She felt she was blushing.

"Mr Darcy…"

"Miss Bennet…I was hoping you would come…"

"So was I," she confessed.

"I am glad to hear that…and I am glad to see you more at ease than yesterday…"

"I feel more at ease, sir."

"I am glad to hear that…I am sorry, I keep repeating myself. It seems I have lost the ability to carry on a decent conversation."

She smiled, amused. "It is fortunate that I have never considered the ability to converse as your main quality."

"I trust this is something I might learn from my future wife," he said, and she smiled, this time her cheeks burning.

"I am not sure you need it, sir. I think that, in essentials, you know everything you need to," she said teasingly. "I hope to learn from you, as I lack the knowledge and skills needed to fulfil the responsibilities attached to the position of your wife," she ended in earnest.

"Miss Bennet…Elizabeth…in essentials, you are everything I wish you to be, and you have everything you need to fulfil any responsibilities. The knowledge you lack, you will easily acquire," he replied with apparent seriousness. Saying her name made his face colour as much as hers.

"Thank you. You trust me more than I trust myself, Mr Darcy. May I know your name?"

"Yes, of course…how silly of me. My name is Fitzwilliam. I was named after my mother."

"Fitzwilliam…is a long, strong name. Just like you."

"And dull...just like me."

She laughed openly, and his smile broadened.

"I am sure that is not true. But you seem to be begging for compliments, Mr D— Fitzwilliam. It must be a bad habit caused by Miss Bingley's constant flattery. Speaking of Miss Bingley, may I ask how she took the news?"

"As badly as I expected. Fortunately, I did not witness it. Bingley informed his sisters, and I have not seen them since. And your family?"

"As well as I expected. Unfortunately, I did witness it," she joked. "But I cannot blame them. Everybody who hears of our engagement will respond with surprise."

"I imagine. Poor Bingley was stunned too. He blamed me for acting as hastily as I accused him of acting. But he was quite happy in the end. Mr Hurst also sends you congratulations and his best regards."

"Mr Hurst? What a lovely surprise," Elizabeth said.

"It was. Even the admiral was impressed by how different he is without his wife around."

The discomfort between them was slowly ebbing away, and the conversation, teasing and pleasant, delighted them both.

"I also spoke to Wickham and his two accomplices yesterday. I believe our news affected them as much as I hoped."

"I hope it did. And what now for Mr Wickham?"

"Wickham will leave Meryton tomorrow, too. He will stay at an inn in London until next week, when he is set to leave England. He will sign a settlement and will have a cabin purchased and the means to start a new life."

"That is generous of you. What if he refuses?"

"If he does not accept this choice, he will spend a long time in debtors' prison. My decision is made, and it will not be changed under any circumstances."

"I would be pleased to never see him again, but I still hope he will attempt to improve his life. Though I doubt it."

"I do, too. But this is the last time he will be my

responsibility."

"Strangely enough, Mama and Aunt Phillips guessed rather quickly who had spread the rumours, although their reasoning was utterly wrong."

"Oh…so the rumours were already spread in Meryton?" he asked with a frown.

"Yes…since yesterday. Fortunately, my mother and aunt assumed we had an understanding some time ago, and so the gossip was simply malicious."

"Which is true," Darcy said. "I shall be happy to support your mother's belief."

"She will be happy with any approval from you. Shall I see you at dinner tonight?"

"Of course. Together with Bingley and the admiral. We all look forward to it."

"Mama is preparing a grand feast and hopes to please you."

"I would be pleased with some simple fare and good company," he answered.

"But she would not," she joked. "I must warn you that you might hear things that will astonish you, and not in a pleasant way. You still have time to break the engagement."

"Break it? I intend to obtain a licence tomorrow so we can be married in a week or so…if you approve of it, of course. We can wait…"

"In truth, I would rather be done with all this turmoil. Considering we have already discussed the arrangements," she said with slight embarrassment.

"I am happy that you approve of it. If there is something we have not arranged yet, it will be as you wish. That is a promise. I shall send your father the settlement the day after I arrive in London. You may add or change anything in it."

"Thank you…I have no concerns in regard to the settlement. I do not even need to see it to know it will be fair."

"Do you have any concerns in regard to something particular?"

"Yes. My main concern is how will your sister bear the

news of you marrying a stranger? I know the rest of your family will oppose it, but your sister's opinion matters the most to me."

"You should not worry about Georgiana," he said, with more warmth in his voice. "She will be surprised, but she will become fond of you immediately. She is sweet and kind, and I think she will be happy to have a sister. Besides, you are no stranger to her."

"I am not?"

"No…I wrote to her about you when you stayed at Netherfield."

"You did?" she asked, incredulous.

"Of course. Since I had already confessed my admiration for your fine eyes to Miss Bingley, how could I not have mentioned you to my sister?" He was smiling, and she felt the warmth of pleasure.

"You are becoming quite proficient at teasing, Mr… Fitzwilliam."

"I have learnt from you, Elizabeth. And from your father and the admiral. Among so many witty people, I had no chance of remaining my old, tedious self."

She laughed again, and he continued, "As for the rest of my family, my cousin Richard, the colonel, will approve of you immediately. He might envy me too. His brother, the viscount, will be surprised but will not express it. My uncle and aunt will be amazed, upset, disapproving, and will probably need time to accept my decision. I hope they will, since I am fond of them, but I do not need their acceptance. The admiral's support will ease things with them."

"And Lady Catherine de Bourgh?"

"I can honestly say that I expect the most unreasonable response from her, and I doubt she will ever accept my marriage to anyone but her daughter. But you must not fear. I shall protect you from any unpleasantness."

"I have no fear, Fitzwilliam. I am grateful for your protection and care, but I trust I shall be able to handle any disagreeable situation by myself."

"Seeing your discussion with Bingley's sister, I have no doubts," he concluded, his smile increasing the warmth inside her.

"I shall leave tomorrow morning and will send you news. I shall ask my housekeeper, Mrs Clifford, to prepare the mistress's suite."

Her face was flushed again, but she held his gaze.

"I hope you do not worry about me not keeping my promise. We shall live in adjoining apartments, but you may lock your door and open it only when you want to."

"I doubt I shall ever lock the door, sir. And I do not doubt your word."

"Thank you. You will be free to change the apartment in any way you wish. Furniture, carpets, or anything else," he continued, and she gently touched his arm.

"Please do not worry in that regard. I doubt I shall want to do that either. Now, I must return home. My mother will soon wake up and start the preparations anew."

He brought her hands to his lips and placed a soft kiss on each.

"Do you still have scratches on your hands? I see your face is healed."

"Just a few," she replied, taking off her gloves.

He took off his own gloves and took her hands in his. The feeling of his bare skin on hers was so powerful that she quivered, and her fingers trembled in his palm. He touched the scratches with his thumbs, then placed more kisses on each. The touch of his lips thrilled her, and the warmth grew unbearable inside her — so much that she felt dizzy.

Then he put her gloves back on, still holding her hands.

"I have spoken to the housekeeper of Netherfield — the puppies will remain there, as they are, with the rest of the dogs, for the next three months. Afterwards, you will decide what you wish to do with them."

"I would like to keep them, since we share them...if you approve."

Her timid smile met his. "Most heartily, Elizabeth."

They separated moments later, Elizabeth's heart pounding with joy. She returned home and spent the rest of the day in a dream. She obeyed her mothers' requests until dinner time, when the guests arrived.

After two days of utter perturbation, Mrs Bennet's rapture diminished in the presence of Mr Darcy, and she timidly welcomed and embraced her future son-in-law. Emotions seemed to overwhelm her, as Mrs Bennet spent most of the time enjoying Mr Darcy's compliments on the tasty dishes and his gratitude for all the trouble, while she stared at him in awe and adoration, disregarding Mr Bingley and the admiral almost entirely.

Elizabeth had no private conversation with her betrothed that evening, as he was mostly engaged in conversation with her father and the admiral, while Mr Bingley spoke mostly to Jane.

They only exchanged glances and smiles over the table, and she did not need more. They had already discussed and agreed on the most important things, so she looked forward to her new life with confidence. And with anticipation and eagerness, as she recollected the sensation of his lips touching her skin.

The next morning, the Netherfield party returned to London, taking with them the tranquillity of three ladies of Longbourn.

Chapter 21

The week following Miss Elizabeth Bennet's engagement to Mr Darcy was one of the most eventful ever known in Meryton.

Despite the gentleman being absent, his actions caused consequences.

Two days after his departure, Longbourn was visited by Dr Talbot, Mr Darcy's physician from London. He examined Mr Bennet — whose state had slightly improved but remained worrisome — and remained three more days for further examinations. Despite his intention to stay at Netherfield, Dr Talbot was invited to remain at Longbourn for convenience. Mr Bennet's health was eventually declared satisfactory, but precautions were required, and medicine was sent for that it was recommended he take for several months.

As one gentleman arrived, Mr Wickham — the entire town's favourite — left the regiment. He informed everyone who wished to listen to him that he had been offered a new, more advantageous commission, which would provide him with a better situation in life.

Nobody knew the truth in regard to this sudden departure except for Elizabeth and her father, who only disclosed it to Jane. Elizabeth's resentment towards Mr Wickham was so strong that she could not see him nor speak of him again. As soon as Mr Wickham left, some reports about his actions arose. People spoke of debts, deceptions, and seductions of at least two shop girls. Such news only made Elizabeth angrier with herself for her foolishness that could have had regrettable consequences, and despite the fortunate outcome, she needed more time to forgive herself.

Some people regretted him, but many were relieved to see him gone. Mr Denny, who had recommended the man to the regiment, was scarcely seen in public at all after the ball. One day, the two officers who, in addition to Mr Wickham, had caused such a disturbance came to Longbourn with Colonel Forster and had a private meeting with Mr Bennet in his library. Of the ladies, only Elizabeth was present. The men expressed their apologies, which Elizabeth and her father acknowledged with little interest.

Although some rumours were still circulating in Meryton, any suspicions over the relationship between Elizabeth and Mr Darcy were washed away.

Caught up as she was in these life-changing events, Elizabeth almost forgot about her friend Charlotte Lucas and her engagement. She felt disappointed that Charlotte had settled for so little, but in light of her own unexpected decision, she dared not say much. She even felt sorry for Charlotte, as her engagement passed almost unnoticed in Meryton, and every time Lady Lucas mentioned it, Mrs Bennet reminded her that Elizabeth was marrying the nephew of the patroness of Charlotte's future husband. For the first time ever, Mrs Bennet had something — her future son-in-law — which was far better than Sir William's title and presentation at St James's, and she made the best of it.

The next day, after Dr Talbot's departure, Mr Bennet received a letter from Mr Darcy. Inside it was the settlement for Elizabeth and news of the licence.

Please study the settlement and present me with any changes or additions you deem appropriate.

I would also kindly ask Miss Elizabeth to consider how she would like to spend Christmas. I know your family have always been

*together at such a time, and I do not want to deprive her of that joy.
My sister and I have spent the winter in London in the last few years,
but I am willing to do my best and accommodate Miss Elizabeth's
wishes for the occasion.*

*I shall have all my affairs completed and shall return to
Hertfordshire with Bingley in five days' time. Due to the bad weather
and short notice, of my relatives, only the admiral and my cousin
Colonel Fitzwilliam will join me.*

*My sister has expressed her delight and eagerness to welcome
Miss Elizabeth into the family as well as her joy to have a sister.*

There were several other things in the letter, but Elizabeth
was not interested in them.

"Upon my word, Lizzy, I wonder if this settlement is real or
a mistake."

"Why, Papa?"

They were alone in the library, as Mr Bennet was reluctant
to involve the rest of his family in matters regarding Mr Darcy.

"According to this, you will have more pin money in a
month than you and all your sisters had together in a year. There
are also some descriptions of the jewels you will receive, some
legal matters in the case of Mr Darcy's sudden death—"

"Papa, what are you saying?"

"My dear, rich people put all these eventualities in writing.
As I said, there is also a promise that Mr Darcy will allow you
to use his means to support your family in any way you find
appropriate. So, you can buy us another house if you want. And
more books for me. I shall send him our acceptance immediately
before he changes his mind."

"Papa, please be serious. This is all exceedingly generous
of Mr Darcy. Perhaps too generous, so please do not mention
the extent of it to Mama or Lydia and Kitty. I cannot bear more
discussions about Mr Darcy's wealth."

"My dear, I have no intention of sharing such details with
anyone except my brother Gardiner. You must not worry in that
regard."

"Thank you. I am a little worried that I shall have to marry in seven days. But it might be for the best. The sooner the wedding takes place, the sooner all this will be done, and hopefully, there will finally be a little peace at Longbourn."

"My dear, there has been no peace at Longbourn since the day Kitty was born and your mother's nerves became delicate. In regard to the wedding, the letter says you may postpone it if you have doubts or if you want to stay at home until January. Mr Darcy has allowed you the liberty to decide."

"Mr Darcy is all kindness, but I have decided. We shall have the wedding on the suggested date. I shall inform Mama."

"My dear, and what about Christmas? If you return to London, you will be alone there."

"I must consider it carefully. But since the wedding will be so close to Christmas, it is too late for any special arrangements. I must be with my husband, and he cannot leave his sister alone, nor can she travel. So, I only have one choice. It is part of my responsibility, and since Mr Darcy has showed such consideration for my family, I shall show the same for his."

As she spoke, Elizabeth felt more and more at ease. She had made her decision, and her immediate future was clear, so there was not much room for worry, at least until the wedding.

In his letter, she observed that Mr Darcy had mentioned nothing about the rest of his family, which led Elizabeth to conclude that the news of their engagement had not been met with joy. Of that — and probably many other issues — she had enough reasons for concern but would not have to deal with them for the time being.

The details of his return and the wedding day stirred new feelings inside Elizabeth. She realised she missed him and that she was waiting for his return with eagerness but also some reluctance. In seven days, she would become his wife and would be beholden to him. In seven days, there would be no Miss Lizzy Bennet, only Mrs Elizabeth Darcy.

Her thoughts also turned to Jane, who would be overjoyed to hear that Mr Bingley would return too. There was no mention of his sisters, so it was still a mystery where he would spend Christmas. But his decision to return so soon proved that he wished to be in Hertfordshire, hopefully close to Jane.

The news of the wedding date threw Mrs Bennet and the entirety of Longbourn into further chaos, just as Elizabeth had feared. Her mother started to cry and whine, incapable of being calmed or consoled.

"Seven days from today? A wedding? You have no clothes! You cannot go into Mr Darcy's house looking like a beggar!"

"I shall write to Aunt Gardiner and ask her to purchase me a few things and send them to me. Or perhaps she will come for the wedding and bring them with her."

"But your aunt does not know what you need! And I must prepare a meal for the guests! Hill cannot do that alone! I need to hire some more help! Maybe my sister's cook and a maid… We have no proper clothes either! This is not to be borne! You must postpone it for at least a fortnight!"

"Mr Darcy suggested the date. I believe he has some business that requires his presence in town, so it cannot be delayed. Besides, he is to bring his cousin, who is Lord Matlock's son, and Admiral Pembroke. I cannot ask them to change their plans, can I?"

The answer disconcerted Mrs Bennet and silenced her momentarily.

"No, you cannot. These important people cannot waste their time like the rest of us. Then go and write to your aunt! Tell her to purchase everything that a newly wedded woman needs! And two gowns, the best she can find, for the wedding day. And tell her to come here quickly, as I need her!"

"Very well, Mama."

"And when will Mr Darcy return?"

"Two days prior to the wedding. Mr Bingley will also travel with them."

"Mr Bingley! Did you hear that, Jane? Dear Lord, what a blessing! If Mr Darcy, who is richer and more important than Mr Bingley, is marrying Lizzy, who is not as pretty as Jane, I am sure

Mr Bingley will propose to Jane too!"

"Mama, we do not know—" Jane tried to temper her, but Mrs Bennet pushed her away.

"Do not get in my way, Jane! I have much to do! Kitty, Lydia, go and deliver this note to my sister Phillips. She must come and help me!"

Throughout that day and those that followed, Mrs Bennet found no rest. She dismissed any advice or suggestion, claiming that nobody in Meryton had ever married such an illustrious man, so nobody could know what was best to be done. She only trusted her sister Phillips, who was the only person who listened to her and approved of her every decision.

Elizabeth chose to distance herself from the turmoil, knowing that contradicting her mother was of no use. She spent time talking to Jane and making plans for their reunion, then with her father, whose health she watched closely, and also with her younger sisters. During the nights, she hardly slept in her maidenly bed, which she would soon leave. She imagined her future bed and her future apartment, as well as his. She wondered about her time alone with her husband and what sort of clothes he would wear in the privacy of his apartment.

She rested little during the night, and her agitation was exhausting during the day. At times, she escaped and went for a stroll in the garden, but she did not enjoy it as much as before, as though something was missing. Or someone.

On the day of Mr Darcy's return, Elizabeth woke up at dawn. It was cold and raining, and soon it turned into sleet. Worries overwhelmed her, as she imagined how difficult such a journey might be in the winter. She was aware that in three days' time she would have to leave with him, in the same sort of weather, but strangely, she was not as concerned for her safety as she was for his.

The gentlemen arrived around four o'clock, and their first stop was at Longbourn. Mr Bingley and the admiral entered with their usual amiability and introduced Colonel Fitzwilliam — whose manners, uniform, and appearance were immediately admired. He addressed a few words and some friendly congratulations to Elizabeth, showing his approval for the upcoming wedding.

Mr Darcy was more restrained and, after everyone had moved towards the drawing room, he remained a few steps behind. Elizabeth did the same, realising how loudly and quickly her heart was beating and how pleasantly disturbing were the chills that ran down her spine.

They exchanged greetings but nothing more, since the others were calling for them.

"I hope Miss Darcy is in good health?"

"Yes, very much so. She looks forward to meeting you."

"And your other relatives?"

"They are in good health too," he replied, and she did not insist further.

"Everything is prepared for you," Mr Darcy added.

"Thank you. I am glad that you arrived safely," she whispered. "I was worried about you travelling in this weather."

"You have no reason to worry. I am accustomed to travelling long distances in any weather. My concern is for your discomfort when we return to London."

"You have no reason to be concerned," she answered, smiling at him. He smiled back.

"I missed being here and talking to you. Very much."

"And you have been missed. Very much," she replied.

He took her hand to his lips, but only briefly.

"I am glad to see we are in agreement, Elizabeth."

"So am I, Fitzwilliam," she ended, as her mother's voice called to them.

Instead of going to Netherfield, the gentlemen remained at Longbourn for dinner. The dishes were tasty, the guests were hungry, and the company was pleasant for everyone. The ladies were mostly entertained by the colonel and Admiral Pembroke, and Mr Bingley sat close to Jane, paying attention to little else except her. Darcy was caught up in conversation with Mr Bennet, but his glances often turned towards Elizabeth, who was talking to the colonel. As charming as Colonel Fitzwilliam was, Elizabeth felt flushed each time she felt her betrothed's eyes upon her.

The evening progressed better than she expected. Her mother and sisters — including Mary — were so enchanted by the colonel that they all behaved reasonably well.

When the guests were preparing to leave, the admiral approached Elizabeth and said, "Miss Elizabeth, I must tell you that you look beautiful. It seems this engagement has not distressed you as much as we both assumed and feared."

"It has not. Quite the opposite, I would say," she said with a smile.

"I am glad to hear that. And relieved. I have great hopes that all will turn out well in the end."

"So have I, sir."

Farewells were taken, and Elizabeth had a short moment of privacy with Mr Darcy, even though they were in a room full of people.

"There is something I would like to speak to you about tomorrow. And I have something to give you. Your father has promised to bring you and Miss Bennet to Netherfield tomorrow so we can talk more privately."

She only nodded, as he was holding her hand, and she was not quite composed.

"My uncle and aunt from London will arrive tomorrow afternoon," Elizabeth said.

"Yes, I know. We have been invited to dinner at Longbourn tomorrow to meet them."

"Oh, have you? I had not heard."

"I noticed you were a little distracted by your conversation with my cousin. He is skilled at charming people," he said, and she detected a trace of jealousy in his voice.

"Colonel Fitzwilliam is the second most charming officer I have ever met, after the admiral. But it was not him who had me distracted," she whispered, trying to tease him but blushing instead.

He bowed his head, brought her hand to his lips for an instant, and then left, leaving her with a mixed sensation of regrets and thrills.

Chapter 22

Darcy was alone in the Netherfield library, looking absently at a book and a box of jewels. It was a set of gold and emeralds that had been left by his mother for his future wife. He planned to give it to Elizabeth prior to the wedding, so she could decide whether she wished to wear it.

He smiled just thinking of her. She had looked more beautiful than ever last evening, and her eyes had been sparkling with mirth. She had said that she had missed him, and her sweet teasing, as well as her glances, had given him hope that it was true. He found it hard to believe that only one day separated him from the moment she would be his wife. Whilst he was in London, the image of their life together had become clearer, and he could not believe that he had previously considered such a marriage unsuitable.

Sharing the news of his engagement with his family had been as daunting as he expected. Georgiana had been surprised, even fearful, but in the end, she had accepted it. Darcy knew he still had to tell Elizabeth about the failed elopement in Ramsgate. He had not found the right moment for such a confession yet, but he would. With the scoundrel removed from their lives, he could wait a little longer. Wickham had been shipped — like useless merchandise — the day before Darcy returned to Longbourn. He was at peace with his actions, and he could enjoy his felicity without further interruptions in that regard.

He expected other interruptions though, as soon as he was married. Lord and Lady Matlock had been stunned and had raised many objections to his engagement, which he had dismissed calmly and decidedly. In truth, the admiral had been helpful, since he had taken upon himself the burden of arguing with the Matlocks, as Colonel Fitzwilliam had revealed. Being fond of the Matlocks and valuing their affection, Darcy hoped for their acceptance, in order to avoid a breach between them. He did not want to choose between them and Elizabeth, but if he had to do it, his choice was easy. He had visited them once after the announcement, and they had still been upset, still trying to change his mind, but their arguments were less vehement.

His greatest concern was Lady Catherine, to whom he had sent a letter two days prior to his return to Hertfordshire. He had contemplated the notion of going to Kent and telling her in person, allowing her the opportunity to unleash her anger; but time had been short, and he could not afford to waste two days, so an express had seemed like the best choice. He had not received a reply before he left, but he expected to find one waiting for him on his desk.

The colonel's decision to attend the wedding did not surprise Darcy; he had always received his cousin's friendship and support. His other cousin, the viscount, had said he would like to attend too, but he had other urgent business — something that Darcy easily understood.

After the wedding, he and Elizabeth would travel to London immediately. The colonel and the admiral were uncertain whether they would join them — in another carriage, as Admiral Pembroke made clear — or would stay a few more days to keep Bingley company. Poor Bingley had no support from his sisters, and he was struggling with the decision to propose to Miss Jane Bennet. The admiral teased him that with Darcy marrying Miss Elizabeth, Miss Bennet would be in town often and would surely draw the attention and admiration of many eligible men.

Netherfield was peaceful that morning. After breakfast, Bingley had taken Colonel Fitzwilliam to Meryton to introduce him to Colonel Forster, and the admiral had withdrawn to his room to rest until Mr Bennet and his daughters arrived. Darcy was amused by how exhilarated he felt at the notion of seeing Elizabeth again. The fluttering in his stomach was something he had never felt before.

Darcy's peaceful reflection was interrupted by the sound of a carriage, and he assumed Bingley and the colonel had returned. He placed the box of jewels in his pocket, as he wanted Elizabeth to be the first to see them. He also noticed that, lost in his thoughts, he had allowed the fire to die down, and he placed two more logs on it, then went in search of his friends.

When he opened the door, he found himself face-to-face with Lady Catherine de Bourgh, of all people, glaring at him. His moment of stupefaction allowed her time to push past him and enter, waving her cane.

"Lady Catherine? What are you doing here?" he enquired in dismay.

"You know too well what I am doing here, Darcy! I have searched for you throughout London, and Georgiana said she did not know where you were! That girl has turned out to be as dishonest and disrespectful as you! Luckily, my brother told me you were already here, signing your death sentence! I have come to try to save you, before it is too late!"

"I am sorry you took so much trouble and travelled so far in such weather. You must be tired. Please take a seat, and I shall order some tea while we speak calmly. May I ask, where is Anne?"

"I do not need tea!" the lady shouted. "And yes, I took the trouble to come and see with my own eyes how it is possible that you could have lost your mind! Anne remained in town, as she was exhausted by the journey from Kent. How ironic that you remember Anne now, since you cast her off in order to satisfy some passing desires that have made you forget about your family and your duty!"

"Lady Catherine, I beg you to mind your words if you want

to continue this conversation," Darcy replied, barely holding his temper.

"Mind my words? Why would I, when you have not minded your actions?"

"I assure you, I have carefully pondered my actions, which you seem incapable of doing. I still insist on continuing this conversation in a civil tone or ending it now."

"You pondered your actions? Wandering in the woods with a country nobody? Is this what you do now? Why not hire a courtesan, as all men do? And to now marry her? No man in his right mind would do that! She tricked you and trapped you, so you were forced to marry her, like the biggest fool!"

"Catherine? What on earth are you doing here? And why are you yelling? You woke me and the entire manor!"

Admiral Pembroke was staring at them from the door, then he entered, still looking at the lady in shock.

"Well, well, Thomas Pembroke, you are here too. Of course you are! Nothing bad ever happened in this family without you being involved! Thank God you have been on the sea for thirty years, or else, God knows, you would have ruined this family!"

"I am pleased to see you too, Catherine," the admiral replied with mockery. "I have not seen you in three years now, but you have not changed a bit. You are still handsome and still irrational."

"Oh, shut your mouth! I have nothing to say to you, you are nothing but a miserable sailor! Darcy, we must speak, now! You cannot possibly do something so imprudent! I am sure you can pay the Bennets a reasonable amount of money and break this dreadful engagement. I am sure that woman used some arts and allurements to make you lose your mind. Mr Collins told me she is not to be trusted! Her mother tried to marry her to Mr Collins first, but he was wise enough to choose better! Can my own nephew be more of a fool than my clergyman?"

"You have said enough, madam!" Darcy replied harshly. "I shall leave you now before I say or do something I shall truly regret. As for breaking my engagement, why would I do that, when I had to work so hard for it? I had to propose to Miss Bennet twice, since she rejected me the first time, and I had to use all my powers of persuasion to convince her! She is truly the most remarkable woman I have ever met and the only one I have ever wanted to marry."

At that, Lady Catherine's eyes widened in disbelief, and she seemed to struggle for air; she sat on a chair, blinking and gulping, while the two men watched her.

"You…you…" she mumbled, then stood up shakily. "You are worse than your father! Much worse! He polluted the shades of Pemberley with his mistress, and you want to place an unworthy nobody there to take your mother's place! Anne would turn in her grave. She would die again if she could see her son's horrible betrayal."

The lady was suffocating with rage, while Darcy listened with horror and dismay.

"Excuse me?" he shouted. "How dare you accuse my father and insult his memory? This is despicable, even from you! You will leave this very moment! I have nothing else to say to you. Yes, my poor mother would certainly turn in her grave if she could see you!"

"Not so hasty, young man! I still have much to tell you! I hoped you would be different, that you had inherited the Fitzwilliams' sense of duty and honour, and Anne's discretion and decency. But you are all your father! He should have been grateful that she married him, and grovelled at her feet! Instead, he had no scruples in deceiving her. She was ill, and he still left her with child, which caused her to die! And all the while he kept another woman for his pleasure!"

Lady Catherine's tirade — long, loud, and barely understandable — devastated and defeated Darcy. He felt his strength ebb away and looked at the admiral, who was standing in silence, waiting for a retaliation that did not come. The woman continued, even angrier, pointing her cane at the admiral.

"Yes, ask him, he knows too well what I am talking about!

But at least George was clever enough to keep one woman for what she was meant for and marry the right one. Why not marry Anne and do the same with this country nobody, as any man would do? I am sure you will be tired of her after a couple of months!"

"Lady Catherine, leave now, or I shall not be responsible for my actions," Darcy replied in a low voice, his fists clenched hard at his sides. "Or better still, I shall leave you. I have nothing to say to you and do not wish to ever see you again," he said, hurrying to the door. It was partly open, and in the doorway stood Elizabeth and her father, both looking petrified and pale.

"Yes, leave, since you cannot bear the truth!" Lady Catherine yelled, walking after him before she noticed the two unexpected witnesses. When she did, her eyebrows lowered, her eyes and lips narrowed, and she took a step closer.

Immediately, Darcy stood beside Elizabeth to protect her, while the admiral held Lady Catherine's arm. She pulled it away angrily and said, "You must be the infamous Miss Elizabeth Bennet. I recognise you from my clergyman's description. You are just as I imagined you — an ordinary country girl, with nothing to recommend you. God knows how you succeeded in capturing my nephew!"

Darcy's first instinct was to push his aunt away, but, to his amazement, Elizabeth touched his arm and took a step forwards.

"And you must be Lady Catherine de Bourgh. I also recognise you from Mr Collins's description, and you are just as I imagined you — disrespectful, arrogant, and irritating. It is good to finally meet you, my lady," she concluded with a wide smile.

Lady Catherine looked even more enraged, but Darcy's fury was suddenly soothed by his pride and admiration for Elizabeth's wit and self-control. She had told him as much, and she had proved it: he may protect her, but she was perfectly capable of dealing with any unpleasantness by herself.

"You…you nothing! How dare you? Your marriage to him will never be recognised! Do you think my brother will give you a penny? He has not said it in so many words, but he thinks the same! The whole of society will resent you, and you will bear the contempt of the world! You are worthless to everyone!"

"Enough, madam!" Darcy shouted. "She is worth everything to me," he added, bringing Elizabeth's hand to his lips in a gesture as romantic and tender as it was improper in public.

Elizabeth smiled. "That is all I wish to know, Fitzwilliam. As for society's contempt, being your wife will certainly provide me with such extraordinary sources of happiness that I am sure I shall have no cause to repine."

"Your extraordinary happiness is a goal I shall strive to accomplish," Darcy said, his back now turned entirely to his aunt, who was breathless with rage.

"Admiral, please see Lady Catherine out this very moment, or I shall ask the servants to do so. And please let her know I shall never see nor speak to her ever again. I am ashamed to be connected to her in any way."

"How dare you! I am your closest relative!" Lady Catherine yelled again, while the admiral dragged her out of the room.

A moment after she was gone, Darcy closed the door and took a deep breath to regain some composure.

"Mr Bennet, Miss Bennet, I cannot apologise enough for what you have seen...and heard. I do not know what I can say to beg your forgiveness..."

"There is nothing to be said on that subject, Mr Darcy. I believe a drink will do very well," Mr Bennet said. "I am pleased to see my daughter has become proficient in taking revenge. You two seem to be of the same mind, at least in this aspect."

"Miss Elizabeth is remarkable," Darcy replied, with a glance at Elizabeth. "I cannot express either my admiration or my regret properly."

"Mr Darcy, let us calm down, and please do not apologise for what is not your fault," Elizabeth suggested, returning to the proper form of address in the presence of her father.

"You are right, of course," Darcy replied humbly. He was burdened by the offence Elizabeth had been forced to suffer from his aunt and devastated by the accusations thrown at his father.

His head was aching, and he could not think properly, only pray that such claims were untrue. But how could an angry, resentful woman invent such a story in the moment? He had had no time to look properly at the admiral, but there had been no denial from him, and this made the situation even more concerning.

While he poured some drinks with trembling hands, the admiral returned. Darcy scrutinised him and noticed a shadow of discomposure, as well as signs of embarrassment that he could not remember ever seeing before on the brave man.

"Forgive me. I do not want to intrude...or bother you. Darcy, do you want me to stay or leave?"

Admiral Pembroke's question was hesitant and fearful, and Darcy had the final proof that something truly shocking had been revealed; otherwise, the admiral would have laughed and mocked Lady Catherine.

"I would appreciate a private conference with you later, Admiral, as I feel there are significant matters that need to be urgently clarified."

"Of course," the admiral admitted, still with a restraint that was unlike him.

"Then I shall send you word." Darcy dismissed the admiral politely but decidedly. He knew he was being rude to a man who had always shown him support and affection, but the threat of a dreadful secret that the admiral might have been involved in was too much and would not allow him to pay proper attention to his betrothed.

"At present," Darcy continued, "I would like to conclude my conversation with Mr and Miss Bennet. I invited them here to clarify some issues regarding additions to the settlement and also to make some plans for a family gathering. Unless they have changed their minds and decided to not be connected with my family, which I could well understand," he concluded bitterly.

"That is not the case, I assure you, Mr Darcy," Mr Bennet interjected. "I am not sure what you have added to the settlement, since Lizzy and I already declared it was too generous. As for the family gathering, after meeting your aunt,

I thank God for granting me Mrs Bennet, to whom I shall deeply apologise for all my mockery."

The admiral left the library before Mr Bennet had time to finish his statement.

Chapter 23

Behind him, Elizabeth and Darcy exchanged some glances, and at that moment, Darcy realised Elizabeth had been at the door long enough to hear the accusation in regard to his father too.

As though she had guessed his thoughts, Elizabeth said apologetically, "Mr Darcy, please forgive our intrusion. We did not know that you had company. We came to talk to you as we planned. Mr Bingley and the colonel are at Longbourn. My aunt and uncle have just arrived. The servant told us you were in the library. I am truly sorry. We should have left immediately, but I heard the argument about the wedding and…I could not walk away."

Elizabeth spoke hurriedly, her distress apparent; unlike earlier, when she had confronted Lady Catherine, now she looked grieved.

"I am truly sorry you heard those dreadful things," Darcy said. "I beg you not to take offence at my aunt's words. She is no better than Wickham in speaking falsehoods. May I ask, did you hear what she said about my father?"

Elizabeth nodded with mortification.

"I am so sorry," she repeated.

"Perhaps it is for the best. You have the right to know that the family you are marrying into might not be as perfect as I claimed. There is still time until the wedding. You still have time to change your mind," he said, his heart so heavy that he could barely find the words.

"Mr Darcy, you keep repeating that we may change our minds," Elizabeth said decidedly. "I must ask, have you changed yours? Would you like to postpone the wedding? Or to cancel it, perhaps?"

Darcy gazed at her, bewildered.

"Why would I change my mind, Miss Bennet? Why would I postpone the wedding?"

"Then why would I, sir? Do I not deserve your trust in my decision?"

The question was harsh and carried a trace of offence, which Darcy did not miss.

"Forgive me. I know I sound foolish. But considering what happened… In truth, the wedding is the only certainty I may count on at this moment," he admitted.

"You may count on me at this moment, tomorrow, and in the years to come, Mr Darcy. I do not change my mind easily, and certainly not because of some improper intervention."

"Thank you," he repeated. At that moment, he felt she was the stronger one, and she could protect him in ways he did not know he needed.

"I never suspected anything other than the deepest affection and respect between my parents," he confessed. "What Lady Catherine said… I doubt it can be true… This is the first time I have heard…"

"Mr Darcy, I would suggest you not give much credit to a resentful woman who would have done and said anything to make her point. I did not have the pleasure of knowing your parents, but usually, things are not quite as children assume. It is always the same, regardless of wealth and connections. Do not allow some spiteful words to tarnish your memories of your parents."

"Thank you for your kind advice, sir. I shall keep it in mind, though I doubt I shall be able to follow it easily."

"Here is my other suggestion. Lizzy and I should leave now. We all have a long day tomorrow, and we have already endured a horrible one today. We can see your torment, and there is no reason to detain you any longer. I believe you should speak to the admiral."

"That is truly generous of you, Mr Bennet. There is still something that I would like to give Miss Bennet... A set of jewels."

He fumbled in his pocket, so distressed that he struggled to grasp the box, as large as it was.

"Mr Darcy," Elizabeth said, gently touching his agitated hand, "I am grateful for your generosity, but I do not need jewels for tomorrow's wedding. If you wish, we may speak more tonight at dinner. Will you still join us?"

Darcy was surprised by the question, as he had completely forgotten everything else.

"Yes, of course. I look forward to meeting Mr and Mrs Gardiner. And I want to keep this fight secret from anyone else, including Bingley and my cousin."

"You may trust our secrecy, sir," Mr Bennet assured him. "I wish you all the strength to settle this matter with as little pain as possible."

Elizabeth did not say much, but in the hall, she gently touched his arm again.

While gazing after the carriage and gathering the courage to find the admiral, Darcy realised there was someone else who might bear the deepest distress: Georgiana, who Lady Catherine had accused of dishonesty. He wondered what Lady Catherine would do, and he feared the worst. With increasing worry, he wrote a note in a hurry and had it delivered by express. He would be home the following day, but it seemed an eternity until then.

Half an hour later, Darcy was sitting in a chair, watching Admiral Pembroke pacing the room. He had locked the door and instructed a servant to not allow even Bingley and the colonel to interrupt them.

"Is it true?" Darcy asked coldly.

"In a way…but not in the way Catherine presented it."

"Can the truth be presented in different ways, Admiral?"

"Yes. Only a day ago you presented the news of your engagement in a particular way, from a particular point of view. Do you remember?"

"Please do not twist my words, sir, when everything I knew about my life is about to be shattered. A day prior to my wedding, instead of looking forward to the future, I have discovered that my past has been a lie, that I have lived a deception, and everything I thought I knew was false. My entire life, I heartily believed that my parents loved and respected each other. That I was a child born from an exemplary marriage."

"Everything you knew and you lived was true, Darcy. There was no lie and no deception that affected you. You were loved by your parents, two of the most excellent people I had the honour of meeting in my life. And they shared a life of mutual respect and understanding. Of the many marriages I knew, theirs was one of the best."

"Do not repeat that, Admiral. I shall ask directly — is it true that my father kept a mistress? Yes, I know many men do. I am neither naïve nor a saint myself. It surely sounds ridiculous that at my age I am appalled by such a notion. But I never expected him to disrespect and disregard my mother's illness and keep a woman for his amusement."

"No, no, no!" Admiral Pembroke shouted, so loud that Darcy was startled.

"This is a complete falsehood, and I shall not allow you to tarnish your father's memory for even a moment with such suspicions."

Darcy stood up and paced the room together with his companion.

"Then tell me what is true, so I know which of Lady Catherine's statements was false. If she knew, it must have been public knowledge."

"No, no!" the admiral repeated. "Very well, I shall tell you.

Perhaps you should have been told a long time ago, but George insisted he would tell you at the right time. His death was so sudden that many things remained unsaid, and I did not have the strength to decide when and if I should tell you."

"Apparently, fate has intervened again and left you with no choice, Admiral. Tell me now."

"Your father and I were friends since we were at school, and we had known each other from infancy. Our families were connected, and we all were well acquainted with the Fitzwilliams too. George had always been as responsible as he was generous and kind. At that time, Pemberley was not as successful as you remember it, so George worked diligently to improve the Darcys' situation."

"All this I know, Admiral."

"Your grandfather had a niece who was also his pupil. Her name was Elinor, and she sadly died when she was ten. A sweet child who had been ill her entire life. Elinor had a governess, Miss Julia. That is what we all called her. She was the illegitimate daughter of a Colonel Morton, born in India."

"I have never heard of him."

"I imagined as much. The girl was brought to England when her mother died. The colonel provided her with a good education and a modest income, but he never officially recognised her as his daughter. When he died, Miss Julia was left alone, with an impeccable education, flawless manners, and perfect beauty, but no name and no connections. Through her father's friends, she found employment as a governess. That is how she came to Pemberley."

Darcy felt a tightness in his chest as the story unfolded. He felt like he was intruding into his father's secrets, and curiosity mixed with grief.

"Needless to say, George fell in love with Miss Julia, and it was no wonder. She was one of the most accomplished women I have ever met. She loved him too, which was still no wonder, as everybody loved him. They were both aware that such a relationship could only progress in one way, so when little Elinor died, Miss Julia left Pemberley and moved to Ramsgate. She loved the sea, George said. He rented a cottage for her as well as a house in London."

"So, their relationship continued?"

"Yes."

"But my father married my mother."

"Yes, as it was expected. Thirty years ago, their families decided that he should marry Lady Anne Fitzwilliam, the daughter of an earl who came with a substantial dowry that would be of great help in improving Pemberley's income. And it did, due to George's efforts over the years."

"So…my father loved one woman but agreed to marry another?"

"Come now, Darcy. Most men would have done the same. Let us be honest with each other. George and Anne were already friends, and the union was readily agreed upon. Everybody at the time declared it was a marriage that was to the advantage of both," the admiral concluded, and Darcy felt a sharp blade cutting his heart.

Those words had been used by the admiral when he had spoken of Darcy's marriage to Elizabeth too.

"George always treated Anne with the utmost consideration and affection. He would have done anything for her comfort, and he actually did. He never refused her anything, and when she fell ill, he found the best doctors. As for Georgiana…it was your mother's great wish to have another child. George feared that it might worsen her health, and he lamented that decision for many years."

"That is why he was always restrained with Georgiana?"

"Probably. He loved her, though. I hope you know that."

"So…my father kept this woman all those years? I assume she was a good distraction while my mother was ill," Darcy said with a bitterness he then regretted.

"Miss Julia died a few years before Lady Anne," the admiral whispered. "Catherine speaks only nonsense. She always has. She saw George with Miss Julia one day in London. They avoided the places where they could be recognised, but it was an unfortunate accident. She recognised Miss Julia and confronted George."

"Do you think she told my mother?"

"I am not sure. But even if she did…I know I might sound cynical, and you might despise me, but you know too well such arrangements are rather common. Even you might have ended up in one, if you had married Anne de Bourgh."

"That is precisely why I did not marry Anne," Darcy replied coldly.

"I admire your strength, Darcy, but the circumstances are different. Your father had not as much liberty of choice as you have now. And Miss Elizabeth's situation cannot compare to Miss Julia's."

"I did not even compare the two situations, Admiral."

"I did not imply you did. To conclude, that was a situation agreeable to all parties. No woman I know would mind her husband having such an arrangement, as long as he showed prudence and treated her properly so she could be happy within her marriage. George treated Anne more than properly. He truly tried to provide her with everything she needed."

"Except for loyalty and true love," Darcy said.

"You are being unfair, Darcy," Admiral Pembroke said severely, and Darcy laughed bitterly.

"Forgive me, sir, are we speaking of fairness? Really?"

"I do not appreciate your tone, Darcy. Neither I nor your father deserves it."

"Did my father have any children with that woman?"

"Yes." The answer came hesitantly. "A daughter. Born before George married Anne."

"A daughter? Older than me?"

"Yes."

"Is she alive? What happened to her?"

"She is very much alive. She is a widow with two small children. Her husband was one of my men. He died in battle two years ago. An exceptional officer and a gentleman, truly."

"So you have maintained an acquaintance with her all these years?"

"Yes. George asked me to."

"And where is she now?"

"She kept the two houses. George purchased them for Julia at some point."

"And what is her name?"

"Laura Moore. After her husband."

"I see."

"Try not to judge your father too harshly, Darcy. I know this has all happened so suddenly, and you are hurt and angry with him and with me."

"I am mostly hurt on behalf of my mother, Admiral. You keep saying she was happy and content and accepted the situation. How can you know that? You were my father's friend, and your loyalty was to him. You wish to believe she was happy, so you can palliate your conscience and diminish my father's guilt."

He spoke with bitterness but could not control his tone, his words, or his feelings.

The admiral paused his pacing and stared at him for a long moment. He looked hesitant, turned his back to him, paced again, and finally said, "I know because I watched over her. And because, before she died, she gave me her diary and revealed her soul to me. It was the most valuable gift I have ever received."

Darcy's astonishment increased, while the admiral seemed overwhelmed, his voice trembling and his countenance altered as if he was on the verge of tears. A desolate image of grief that Darcy had never seen before.

"You see, Darcy, Anne Fitzwilliam was the love of my life. I loved her so deeply that it hurt my soul forever. We were very young, and as a second son, I had neither the means nor the strength to fight for my love. When I gathered my courage to confess my feelings to her, I heard the news of her engagement to George. You cannot understand the pain of a broken heart until you really feel it, Darcy. When she married my best friend,

I joined the navy and went to sea."

He paused, struggling to keep speaking, and his voice became lower and weaker.

"When she gave me her diary, two days before she died, I discovered she had also loved me all her life."

Frozen in shock, Darcy stood still in the middle of the library, while Admiral Pembroke left and shut the door behind him.

Chapter 24

The discussion with the admiral left Darcy in a state of profound perturbation. The unveiled secret of his parents' marriage — a lifetime of repressed feelings disguised as happiness — was devastating and brought him to the edge of tears, which had not happened since the day his father died unexpectedly.

The admiral's turmoil at the end of his narration was heartbreaking, and seeing a friend in suffering, Darcy's first impulse was to go after him. After a few steps, though, he returned to the solitude of the library. The admiral had left his company because he did not desire it, and following him would mean disregarding his wish.

He sat in a chair, mourning over the painful revelation, but he had not much time for sadness, as the colonel and Bingley returned in an excellent disposition that opposed Darcy's dark mood. Since he did not wish to share his distress, he was forced to change his countenance and listen to their narration with apparent interest.

"The visit to Colonel Forster was quite pleasant. He seems a good man and a responsible officer, but I fear he married a woman too young and too pretty for his own good." Colonel Fitzwilliam laughed. "And it was amusing that I saw those two fools. I mentioned that you were still thinking of a way to get satisfaction from them, and I mentioned that nothing builds a man better than some time spent at war. You should have seen their faces! I would not take either of them to war, not even as bait."

"I agree," Darcy replied.

"And the Gardiners — they are a true delight. Rather young, fashionable people, handsome and witty. A pleasure to be around."

"I am glad to hear that. I shall be happy to meet them at dinner tonight."

"Darcy, I spoke to the colonel… After your wedding, I shall propose to Miss Bennet. Jane Bennet," Bingley said with an enthusiasm that at any other time would have amused Darcy.

"Congratulations. I am sure you will be very happy," he offered.

"Jane Bennet is a beautiful woman, and she seems sweet-natured and kind. And I am amused by how she looks at this young man." The colonel laughed. "You are fortunate that you can choose to marry the woman you love, Bingley."

"Very fortunate indeed," Darcy agreed.

"And you, Darcy, how have you been? How do you feel on the last day of being a single man? Miss Elizabeth and Mr Bennet returned quite quickly. Is everything settled, then?" the colonel teased him.

"I had little time to think of that. I assume I would have felt quite well if not for Lady Catherine's visit."

His two companions looked at him, puzzled, and the colonel burst out, "Lady Catherine was here? Why the… Why on earth did she come all the way here? She has lost her reason entirely."

"You know why," Darcy responded. "And indeed, she cannot see reason at all."

"I am sorry I was not here to welcome her," Bingley said. "I have not had the pleasure of being introduced to her yet."

"I doubt you will have such an opportunity any time soon. At least not from me. Today I stopped calling Lady Catherine my aunt."

"That has certainly ruined your day," the colonel uttered. "I can only imagine the fight you had."

"No, Richard, you cannot imagine. And the worst part is that Mr Bennet and Elizabeth happened to hear her. The things she said…the offences…I am amazed that Elizabeth still wishes to marry me."

"Dear Lord!" Bingley exclaimed.

"Fortunately, Elizabeth is even more astonishing than I believed. She replied to Lady Catherine as she deserved. Quite harshly, I would say, since she called her uncivil and irritating. But, to her credit, she did it graciously and even curtseyed."

Bingley and the colonel listened with their eyes and mouths open, and at the end, the colonel started to laugh.

"Now that was a moment that you will cherish your entire life. I would have done anything to witness it!"

"I am glad you were not here, Richard," Darcy answered in earnest.

"Shall we go and prepare for dinner? We must return to Longbourn in two hours. Where is the admiral?"

"Yes, we should. The admiral is in his chamber, I assume," Darcy answered.

"I have decided to stay a few more days with this young fellow, at least until he becomes engaged. I hope the admiral will remain too. He said he would."

"Very well," Darcy said, still absently. His mind was too filled with worry to even listen to what was being said. Even his joy at seeing Elizabeth was slightly shadowed. Thinking of her, before he went to his room, he took a stroll downstairs to check on the puppies, so at least he could bring her some good news.

Elizabeth sat on a chair, gazing into the mirror while her aunt Gardiner arranged her hair and they spoke of the latest events. To her amusement, Mrs Gardiner's enthusiasm almost matched her mother's.

"My dear Lizzy, I am not sure if you realise your

extraordinarily good fortune. I grew up in Lambton, only five miles from Pemberley, and I can tell you two things: Pemberley is the most wonderful estate I know — and I have seen plenty — and the Darcys were the most excellent people, everybody admired them. Lady Anne was beautiful and kind and gentle. Everybody who knew her grieved her loss. Mr Darcy was such a handsome man. I still remember him riding on his impressive stallion. He was the best master and the best landlord — people said so. At times, his son rode with him, but I can hardly remember the young master. I cannot believe I shall meet him tonight, and he will marry my niece!"

"My dear aunt, you sound like Mama!" Elizabeth laughed. "You only have to mention Mr Darcy's income of ten thousand pounds."

"It is not about his income but about you becoming part of such a wonderful family! The fact Mr Darcy proposed to you — considering all the heiresses he must know in town — is amazing. And that you refused him, and he insisted, is beyond words, truly."

While her aunt praised the Darcy family, Elizabeth recollected Lady Catherine's horrible accusations and Mr Darcy's turmoil when he asked whether she still wanted to be part of his family. Any offence Lady Catherine threw at her, Elizabeth easily dismissed. The spiteful woman had no decency and no respect for her own family.

She felt satisfied for returning the offence and equally pleased and proud of how easily Mr Darcy had entered into her game and they had united their forces to defend their union.

Elizabeth also felt sorry for Charlotte, who would have to suffer not only a life with a man whose wit was wanting but also accept Lady Catherine's rudeness and Mr Collins's worship of such a woman.

"If I could visit Pemberley in a small phaeton, with my niece as the mistress of it, I would call it a dream come true. But please, do not mention it to Mr Darcy! I do not wish him to believe we are abusing his generosity," Mrs Gardiner said.

"Dear aunt, have no worries. I promise you will visit Pemberley as much as you like. Now, let us go downstairs. I think I heard a carriage."

Elizabeth was rather unsettled while she waited for the guests. When they finally arrived, the first thing she noticed was the admiral's and Darcy's frowned countenances and their forced smiles while they were introduced to the Gardiners. They avoided looking at each other, and while both made apparent efforts to be amiable, Elizabeth had come to know them too well not to recognise the truth.

The effects of Lady Catherine's accusations had not passed yet, and the traces would probably last a long time.

The colonel and Bingley's genuine gladness accentuated the other two gentlemen's low spirits even more.

Elizabeth caught Mr Darcy's gaze a few times; he was engaged in conversation with Mrs Gardiner, while Mr Gardiner was talking to the admiral and her father. When they moved to the dinner table, she went to him directly.

"Mr Darcy, how are you feeling?"

"Reasonably well. Especially now I have seen you. I must tell you that I visited the puppies earlier. They look healthy and grow every day. I believe we could take them in two months."

"How wonderful, thank you! How sweet of you to be so thoughtful when you have so much on your mind."

"I enjoy your compliments even if I do not deserve them, Miss Elizabeth," he replied teasingly. "And how are you? I hope you feel at least half as well as you look. I know my aunt—"

"Please, do not mention it again. I feel quite well. Almost as well as my aunt, who is overjoyed to have met you," she teased him.

"I am happy to have met her, too. It is a pity we have only such a short time to get to know each other, but perhaps we can meet again when they return to London."

"I would love that, and I am sure they would too. But Admiral Pembroke? I can see he is troubled. And so are you."

"We are…but this is not the proper time or place to discuss

this. Perhaps tomorrow, during the journey to London. We shall have time and privacy to speak of anything you like."

With that, their little interlude ended. At the table, the admiral was seated between her father and Mr Gardiner, and she chose a seat close to them.

The evening passed remarkably well, much to Mrs Bennet's utter delight. She received so many compliments that she blushed all the time, like a young girl.

Elizabeth did not even attempt to approach Mr Darcy again; she was only content and grateful to watch him speaking to her uncle and aunt, as well as her mother. He appeared warm, friendly, smiling, and engaged in conversation, although she knew too well that his soul was weighed down by a heavy burden.

The next day, she would marry him, and they would travel together to London, to their new life. Alone for hours, in the carriage. Tomorrow evening, she would be in her new apartment, separated from his by only a door. She would have to wear one of the three nightgowns her aunt had purchased for her — silky, soft, and too revealing, even with a robe worn over them. Mrs Gardiner had teased her that a nightgown had to be revealing, which was probably true, since her aunt must know better than her.

She did not expect to consummate her marriage on her wedding night; of that, she was certain. However, she found herself wondering whether he would at least visit her apartment. Kiss her. Touch her. She had already enjoyed the feeling of his touch, of his lips on her hand. How would it feel on her lips? On her skin?

Such thoughts, troubling her in the middle of the dinner with her family, made her shudder and blush, even more so as she felt Mr Darcy's gaze upon her, and she feared he could guess the subject of her reverie.

The dinner ended at a reasonable hour, considering the events of the following morning, but the exhilaration remained at Longbourn.

"Upon my word, I can safely say this was the most successful dinner ever hosted in this neighbourhood," Mrs Bennet declared. "To have a colonel — the son of an earl — an admiral, Mr Darcy, and Mr Bingley all gathered round my table, and all complimenting my food, is beyond my wildest dreams. Wait until I tell my sister Phillips, Mrs Long, and Lady Lucas! I am sure they will all be at the church tomorrow, to see with their own eyes."

"It was a huge success, indeed," Mr Bennet agreed in a serious tone that puzzled his wife. "I thank you for taking such trouble all these weeks."

"Mr Bennet, are you mocking me? If you are, you should know you cannot ruin my disposition."

"I am not, Mrs Bennet, and I shall refrain from doing so again, if possible. I truly appreciate your efforts in assuring our daughters' happiness," he said. Elizabeth knew that he was serious, as well as the reason behind it, but Mrs Bennet watched her husband doubtfully, incredulously, then turned her attention to her sister Gardiner.

"It was a perfect dinner, Sister," Mrs Gardiner approved. "And I was shocked at how kind and amiable Mr Darcy is! Lizzy wrote to me last month that he was proud and disagreeable, but I saw nothing of it."

"Lizzy was wrong, Sister! And so was I! You do not know how much we despised Mr Darcy! I almost forced Lizzy to marry that horrible Mr Collins, and she was almost smitten with an officer — Mr Wickham. But all is well that ends well. I thank the Lord for that!"

"I was not smitten with anyone, and I would certainly not have married Mr Collins," Elizabeth explained. "It is true that Mr Darcy and I had a rather challenging start to our acquaintance. The behaviour of us both was wrong, and we both admitted it and are trying to make amends to remedy the errors."

"Well, since he will marry you tomorrow, he does not have to remedy anything else!" Mrs Bennet concluded. "We should go to bed now. It would not do for you to look tired and plain. He can still change his mind and leave you, you know."

"I am quite sure that will not happen," Mr Bennet intervened. "But yes, it is time to go to bed."

Even after her parents and sisters withdrew to their rooms, Elizabeth was far from desiring to rest; she spent another hour talking to her aunt. And even afterwards, although she felt exhausted, she could not sleep until dawn.

∞∞∞

At Netherfield, Bingley suggested staying up for another drink, which the colonel happily agreed to. Admiral Pembroke, however, excused himself and withdrew to his room. After a brief consideration, Darcy followed him and caught him when he was just closing the door behind him.

"What is it, Darcy? I am very tired. I need to rest."

"Forgive me. I do not want to bother you. I just wish to thank you, sir, for telling me the truth. And to apologise for my arrogant and selfish response."

The admiral hesitated for a moment, then invited him in.

"Sir, as my father's son and your friend, I felt betrayed, deceived for being kept ignorant of such an important secret. I felt like I had lost my entire childhood. If I had heard it from my father or from you, it would have been less painful than Lady Catherine's spiteful accusations."

"Yes, I realise that. I was wrong, and so was George. We should have presumed that you might find out one day."

"I know I have no right to judge my father's actions, as long as he fulfilled his duty to me and to my mother. But even though I know they are almost a custom, I cannot approve such arrangements in marriages, for too many obvious reasons that I shall not even mention. But it is an arrogance to presume I know how I would have acted if in his place in similar circumstances. Or in your place…"

"We both need time and proper consideration before we

speak of all this again, Darcy. And as much as you are hurt by the past, it cannot be changed. I would suggest that for now, you should concentrate upon the present. Upon your marriage."

"I shall…but I would appreciate it if we could speak more. There are still things that are unsettled…"

"We shall. About your father, not about me. My confession was not meant for any other living soul but you, and I shall not speak of it again."

"As you wish. And, sir, one more thing. Elizabeth heard Lady Catherine's accusations. I am sure of her discretion, but we have been open and honest with each other since we decided to marry. I would not want her to start our new life with suspicions. I would like to tell her if you approve of it. About my father, not about your secret, sir."

The admiral looked at him in silent contemplation, as though he was trying to ponder his answer.

"You may tell Miss Elizabeth whatever you find appropriate, Darcy. She will be your wife, and if you want to keep no secrets from her, I applaud you. Honesty will only help you to ensure your happiness in marriage. And I truly believe your marriage could be a happy one, not only in appearance but also in truth."

"Thank you, sir. I must also consider if and what to tell Georgiana. I fear she will be deeply hurt, but I fear even more that she might find out from another source."

"I am sure you will decide to her benefit, Darcy. Is there anything more for now?"

"No… Will you stay a few more days at Netherfield, with Richard?"

"I must. I promised Bingley, and I do not want to disappoint him."

"Admiral, when you return to London, please call on us."

"I shall send you a note when I return, Darcy. Good-night. I shall see you in the morning."

With that, Darcy was forced to leave, but he remained in the hall for a little while, to gather himself together. Then, he returned to his joyful, carefree friends and became the recipient of their teasing while they all enjoyed another drink.

Chapter 25

While Elizabeth slept little, her mother seemed to have rested well enough. She came to her room when it was barely daylight, sitting on the bed and shaking her, until Elizabeth startled and woke up with a cry.

"Mama? What has happened?" she asked with worry, not realising the time.

"Nothing has happened, my dear. I came to speak to you, as I had no time before, and your engagement was so short. Lizzy darling, do you know what is required from you as a wife? On your wedding night, I mean?"

Elizabeth felt her cheeks, neck, and ears instantly burning, while her mother looked at her with a strange expression.

"I know, Mama," she whispered. "I read books…and I spoke to Aunt Gardiner."

"Oh, good…good. My dear, you have always been a wild child, and your manners are still not suitable for a young lady. Especially one married to such an illustrious man. You must temper yourself. And keep in mind that a man like Mr Darcy… It is your duty to make him happy in any way he wants, if you understand my meaning."

Mortification left Elizabeth speechless, and she only nodded. There was nothing she could say in reply, and opening a debate with her mother would be disturbing and pointless.

"Yes, Mama."

"Keep in mind that you have been fortunate beyond words. I still wonder whether it is true. You must be grateful for your luck and be careful not to lose it."

"Yes, Mama."

"Good. Now let us get you up. You need time to make yourself beautiful. Do you have your luggage prepared?"

"Yes, Mama. Mr Darcy wants to leave immediately after the wedding ceremony. He is eager to be in London today."

"Yes, yes, of course! Do as he says! Now, let me help you. Your hair looks a fright! When you are married, you must wake up before your husband and arrange your appearance, so he does not see you in such a way."

"Yes, Mama."

"I mean, I never did that, but one cannot compare your father to Mr Darcy. Jane, you should get up too. Let us help your sister. I cannot wait to see Lady Lucas's face! I shall be at the church when Charlotte marries Mr Collins — just for comparison."

"Mama..."

"Wait here, I am going to wake up your sisters too. And sister Gardiner — she must come to help you."

With the help of Mrs Bennet, the entire house slowly awoke and turned into an uproar that gave Mr Bennet a headache and made him lock himself in the library until the time for their departure came.

As they were preparing to leave, he embraced Elizabeth tightly, which he had rarely done since she was a child. They were both tearful, as he said, "You will be deeply missed, Lizzy, but I trust that, despite the circumstances, you have found a good husband who will make you happy. A man who, in disposition and talents, will most suit you and who must love you, or else why would he insist on marrying you? I feel, my child, that this union will be to the advantage of you both, as the admiral has said several times. I trust you will do your part, my child."

"I am confident in this marriage and in Mr Darcy too, Papa. And I shall do my part!"

"Darcy has invited me to visit you any time, so you might

see me when you least expect it."

"I shall depend upon it, Papa."

They embraced again, then left the house together, as the others were already in the carriages. Minutes later, they arrived in front of the church, which was full of people, brought there by their curiosity.

When she saw Mr Darcy, Elizabeth's heart pounded, and as she stepped towards him, a sense of utter joy overwhelmed her, dissipating the last trace of worry.

With her family and friends around her, Elizabeth noticed little, as emotions overwhelmed her. She listened to the vicar, but even he and the church — both part of her life since she was born — seemed different.

When the ceremony ended, Mr Darcy led her towards their carriage, the only one leaving for London instead of Longbourn. They were still surrounded by people, all taking their farewells.

Among so many people she loved and knew she would miss, Elizabeth approached the admiral, who smiled at her.

"Congratulations, Mrs Darcy," he said.

"Thank you, Admiral Pembroke. I hope you know how grateful I am to you and how deeply I wish to thank you. I cannot find the right words now, but I shall, next time we meet."

"You may thank me by being happy, Mrs Darcy. I shall be content to watch your happiness, and Darcy's, from afar."

"I wish and pray you will be part of it, Admiral. You must promise me that, since you once claimed I saved your life, and you are in my debt."

The admiral smiled again, and Elizabeth embraced him. She felt he was taken by surprise, but then he closed his arms around her for a moment.

Mr Darcy approached them, and Elizabeth could sense both men were still awkward around each other.

"I was telling the admiral that I hope to see him soon," Elizabeth said.

"I hope so too," Mr Darcy added. "As soon as you return to

town, we should be happy for you to be our first guest for dinner, Admiral."

A brief hesitation followed, and then he said, "Thank you. I shall. You should leave now. It is getting dark very early now, and you do not want to travel at night."

"That is what I intend to do, as soon as Elizabeth has said her farewells to her family." Half an hour later, when everybody was almost frozen through, the newly married couple finally entered their carriage, leaving their friends and family behind.

For the first time in her life, Elizabeth was alone in a carriage with a man who was not her father. She felt uneasy, even though the man was her husband. He sat opposite her, looking not perfectly comfortable either.

"It is very cold, and you stayed out of doors too long," Mr Darcy said. "Your clothes and shoes are too thin for this weather."

"Usually, women's clothes and shoes are too thin for winter." She smiled. "Mama said this happens because usually, ladies stay indoors in bad weather. Except for me, of course. I have the very bad habit of wandering through the fields. Mama says that too."

"I am enchanted by your bad habit, Mrs Darcy. But I must insist you learn to ride too. As soon as we arrive at Pemberley." He was now smiling at her, and his voice was teasing. She should have felt more at ease, but the dimples that the smile revealed on his cheeks had the opposite effect.

"Insist? Have you already become demanding, Mr Darcy?"

"I have. But in return, you may insist on me doing something I do not truly enjoy."

She laughed. "That is a fair enough arrangement."

"How silly of me! You look cold. Let me wrap you in a blanket," he said. Before she had time to respond, he unfolded a soft, thick blanket and placed it around her. In doing so, he leant against her, his arms embracing her. She shivered even more, though she should have been warmer.

"Thank you," she whispered. They were silent for a little

while, then she continued.

"May I ask, what are your plans for the next few months? Shall we go to Pemberley?"

"Yes, but no sooner than May or June. Unfortunately, we shall be forced to stay in town for the Season. At least for a part of it. I believe it will be expected of Mrs Darcy."

"Your voice shows little joy. It sounds like something unpleasant or dangerous."

"It might be both," he replied, and she laughed loudly.

"Then how does it happen that so many people — both men and women — are exceedingly attached to the Season?"

"I cannot understand that," he replied so seriously that she laughed again.

"Shall I have the chance to visit my uncle and aunt when they return from Longbourn?"

"Of course! I look forward to seeing them too. I am sorry I spent so little time with them. I truly enjoyed their company."

Unwittingly, she yawned. "Forgive me, I think I am a little tired. I have barely slept the last few nights."

"I can imagine. It must have been very difficult for you after everything that happened in the last fortnight. All the torment, the sudden engagement and marriage, leaving your family — something you had not even considered before the ball."

"That is true, but I am sure it was not easy for you either."

"And then I insisted on leaving immediately after the wedding. I am afraid this journey is tiresome for you. And you will continue to have a difficult time even after we arrive in London."

"Why?"

"Our housekeeper, Mrs Clifford, has surely prepared a presentation of the servants to you. If only you can spare a few minutes while she introduces them to the new mistress."

"Oh...of course. It will be my pleasure."

"We shall have to spend some time with Georgiana too. I hope she was not too affected by Lady Catherine's visit."

"I look forward to meeting Miss Darcy, and I hope to spend a lot of time with her. But what difficult time do you mean?"

"These...the presentation of the servants and..."

"Why would that be difficult? How many people work in the house?"

"Twenty. And Mrs Clifford and the butler."

"Oh!" She was truly surprised and started to realise the size of his home. "I shall be happy to meet them all."

"You will also have to choose a maid. We may hire a new one, who is trained to be a lady's maid."

"Hire a new one? I had not even considered it. I am sure I shall find someone in the household to assist me."

"As you wish."

There was silence again; she felt uneasy, but curiosity defeated her prudence.

"Mr...Fitzwilliam, forgive me for asking...I know I should not enquire, and I do not mind if you do not answer. I was curious about...have you spoken to Admiral Pembroke?"

His expression changed, and he rubbed his temples before he replied.

"Yes. I do not mind you asking, and I shall tell if you wish to know. Although I would not reveal the story to anyone, not even to my cousin, the colonel. But I believe you should know since you heard the claims...the accusations. I must warn you — it is a painful and disturbing tale, not appropriate for a newly wedded young lady."

"Please tell me. I want to know, since I can see it still troubles you, and it has affected your long friendship with the admiral."

He looked around a few times, then finally his eyes locked with hers, and his hands rested on his thighs. Then he started to narrate, words flowing from his mouth. She did not interrupt him, only watched and listened. His turmoil was betrayed by his trembling voice, hers by her moistened eyes. When he had finished, he leant back and closed his eyes. The sorrow seemed to make it hard for him to breathe, but the weight on his shoulders seemed to have eased, and she knew he had given her part of it.

She wiped her eyes with her handkerchief, and in doing so, the blanket fell from around her.

"I am sorry for burdening you. It was selfish on my part. I warned you it was a distressing story."

"It was not distressing, only incredibly sad. It is no wonder you were so affected."

"First, I was angry, and I felt lied to…betrayed by my father and by the admiral. But then I realised it was not about me. My present suffering means little compared to the happy life I was given and to the long-lasting grief of others. My father deceived my mother, and I completely disapprove of such arrangements — I said as much to the admiral. He asked me what I would do in a similar situation. How can I know?"

"You said that your father deceived your mother, but you also said he was affectionate, respectful, and caring, and he attended to her needs."

"Yes, that is how I remember him. That is why it is hard for me to condemn him."

"If you are to condemn your father, what can I say of my father?"

"Your father? Mr Bennet?"

"Yes. I love him dearly — I am ashamed to admit I love him more than I love my mother — but I am not blind to his faults as a husband. He might not have loved other women, but I have hardly heard anything from him other than jokes and mockery. He rarely spends any time with my mother, except for dinner and breakfast. He makes sport of her all the time. He might have affection for her, but he has no respect, no consideration. She has learnt to pay him no attention. Is such a marriage any better than your parents'?"

She ended with a grieved voice and wiped her eyes again.

"As I see it, Fitzwilliam, your father was loyal to two women his whole life. He loved and respected each of them, and his heart was likely torn all the time. Would I want my husband to have such an arrangement? Certainly not," she said, averting her eyes, avoiding his gaze. "But would I want my husband to treat me as my father does my mother? Most certainly not. I cannot say what is best. I cannot say who suffers more."

∞∞∞∞

Her words left him confused, his turmoil growing even more. They were still facing each other, then slowly, he moved to sit next to her. She glanced up at him and shyly placed her head on his chest. His left arm embraced her shoulders, while his right hand tried to pull the blanket back over her.

"You should cover us both with the blanket," she whispered. "I am sure it will be warmer that way."

He obeyed, and she edged closer to him. The blanket was like a sweet trap, keeping them together, their bodies brushing against each other with the movement of the carriage.

After a while, she put her hands around his waist, first reluctantly, then more daringly. And only then did she sigh with contentment. He smiled to himself and gently tightened his embrace. He felt her shivering and asked, "Are you cold?"

"No. I am warm...perfectly warm. Fitzwilliam, will you tell Georgiana?"

"I am not sure. I know I should, but I do not know how and when. Will you help me?"

"Always."

"There is also something more I must tell you about Georgiana, but it can wait. It is not urgent, since it is in the past and has no consequences."

"As you wish. What about..." She paused and glanced up at him again.

"Yes?"

"What about Miss Julia's daughter? Your father's daughter?"

"I understand she has a comfortable life. I cannot think about her any more at the moment."

"You should do what makes you comfortable. What satisfies your heart and honour."

He said nothing further, only held her tight, and she seemed to find peace in his arms. Soon enough, he felt her breathing steadily, and he understood she had fallen asleep. He breathed in her scent, his heart filled with love for her, and allowed her to sleep, barely moving until the carriage stopped in front of their townhouse.

Chapter 26

"Elizabeth? We are home," he whispered.

She woke up, slightly confused, looking around. Through the window, she saw an impressive building, lit by several torches. The coachman had already opened the carriage door, so the noise from London's busy streets broke the silence. She felt she had slept but could not believe it had been for long.

"How do I look?" she asked, unsettled and slightly worried again. He smiled and arranged her bonnet, his fingers touching a rebellious lock of hair that had escaped from it.

"You look lovely, Mrs Darcy," he said. Stepping down, she took his arm. After sleeping in his arms, his nearness was soothing her nervousness, which increased with each step.

The door opened, and her eyes fell on a large hall. The first thing she noticed was a beautiful young woman, with an older one by her side, and she knew it must be Georgiana Darcy.

Steps behind, the butler, the housekeeper, and the rest of the servants were waiting in line. Mr Darcy greeted them and made the introductions: Georgiana, Mrs Annesley, Stevens, Mrs Clifford.

The housekeeper greeted Elizabeth ceremoniously and asked for the favour of introducing the servants to her. She thanked and took a step forwards, finally releasing her husband's arm. One by one, the servants were presented, as well as their roles. Elizabeth nodded and smiled, trying to remember their names.

"I thank you all for the warm reception," Mr Darcy said. "It is very much appreciated. We are a little tired from the road, but in the next few days, Mrs Darcy and I shall speak to each of you. Please return to your duties now."

The servants slowly withdrew, including the butler; only Mrs Clifford remained.

"Will you have dinner now?" she asked.

"Yes. In half an hour would be perfect. I shall just show Mrs Darcy her apartment."

When all the servants were gone, Darcy turned to his sister again, and she hurried to embrace him.

"Oh Brother, I am so happy you are home! And you too, Mrs Darcy!"

"I am delighted to finally meet you, Miss Darcy. I have heard so many wonderful things about you!"

"And I about you, Miss Bennet. I looked forward to meeting you. Oh, forgive me, Mrs Darcy," the girl said, turning crimson, then pale.

"Please do not worry. I still think of myself as Miss Bennet." Elizabeth smiled. "And I still call my husband sir and Mr Darcy."

"We all need a little time to adjust to each other," Darcy interjected. "Let us start with dinner and a little bit of conversation, and that will do for tonight."

∞∞∞

Two hours later, Elizabeth was alone in her apartment, marvelling at the beauty around her.

Mr Darcy had introduced her to the mistress's suite, but she had barely looked at it, so anxious she felt. After changing her clothes, having a lovely dinner and coming to know her new sister a little better, she felt more composed and could enjoy herself a little more.

She admired the walls, the furniture and the carpets,

and all the elegant and harmonious arrangements. She knew Mr Darcy was only steps away, behind the door that kept drawing her attention. He had been warm, friendly, and considerate during dinner, helping her and Georgiana to become accustomed to each other. By the second course, Mr Darcy was smiling more than usual, Georgiana was trying to overcome her shyness, and Mrs Annesley displayed perfect manners and a gift for conversation. Elizabeth felt almost her usual self until the dinner ended and he escorted her back to her apartment for the night.

A young maid, Janey, likely younger than her, was assigned to serve her that evening, Mrs Clifford mentioning that next morning she would wait for the mistress's instructions in regard to her personal maid.

In truth, Elizabeth felt even more nervous than the maid looked, but she tried to put the girl at ease, while Janey helped her bathe and change for the night. She dismissed the maid, and then she sat on a chair, staring at her image. She was now Mrs Darcy. Not his wife but Mrs Darcy. His promise sounded clear in her mind, but since then, many things had happened. And the intimacy they had shared in the carriage, opening their hearts and minds to each other, sharing distress and comforting each other, had melted her heart. She did not examine her feelings carefully enough to determine and voice the nature of her feelings for him, but she knew that she would not oppose him coming to her that night if he proposed it.

"Elizabeth?"

She had not heard him entering, so she was startled and stood up when she saw him at the door.

"Forgive me. I do not wish to intrude. I have just come to see how you feel. I shall leave you now."

She suddenly became aware of her revealing nightgown, seeing him dressed in trousers, an unbuttoned shirt, and a robe.

"No, please do not leave!" she said, and her voice embarrassed her. He seemed surprised too but stepped in.

"Were you pleased with Janey's service?"

"Oh yes, very much so! She seems kind and respectful. I was very pleased."

"And do you like your apartment?"

"Who would not like it? It is perfect," she whispered, glancing around the room. "Just perfect…"

"I am glad you approve of it. Would you like to see my apartment?"

She blushed, but his voice was calm and friendly, and she found herself nodding.

He opened the adjoining door widely, and she looked inside. At first glance, the apartment seemed similar to hers, only the furniture was of a darker colour and with more sharp, manly lines.

"Would you like a glass of wine?" he asked, still tentative. "It will help you sleep."

"Oh…if you say so…yes, please."

He smiled, returned to his room, and came back with a bottle and two glasses. They sat around a small table by the window. The curtains were drawn, but the noise from the street could still be heard.

"If you need anything, just ring for a maid," he said.

"I do not need anything else for now," she said, sipping from her glass. She licked her lips and felt his gaze upon them.

"The wine is very good, but I might become dizzy from it."

"If you do, you will sleep and rest till tomorrow."

"I slept all the way to London. It must have been uncomfortable for you," she said, blushing at the recollection.

"Quite the contrary; It was the most pleasant journey I ever had," he answered, and she only sipped more wine so she could blame it for her red cheeks.

"Elizabeth, if you are not too tired, may I give you something? I wished to offer it to you two days ago before my aunt's unfortunate visit changed my plans."

"Of course…but you do not need to give me—"

"Yes, I do."

He hurried to his room again and brought back a black

velvet box, which he placed on the table before her eyes. Under her amazed gaze, he opened the box, and Elizabeth gasped, covering her mouth with her hand.

It was a set of jewellery in gold and emeralds — necklace, earrings, and bracelet — so beautiful that she did not dare breathe, much less touch them.

"It was meant for Mrs Darcy, but my mother never wore it. She used to say she did not feel strong or bold enough for these stones."

Elizabeth was silenced in awe, and he continued, emotions altering his voice.

"She gave me the box when she was already in her sick bed. I must have been fifteen or sixteen years old, and Georgiana was only an infant. She told me to choose my wife with my mind and my heart and to find a woman with so much heart and spirit that these jewels would suit her."

Elizabeth looked at him, unable to speak or move.

"That is how I knew my mother never wanted me to marry my cousin Anne. I remember her bits of advice, her words of comfort…" he said, then he stopped and turned his back to her, overcome by sorrow.

"Forgive me. It is hard for me to speak of her, especially now, after…"

"Please do not apologise," she said, taking his hands in hers. Then daringly, she released one of her hands to gently touch his face. He turned his head and placed a kiss in her palm.

"The moment I began to fall in love with you, Elizabeth, my heart knew you were the woman suited for these stones and for me, only my mind needed more time to accept it."

"Fitzwilliam…" she whispered tearfully.

"No, please, do not cry, and do not feel the pressure of my confession. I am well aware that your feelings were different from mine and still are. If fate had not forced us, I would have probably needed more time to propose. Perhaps months. But I would have taken this step eventually. I wonder if you would have still rejected me," he ended teasingly.

"I might have if my feelings would not allow me to accept. But they did, even if the timing of the proposal was forced. I believe the admiral played a small role too. He spoke to me after my rejection, and then we met in the woods… I kept wondering why he insisted on my marrying you when such a marriage was surely only to my benefit."

"He likely insisted because somehow he knew what my mother wanted for me," Darcy responded. He then took her hand, and with their entwined fingers, he caressed the glowing jewels.

"Elizabeth, do you like the jewels? Do you like emeralds?"

"I have never worn emeralds before, nor have I ever touched one," she confessed. "These are beautiful."

"Would you allow me?" he asked, taking the necklace.

She nodded, and he gently wrapped it around her neck. His hand lingered on her skin, and she shivered at the touch of the gold and of his fingers.

"I barely dare breathe," Elizabeth admitted. "How can I ever dare to wear them?"

"Because you have the heart, the boldness, the strength, and the spirit to wear them, Elizabeth. They belong to you."

She truly held her breath, gazing at him from only inches away. The necklace was cold, but it was not the reason why she shivered. She touched it on her neck, while he was still watching her.

Then she raised herself up on her toes, and with shy daring, she pulled his head down a little and touched her lips to his.

The gentle touch was as soft as a barely felt breeze, but it made her dizzy and weak in the knees. She put her hands around his waist, waiting for something that did not come. She opened her eyes and met his gaze, darkened by repressed feelings.

Slowly, his lips returned to hers, and she sighed, leaning closer to him. His arms closed around her, and as his tender kiss turned more passionate, her lips opened for him. The savouring of each other's taste made them both gasp, and Elizabeth felt herself lifted and carried to the bed. Lying against the pillows, her arms encircled his neck, she felt his weight on her, and his lips started a sweet assault over hers. She felt lost, dizzy, and frightened by the sudden waves of warmth inside her.

"Fitzwilliam, please," she managed to whisper, and he suddenly stopped, immediately standing up. She still struggled to catch her breath, and apparently so did he.

"I am very sorry...so very sorry, Elizabeth...I did not mean... Please forgive me. I shall leave you now. You may lock the door."

He turned to leave, his embarrassment apparent, but she called to him while trying to arrange her gown.

"Please, do not leave! I do not want you to leave! I just wanted to...I could not breathe," she said, lowering her eyes in shame. She heard him walking back but spoke further, still avoiding his eyes.

"I have never...you know...and never imagined a kiss could be so..."

She finally lifted her eyes to him to say, "You may stay if you want. I know you promised, but...I would not oppose it."

Her embarrassment was too strong for her to continue, and she lowered her eyes again. He sat next to her, taking her hands in his.

"Elizabeth, please look at me. There is nothing I want more than to stay. And I know you would not oppose it. I would do everything I could for you to...enjoy it..."

His hoarse voice, as well as the words he did not say but implied, made her quiver again.

"But I shall leave now and let you rest. You are tired, exhausted by the torment of the last few days, by the journey, by my confession, by the wine, by the kiss. That is why I shall leave."

She nodded, and he gently kissed her hands.

"You know, Elizabeth, the moment when your lips touched mine...I have never felt so much pleasure, so much joy before. It made me dizzy too."

She smiled, slowly regaining some composure, her hands

still in his.

"This necklace," he said, gently touching it again. "It looks even brighter than usual on your skin. And so do your eyes. Good-night, dearest, loveliest Elizabeth."

He left, and she gazed at the closed door for a few moments, then she blew out the candles, took off the necklace, and lay down on the bed, pulling the blankets over her. The blankets were many, thick, and soft, and the fire was burning, but she still did not feel as warm and comfortable as she had felt in the carriage, in his arms.

Chapter 27

On the second day of her marriage, Elizabeth woke up late. She needed a moment to realise where she was, to recognise the luxurious room, and to remember what had happened on the previous day and night.

She saw the box of jewels on the table, and the memories returned with all the pleasure and the anxiety she had felt. The trace of Mr Darcy's caresses, his scent, the taste of his lips, so strong yet so soft, which had made her as dizzy as the wine. She had wanted him to stay, she had asked him to, but he had still left, while his profession of love had warmed her heart.

She wondered where he was when she realised she missed him.

She left the bed and rang for the maid; Janey entered shortly and greeted her shyly, helping her to prepare for the day.

"The master and Miss Darcy are already in the parlour, waiting for you," the maid said.

She hurried downstairs, looking around as she could not precisely remember the direction, and finally found her husband and sister-in-law. Mr Darcy came to her, took her hand, and kissed it. Her eyes met his, and warmth spread through her body.

"Breakfast is ready," he said. "We shall be only the three of us today. Mrs Annesley will not join us. I was just talking to Georgiana about Lady Catherine's visit and how you responded to her offences."

"Nobody has ever responded in such a way to Lady

Catherine," Georgiana said in a low voice, as if the lady could hear her.

"I am not particularly proud of myself, but there are times when my temper betrays me," she said.

"Which I found enchanting," Mr Darcy declared, and his sister chuckled. "And speaking of Lady Catherine, I have received a note from Lord Matlock. He has expressed his apologies on behalf of his sister and assured us that he and my aunt are looking forward to meeting you."

"How kind of him," Elizabeth said, not without an inward sigh of relief. She was certain the Matlocks had not approved of the marriage either, but she was grateful for their politeness and acceptance, as reluctant — or even insincere — as it might be. Placing Mr Darcy in conflict with his entire family was still something she feared.

During breakfast, the conversation was varied. Mr Darcy encouraged Elizabeth to think of what she would like to do on her first day in London, even though the weather was cold and cloudy. Afterwards, Georgiana left to practise the pianoforte, and Elizabeth found herself alone with Mr Darcy.

"Did you sleep well?"

"I did. Quite late, I am afraid. It is not my habit," she replied.

"Yes, I know. You are used to waking up very early and taking morning walks," he said, much to her amusement.

"And you, sir? Fitzwilliam?"

"Well enough. Would you like to join me in the library? There is something I wish to speak to you about. Privately."

"Of course. In truth, I am looking forward to seeing the library," she said.

"I imagined as much. If you approve, later today we can have a tour of the house, so you can become properly acquainted with it."

"I would like that very much. Would it be possible for me to speak to Mrs Clifford again today? I felt she went to so much trouble to welcome us, and I barely exchanged a few words with her."

"It would be very kind of you, though she is well paid to take so much trouble." Darcy smiled as he opened the door, inviting Elizabeth into the library.

She gasped with surprise, her face beaming with delight.

"This is beautiful! Stunning!" she whispered. "So many volumes! Such a rich collection! Papa would be thrilled to see it."

Her enthusiasm made Darcy smile.

"I hope he will — soon. This library and the one at Pemberley, which is even larger and richer. Come, please sit down. There is something I wish to speak to you about."

"Nothing else has happened, I hope?" she asked, worried.

"No. Last night I could not actually sleep, so I spent the time thinking."

"Oh?" she replied.

"I mostly thought of you," he confessed, his smile twisting the corner of his lips. The lips whose taste Elizabeth still remembered, making her cheeks feel warm.

"Not in *that* way," he said. "Not *only* in *that* way," he added, and her eyebrow arched in challenge.

"Mr Darcy, you have become dangerously fond of teasing, sir. You should know I might retaliate, since you know I am proficient at it."

"I am counting on it, Mrs Darcy. But some of my thoughts were quite serious. I remembered what you said in the carriage in regard to Miss Julia's daughter. My sister. Now that I know about her, I cannot do nothing for her."

The gravity of the subject changed his tone.

"I plan to speak to the admiral and ask for a meeting. Would you come with me?"

The question and its meaning, as well as his worried expression, touched Elizabeth.

"Of course! I am glad and grateful that you asked me."

"I shall not tell Georgiana at first. She is too young and has faced too many problems this year. If necessary, I shall allow her to meet Laura Moore s a simple acquaintance. But not until after

Christmas. We shall see. Until then, I wish to avoid anything that might disturb us. I want to enjoy your company...and to court you, if you will allow me."

She looked at him for a sign that he was jesting, but there was none.

"Court me? But we are married, sir, in case you had forgotten."

"We might well be, madam, but I have not courted you yet," he said, bringing her hand to his lips.

"Then by all means do so if you wish, Mr Darcy. I would by no means suspend any pleasure of yours, sir."

"Nor I yours, madam," he replied, his eyes locked with hers and her hand still near his lips. "And I shall start with something that I know you enjoy, although most people would loathe it in this weather. Would you like a walk in Hyde Park, Mrs Darcy? I would be happy to accompany you."

Her eyes brightened with mirth. "You know my preferences too well, Mr Darcy. That is something I would never refuse."

"I only know some of your preferences, Mrs Darcy, but I strive to discover many more."

The private meeting in the library on the second day of their married life marked the beginning of a strange and delightful mixture of courtship, teasing, and exploration, combined with serious work and learning, sharing knowledge, and acquiring responsibilities. Under Mr Darcy's supervision, Elizabeth started to discover the size of her husband's wealth and of his obligations to the people under his protection. She was eager to learn and willing to put all the effort needed into it, as she had promised. She assumed her role as the mistress of the house, learning her duties and how to fulfil them. She became accustomed to the house — her home — as well as to the people in their service, and she quickly obtained Mrs Clifford's approval, which spread to the other servants.

Elizabeth also spent important time with Georgiana, with whom she formed a strong friendship and whose talent at the pianoforte humbled her, as she confessed to Mr Darcy. On the third day of their marriage, Colonel Fitzwilliam returned from Netherfield, bringing the news that Mr Bingley had finally proposed. Together with the colonel, Lord and Lady Matlock, as well as their eldest son, called to congratulate Mr and Mrs Darcy. The meeting was rather short and slightly awkward, but it was the first step towards an amicable relationship, and it ended with an invitation for Elizabeth and Georgiana to have tea with Lady Matlock.

Admiral Pembroke returned to London and sent a note, as he had promised, but he declined Darcy's invitation to dinner, claiming he had some business to see to. Darcy replied, expressing his intention of meeting Mrs Laura Moore at a time that was convenient to her.

For Darcy and Elizabeth, the days were busy and allowed them little opportunity for privacy. His courtship was tender, considerate, and proper, despite the fact that they were already married. They walked together every day, regardless of the weather, and often came home wet and frozen, then warmed themselves by the fire, with a cup of tea and conversation. Their little games involved kisses, touches, teasing — everything that was allowed for betrothed couples but still innocent considering they were already married.

However, their intimacy increased every day, and their bond grew stronger while their relationship enhanced.

On the seventh day after their wedding, Darcy astounded Elizabeth by offering her — in the middle of the winter — a bouquet of bright yellow roses. She thanked him tearfully, then offered him a tender, sweet kiss, as she was now used to doing. This time, however, her lips lingered on his for longer, while her arms encircled his waist.

Tender at first, the kiss deepened, and her lips parted,

while she struggled to breathe. The shock of his tongue testing, parting, and conquering her lips, shook her. A sigh of delight escaped her, which only increased his boldness. She gasped and held her breath when she felt his tongue slipping inside, taking possession of her mouth. The intimacy of the gesture made her heart skip a beat; she felt almost frightened by such an intimate gesture and by the novelty of the sensations that were growing inside her.

And then, a sudden yet strong knock on the door made them stop, bewildered, breathless, glancing at each other.

"What is it?" Darcy shouted.

"Sir, forgive me," the valet replied, "Admiral Pembroke is here. He says there is an important matter he wishes to discuss with you urgently."

Darcy glanced at Elizabeth, then placed a few small kisses in her hair. With few words, he offered her his arm, and they walked together, finding the admiral in the library.

The gentleman's countenance showed a deep tiredness, dark circles around his eyes, and a pallor that worried Elizabeth. The man she had known only a month ago was nowhere to be seen.

The admiral greeted them, kissed Elizabeth's hand, and then asked them to sit.

"What I am about to tell you is a matter of the greatest importance. I have come to discuss this with you, Darcy, so you find out from me and not from others. I feel I owe you as much. However, please know that, regardless of your opinion, the matter is settled already."

He paused a little, then continued.

"I was pleased to receive your note, Darcy. It is to your credit that you wish to meet Laura. She was flattered and moved by your generosity. I shall introduce her to you, and I hope you will come to appreciate her and to treat her as a friend. Even as a relative," he said, and Darcy frowned.

"Not as a sister but as a friend," Admiral Pembroke continued. "You see, I have been thinking about this for a long,

long time, but I kept delaying my decision, until Catherine's indiscretion brought everyone so much pain and distress. Now, since you already know the truth, I have spoken to Laura, and she at first refused my proposal. It required much effort and persuasion and reference to her children to convince her to finally accept it."

"Proposal? Do you wish to marry her?" Darcy asked, his eyes wide with shock.

"No, I wish to recognise her as my lawful daughter and give her the chances that she and her children are entitled to," Admiral Pembroke said, while two pairs of eyes stared at him in shock.

"Nobody but us will know the truth. I shall never marry and have children, so no one else will be affected by this. I shall make the public announcements and sign all the necessary papers."

"I assume my opinion does not matter, but did she agree? Miss Moore?" Darcy replied.

"Your opinion does not matter to me more than you cared about others' opinions when you decided to marry Elizabeth. I have no doubts that both of us are doing the right thing to ensure our future peace and happiness."

Chapter 28

T he admiral did not stay long; he presented his story and left, while Elizabeth and Darcy remained stunned, bewildered, looking at each other.

They continued to discuss the matter, although there was little to be said. It was obvious that the admiral had considered the matter for longer than the last week, and his decision was not to be changed.

Until dinner, they spoke of little else; even Jane's engagement to Bingley was given little attention, and they only changed the subject when they were joined by Georgiana and Mrs Annesley.

Darcy was thoughtful the entire evening, and Elizabeth felt his pain. He seemed torn between what the admiral thought was right and what his conscience dictated to him.

When they retired for the night, Darcy was still distressed; they separated at the door to her chamber, and then later on, he came to say good-night, as was his custom. Elizabeth was looking at the roses that seemed to smile from their vase, and she smiled at her husband.

"This was not quite a merry anniversary. It seems I am not proficient at courtship." He smiled bitterly.

"It might have not been merry, but it was happy. I am happy, Fitzwilliam, although I know you are now sad."

He embraced her, and she leant her head against his chest.

"I am happy too, Elizabeth. This week since you have been my wife has brought me joy, peace, and hope. I am glad to hear you are happy too."

"Did you doubt it? Could you not see that I was happy? Could you not feel it?"

"I could, but I still feared that I might be assuming more than there was, as I have done before."

"You cannot assume more, as there is already so much," she replied, taking a step away from him so she could see his face.

Then she stepped completely away, and he was ready to leave her, but she blew out the candles, one by one, until only the light of the fire remained in the room. She returned, looked at him again, and placed her arms around him.

"I have been married to you for seven days, but I am not your wife yet. I wish to be, with all my heart. I am not tired, nor dizzy from the wine, but I would like to become dizzy from your kisses," she whispered, her daring words making even her shiver.

He was standing still, looking at her, while her eyes sparkled at him. She removed her robe, and the nightgown revealed her arms, her shoulders, her neck, and her hair falling loosely down her back in heavy curls.

"I am already dizzy, and I have not even touched you yet," he said.

"Please do so," she whispered, sighing with pleasure when his arms imprisoned her, carrying her towards the bed. He set her down against the pillows, while his eyes never released hers.

"I wish nothing more than to be your husband, Elizabeth. I have wanted it for a long time and dreamt of it so often."

His lips captured hers gently, tasting them, but the thirst soon turned from tenderness into a fervour that left both breathless, and only the need for air separated them.

He looked at her as she was lying still, her eyes closed. He leant closer, inhaling her scent, kissing her eyelids.

"Elizabeth? Please look at me, my love."

She smiled shyly, breathing irregularly.

"You must tell me what you wish me to do," she

whispered.

He covered her face with kisses and tantalised her ear, then his lips rested upon hers.

"Nothing special, unless you want to. Or you would do better to tell me what you want me to do..."

She shivered, her heart racing, and leant closer, his body almost crushing her. He supported his weight on his elbows, looking at her from only inches away. Their bodies brushed against each other through the thin fabric of their night clothes.

Their eyes held, their lips almost touching, and she entwined her fingers in his hair.

His lips returned to caress her face, her jaw, her throat; then he stopped and looked at her again.

"I have dreamt of kissing you so many times," he said.

"You have already," she said, breathless.

"Not as I would wish to." He smiled. His face was so near, and she admired his handsome features as he whispered, "You are so beautiful..."

His lips finally met hers, and she abandoned herself to him. She let out a small cry when she felt his legs parting hers and resting between them. He stopped again, looking at her for a sign of disapproval which did not come. Then he pulled up her nightgown, brushing over her thighs, while the passion and eagerness of his kiss never ceased.

He rolled from atop her and removed his shirt, and her eyes gazed at his bare chest. He took her hand and kissed her fingers, her palm, and her wrist, then along her arm to her shoulder, where he lingered for a moment. The sweet exploration continued along her neck, down to her throat, and then he stopped and looked at her again. She gulped for a little air and licked her lips. His eyes held hers as his fingers slowly and gently brushed over her breasts. Her back arched, while she moaned with surprise and pleasure. His hand touched, felt, and caressed the softness of her breasts, closing upon each of them with possessive tenderness. There was no haste in his movements, only a sweet, slow torture that made her head spin.

His hand travelled gently along her body, sliding down along her ribs, lingering on her belly, then caressing her hips. Her body quivered, and her fingers tightened in his hair while his lips found hers again.

She struggled to breathe as his eyes locked with hers, but she could not bear his stare for too long. A smile she had not seen before twisted his lips, and she closed her eyes when his fingers caressed her breasts again, sending waves of warmth through her.

She heard her husband groaning, and she felt his caresses on her thighs. She realised she was now completely naked, and the caresses returned to her lower body, making her lose any coherent thought.

"You are so beautiful," he whispered, kissing her face while his hand continued its conquest. His strokes tantalised her legs some more, then, to her shock, his hand moved higher, to the spot that burned her the most. Her back arched, and her moans increased when his hand began to move, first gently then more daringly.

"I want to kiss you," he whispered, and she wondered what he meant, since he had kissed her so many times already. He showed her a moment later, when his mouth hungrily tasted every inch of her skin that his hand had already caressed.

A trail of warm kisses encircled her breasts, his lips closing upon the soft hardness to capture it. Elizabeth cried out and bit her lip; every stroke left her wanting more, every touch gratified a deep, burning need inside her, sending waves of pleasure through her body. She could not and wished not to open her eyes and meet his gaze.

"Please look at me, my love," he whispered, but she needed some time to gather herself.

"I have dreamt of you so many times. I have dreamt of this," he said.

"I have never dreamt...never imagined this," she admitted.

He tenderly tasted her lips again, while his hands eagerly

touched and caressed her softness. Soon enough, he abandoned her mouth and travelled back to her breasts, while his hand climbed back down to the warmth of her thighs, and she moaned even before she felt his touch. But nothing could have prepared her for the shock of feeling the softness of his lips on the soft spot between her thighs or the unbearable pleasure that overwhelmed her.

He gently conquered her until she knew nothing else and shuddered violently under the countless chills that burned her skin.

Her senses finally returned, but her entire body still trembled. His hands, strong but tender, cupped her face, kissing her tenderly. His gaze darkened when he whispered, "You are becoming my wife now."

He moaned, and her heart nearly stopped as he entered her and his body finally joined with hers, breaking the last barrier between them.

Her nails dug into his back, and she cried out again, while her body stiffened in pain.

He stopped, remained still inside her, and kissed her face. His hands gently caressed her, helping her to calm and relax.

"Does it hurt?"

"Only a little. I knew it would. Please do not stop."

His hands glided between their bodies, caressing the parts of her that already craved his touch. She felt him inside her, invading her body with his passion.

"This is so perfect," he groaned while his thrusts shook her body, gently, slowly at first, then became more intense, stronger, harder, eager, faster.

The pain increased, then dissipated, mixed with a pleasure that slowly enveloped her entire body. His mouth trapped hers, his tongue moistening her swollen, dry lips while her moans mixed with his, her soft cries with his deep groans.

Her hands tightened on his back while her body began to move beneath him, and she completely lost herself until he finally reached the long-desired moment, shuddering in release and spreading warm waves inside her trembling body.

"You are my wife now," he whispered, long moments later, when they could breathe again.

"I am your wife. My body is now yours, as my heart has already been for a while."

He looked at her, incredulous, caressing her beautiful face.

"I know my feelings very well now, Fitzwilliam. Not from tonight but from before. Even when I accepted your proposal, you had my heart, but I did not know it."

She touched his hand and smiled at her own recollections. "When we danced at Netherfield, I knew your touch was something I had never felt before. I believe I knew it even before that, but I could not recognise nor admit it. After all, you called me tolerable and refused to dance with me, remember?"

Chapter 29

On the seventh day of their marriage, Elizabeth and Darcy finally became husband and wife. The following morning found them sleeping soundly, tightly embraced, in Elizabeth's bed. Unlike other mornings, neither Janey nor the valet were summoned until later.

To anyone who observed them, the change brought about by their completed union was visible.

Colonel Fitzwilliam, who came to visit again, and even Georgiana complimented Elizabeth on looking more beautiful than ever, without either of them suspecting the reason for the change, or for Elizabeth's violent blushing.

The fulfilment of their love — finally admitted and acknowledged — brought them a new level of happiness, with no further restraint between them.

In the days that followed, their usual activities were interrupted by little interludes when they would disappear from company to enjoy their privacy. Also, they retired earlier in the evenings and woke later in the mornings than in their first week of marriage.

To Darcy, Elizabeth's passionate nature — which he had recognised before — was slowly revealed day by day. He had once believed that he loved her ardently, but the time he spent with her showed him what ardently truly meant. He learnt it at the same time as her because, despite his experience as a man of the world, his feelings for Elizabeth, the sensations he experienced with her, he had never felt before.

Every day that passed made Darcy wonder about the joy he had felt since Elizabeth had been by his side. His concern about her feelings for him was all gone, as she told him, showed him, and proved to him how she felt every day. Besides their shared passion — about which he teased her saying she had learnt as quickly and diligently as she had learnt everything else — there were countless small things that he would not have even noticed before.

He became accustomed to viewing his life as 'before' and 'after'. Meeting Elizabeth and falling in love with her had been a turning point in his life. Her company brought him immense pleasure, whether it was in the intimacy of their apartment, in the library, or in the music room while Georgiana was playing. He just loved to be with her. He could see Georgiana's amazement at the way he spoke to Elizabeth, at their teasing, and his dear sister needed a little while to become accustomed to his new manners.

The growing friendship between Elizabeth and Georgiana had extinguished one of his other concerns. His wife's friendly nature and kind heart had encouraged Georgiana to open up to her, and only a few days after she met Elizabeth, she confirmed to him that she had already begun to feel like she had a sister.

In one of their moments of privacy, Darcy told Elizabeth about the failed elopement.

"You should have hunted Wickham down that moment, just as the admiral said," she uttered at the end of the story, with a deep resentment that amused Darcy. He placed a kiss on her eyes, which were narrowed in anger. He knew she spoke in earnest, but since the scoundrel had left England, Darcy could treat his distressing memory with more leisure than he used to. It was the last time Wickham was mentioned between them.

About the other culpable officers, Darcy had not much news. His rage and desire for satisfaction and revenge slowly dissipated, as he considered the bliss that the miscreants' indiscretions had brought to him.

The news from Hertfordshire was all good and came

regularly. Bingley's engagement to Jane, described in his letters, which were written carelessly as usual, both amused Darcy and touched his heart. He had no doubt that his friend would find his own felicity in his marriage and was overjoyed for him, just as Elizabeth was for her sister. Darcy teased his wife, saying that the Bingleys would be the second happiest couple in the world but a significant way behind the Darcys. To such a statement, Elizabeth agreed with sparkling eyes.

Bingley decided to remain at Netherfield for Christmas and only returned to town in January. Their wedding was set for the beginning of March, and all the Darcys were eager to attend. Bingley's sisters did not return to keep him company at Netherfield. They also avoided Darcy, and they only met once, by chance, when he was enjoying a walk with Elizabeth. Their fierce glares and cold politeness in greeting them was more laughable than upsetting. With Hurst, Darcy had a most cordial encounter at his club on the only day when he joined his uncle and cousins there, leaving Elizabeth at home with Georgiana. After only one hour, he missed his wife so much that even he laughed at himself and hurried back to her.

Before Christmas, Lady Matlock invited them to dinner, and he accepted, knowing it was another small step towards Elizabeth being recognised as part of the family. He also knew that the admiral must have had something to do with it, and he was grateful to him once again. Admiral Pembroke did not attend dinner and did not visit Darcy again. During his brief call, he had looked like a changed man, as though bringing back the past had altered his present. The friendship that Darcy had always cherished and the affection he had felt from the admiral all his life were now changed and missed.

His growing love for Elizabeth helped Darcy to better understand the anguish the admiral had suffered for twenty years, loving a woman who was married to his best friend, and the excruciating pain he must have felt when he read her diary and found he had her love too, only to lose it for good days after.

He also looked at his father's life with less severity. The

first person who had offered him a different perspective was Elizabeth, on their journey to London, when she spoke of her parents' marriage. Most of the marriages he knew were either like his parents' or the Bennets' or somewhere in between. Being blessed with a different sort of union made him more generous with his compassion and more restrained in his judgments.

The dinner at the Matlocks' was as he expected.

The colonel was there, amiable and supportive. His uncle and aunt, as well as the viscount and his wife, displayed rather cold politeness; they asked Elizabeth questions, which she answered lightly, with wit and confidence. There were small details that could have offended Elizabeth, and Darcy immediately noticed, but Elizabeth wisely chose to disregard them, just as she elegantly overlooked any reference to Lady Catherine.

"As forgiving and kind as Elizabeth might be, I shall never forget Lady Catherine's behaviour. I have only one aunt now, and nothing will change that. I shall not permit anyone to offend my wife, and if I must choose between my wife and anyone else, my decision is clear and easy," Darcy declared with repressed anger when his uncle tried to justify Lady Catherine's behaviour.

His outburst almost ruined the dinner, but Elizabeth and the colonel masterfully changed the subject and turned the conversation down a less dangerous path.

When they returned home, in the comfort of their apartment, Elizabeth told him that she understood the Matlocks' reluctance to accept a stranger who had suddenly become Mrs Darcy and taken a place so desired by many.

Christmas was a rather small, intimate affair. It was only Darcy and his wife, Georgiana, and Mrs Annesley. The Gardiners were still at Longbourn, the colonel had other plans, and the admiral refused the invitation, mentioning he already had a fixed engagement — one which Darcy believed he could guess.

Elizabeth wore the emerald and gold set and shone in it, but to him, her eyes were brighter than the jewels, and he knew — she told him as much — that it was her happiness that made them sparkle.

On Boxing Day, together with Elizabeth, he offered the usual gifts to his servants, and afterwards, they took a long walk through the frozen and empty Hyde Park. They returned home cold, dirty, their shoes and clothes wet, and warmed themselves in each other's arms until they fell asleep in delightful tiredness.

Three days after Christmas, Darcy received an invitation for him and Elizabeth to Admiral Pembroke's house. He knew the reason, and emotions overwhelmed him, as he confessed to Elizabeth. He needed time to prepare for a meeting that would be the clear and undeniable proof of a hurtful past.

He had never asked the admiral what the woman looked like, but the moment he saw her, he needed all his strength and self-control not to run away. The beautiful young woman was the living image of George Darcy, only her skin was slightly darker and her features softer.

The introduction was painful and uncomfortable for Darcy, as well as for Laura. The two mostly stared at each other in silence, while the conversation was carried by Elizabeth and the admiral. They discussed Hertfordshire, Bingley and Jane, Elizabeth's time in London, and some upcoming performances which Elizabeth would like to attend.

As much as Elizabeth tried, Darcy could not open himself enough to become pleasant company. He observed Laura carefully, scrutinised her gestures and her features, and had to admit — from the little she spoke — that her good education and elegant manners were obvious.

The visit ended rather quickly but in a better spirit than it had started.

"Mrs Darcy, whenever you have a little bit of spare time, we would be happy to see you again," Admiral Pembroke said.

"So would I, sir," Elizabeth assured him. "There are few people in the world whose company I enjoy as much and to whom I am so grateful, sir. Mrs Moore, it was a pleasure to meet you, and I hope to see you again soon."

"Thank you, Mrs Darcy. You are very kind. The admiral's

praise of you was not at all exaggerated."

"I am sure it was," Elizabeth said lightly. "But I am still grateful to him, and I look forward to our next meeting."

To such a warm good-bye, Darcy only added a few polite words and a proper bow.

In their carriage on the way back home, Elizabeth held Darcy's hands, trying to comfort him.

"Laura is beautiful," she said. "And she seemed so kind, so amiable, and so accomplished. Her daughter is seven and her son five, I believe?"

"She is beautiful...and well educated, it appears. A father would be proud of her...and so should an honourable brother be. But I am still too grieved to feel anything, although I know it is not her fault."

"My love, you must not be so severe on yourself. You have done something remarkably difficult by meeting her. Your feelings will change as you heal."

"She knew of me but never contacted me. She could have exposed our family to scandal if she wished to."

"Why would she have done that? She loved her father, and she felt loved and taken care of. She said as much, did she not? She was content with what he gave her, and so was her mother," Elizabeth said.

"She loved my father and considered him generous. I consider him disloyal, as much as I loved him. The admiral was right — it all depends on the point of view. My heart is still grieving, but I am glad I met her...and I intend to see her again. Perhaps one day, I shall allow Georgiana to meet her too."

Holding his wife's hand, he kissed it and confessed in a voice saddened by sorrow, "I cannot imagine the pain of a man having to leave the woman he loves. I cannot imagine the pain of ever having to leave you, Elizabeth."

"You will not have to, I promise you, my beloved. But I would never accept sharing your love with anyone," she whispered.

"You will not have to, I promise you." He repeated her

words, and he claimed her lips for a sweet kiss to seal their vow, a kiss which soon turned from gentle to passionate — as always happened.

∞∞∞

In the following two months, Mr Darcy and his wife remained in London, and they were seen more and more in society. They seemed to enjoy the theatre, the opera, and — strangely — long walks in Hyde Park.

They were often in the company of Miss Darcy or Colonel Fitzwilliam, sometimes the admiral, and occasionally the Matlocks. Mrs Darcy was the object of the public's interest, and many were ready to criticise her and find fault in her every gesture, as well as in her figure, which was declared not as perfect as Mrs Darcy's should have been.

Of all this, neither Mr or Mrs Darcy cared much, as they were always seen in good spirits, arm in arm, and the gentleman who was once considered proud, arrogant, and always proper in manners, was seen holding his wife's hand and even kissing it.

In January, the Gardiners returned to London, and regular visits were exchanged between them and the Darcys, which strengthened their friendship. Darcy came to value them as much as Elizabeth, and they became his family as much as hers.

Elizabeth and Darcy also visited Admiral Pembroke, seeing Laura again and even meeting her children. Unlike his wife, Darcy was still far from comfortable in Laura's company, but his efforts did not go unappreciated, as the admiral told him.

At the end of February, Mr and Mrs Darcy returned to Hertfordshire, together with Miss Darcy, to attend the long-awaited marriage of Mr Bingley to Jane Bennet. Their arrival was the happiest event in Mrs Bennet's eyes, and it raised the interest of the entire town. Upon seeing the couple, everybody admitted that Mrs Elizabeth Darcy looked more beautiful than they remembered and Mr Darcy more handsome and less arrogant than they recollected.

Charlotte Lucas, who had married Mr Collins a month prior, was completely forgotten, despite Lady Lucas's repeated mentions of her daughter's felicity.

The Darcys stayed at Netherfield, as Longbourn was already crowded with the addition of the Gardiners, but they were all at Longbourn every day, a place that, despite the din and uproar, even Miss Darcy learnt to enjoy.

Elizabeth spent quite some time with her father, removing his worries and doubts in regard to her hasty marriage. She, however, was still concerned about his health and insisted on him following the doctor's orders.

"Do not bother me with this, Lizzy. Let me just enjoy your presence. Your husband keeps sending that poor Dr Taylor to examine me for no reason. It is good that he is a pleasant man, and I hope he is well paid to waste his time on the roads."

"He is well paid." Elizabeth laughed, kissing him. "But please know that nothing is more important to me than to know you are in good health, Papa."

"Do not worry, child. I have no intention of dying before spending enough time in Darcy's library. Besides, your mother would never forgive me if I died and let Mr Collins take Longbourn. Come, let us talk. Tell me more about your life as such a rich lady. Do not worry, your husband is in good hands — your mother has long desired to express her adoration to him, and she now has the chance. You know, when she speaks of Mr Darcy, your mother sounds almost like Mr Collins when he is worshipping Lady Catherine de Bourgh."

In such a way, a week passed, and the anticipated wedding took place. Two days later, the Darcys returned to London. They took with them two joyful English setter puppies — both boys — the little souls that Elizabeth had saved and shared with the man with whom she was now sharing everything.

In the middle of May, before the Season started, the most astonishing news broke in London society: Admiral Thomas Andrew Pembroke, a man widely known across the country and much admired, made a public announcement that he had a daughter and two grandchildren.

A scandal arose, shaking the Fitzwilliam family, with Lady Matlock barely wanting to see her brother again.

Nobody knew the truth, except for Elizabeth and Darcy, and no connection was made to the late Miss Julia. However, that did not make the admiral's announcement any easier for the family to bear.

The existence of illegitimate children was a fact of no importance and would not surprise anyone, but the recognition of such a burden, the public exposure of a forbidden relation, and the presence of a daughter of questionable origins and dark skin was something not to be borne, nor to be accepted and forgiven.

The admiral's daughter was rarely — if ever — seen in public during those trying days. However, a shocking report revealed that the newly wedded Mr and Mrs Darcy — and even Miss Darcy — were regular visitors at the house.

Darcy showed his unrestrained support to the admiral, as he knew it was needed. He had a long and painful conversation with the Matlocks, assuring them of his and Elizabeth's utmost respect and consideration but declaring their support for the admiral, to whom they were both deeply and forever grateful.

When the Season began, the gossip about Admiral Pembroke's daughter was one of the main subjects of conversation at parties and balls.

The Darcys received many invitations — most of them out of pure curiosity — and they accepted only a few.

They also hosted a dinner party when Mr and Mrs Bingley came to London. At that party were also the Matlocks and the Gardiners. An invitation was sent to the admiral but was declined.

Another dinner took place two weeks later, just before the Darcys' long-planned journey to Pemberley, in Admiral Pembroke's house, with the Darcys and the Bingleys as well as Colonel Fitzwilliam. It was the first time Darcy locked eyes for more than an instant with Laura and engaged her in conversation.

At the end of the Season, the gossip about the admiral had already faded — though it still continued in certain circles — as other sensational reports caught society's curiosity.

At the beginning of June, the Darcys left the bustle of town for the beauty and peace of Pemberley. The three of them, along with Mrs Annesley, left together, but only a month later, they were joined by Mr and Mrs Bingley, the Gardiners, the Bennets, as well as Colonel Fitzwilliam. Darcy extended an invitation to the Bingley sisters too, but their brother did not even mention it to them.

The first month spent at Pemberley was pure bliss for both Elizabeth and Darcy. By the time the other guests arrived, Elizabeth had become accustomed to everything and everyone at her new home. The two puppies were now grown up and quite spoilt, taking ownership of the house and grounds.

Among many other responsibilities she had to learn, Elizabeth surrendered to her husband's plea and learnt to ride — a decision with provided her with more liberty to enjoy all the beauties of which she had become mistress.

The large party stayed at Pemberley for two months, a time as joyful as it was challenging for Elizabeth and Darcy, who struggled to find the intimacy they so desired. As with any challenge, it was eventually resolved, much to their satisfaction.

Elizabeth did not forget the take her aunt for several rides in the phaeton, and Mr Bennet did not hesitate to make the library his favourite room, which he rarely left.

Epilogue

Pemberley, December, three years later.

D arcy watched the large gathering, his eyes falling upon his wife, as usual. Elizabeth's beauty and her presence still took his breath away. She glanced back at him, holding their son — a beautiful baby who had just turned one year old.

With her was Jane, holding her beautiful daughter of the same age.

Elizabeth was surrounded by their extended family, as happened every year, in summer and for Christmas.

Amongst all the others, one special addition had shyly accepted the invitation issued after a long hesitation.

Lost in his thoughts, Darcy heard Admiral Pembroke's voice and turned to him.

"Thank you, Darcy."

"You thank me, sir? I have reasons to thank you for at least two lives," Darcy said.

"I know it was not easy for you to invite Laura and her children to Pemberley."

"It was not. I admit to my heart still feeling heavy. But not because of her. It is my burden, and I must learn to carry it."

"And that is why I thank you. The scandal around my daughter has finally calmed down, and even my sister has put aside her grudge. Elizabeth's support has been of great help to Laura and to me. Only Catherine will never forgive either one of us."

"That subject is of no concern to me, sir. Whilst I often send my regards to Anne, through Richard, I only have a cousin in Kent, not an aunt."

The admiral laughed. "Yes, I know you are resentful and that your good opinion once lost is lost forever. Elizabeth teases you often about it."

"She does, and it is well deserved. I hope my son will resemble her more than me."

"You mean my godson Andrew? Yes, I hope that for him too!"

They watched the scene before them in silence for a few moments, then Darcy said, "Admiral, do you remember when you told me that I should marry a woman who delights all my senses? Years ago, when we were at Netherfield."

"Yes, of course."

"At the time, I did not know what you meant, but now I do. I have felt it every day of my life since I married Elizabeth."

The admiral smiled bitterly.

"I am happy for you, Darcy. Few men know what it means, and even fewer are blessed with feeling it. I am one of those who does not know, as I have never felt it."

"I am sorry to hear that, sir."

"Do not be. Just be happy for you and Elizabeth. So, you agree that, in the end, your hasty marriage was to the advantage of both?"

Admiral Pembroke smiled.

Darcy glanced at his wife, then looked back at his companion. "I do agree, Admiral. Most heartily!"

The End

Printed in Great Britain
by Amazon

31313643R00155